The Devil's Dance

BRETT McKAY

---

1.   http://StreetlightGraphics.com

For Grandpa

Author's Note

The Paiute people play a significant role in this narrative. While I conducted extensive research to portray their culture with respect and accuracy, I acknowledge that I may have made mistakes. My intent is not to misrepresent or appropriate Native American traditions, but to honor them. I hope this story reads as a tribute to the Paiutes and Native American heritage as a whole.

This story takes place in Utah and references a mix of real and fictional locations. I intentionally took creative liberties—merging actual places with imagined ones—to evoke a growing sense of disorientation. As the characters delve deeper into the canyons, the landscapes become increasingly surreal. Readers familiar with the region may notice certain areas seeming out of place; this is by design.

Cult:

A cult is a group which is typically led by a charismatic and self-appointed leader, who tightly controls its members, requiring unwavering devotion to a set of beliefs and practices which are considered deviant. – *Wikipedia*

CHAPTER ONE

Bourbon splashed over the rim of Chase's glass as his drinking hand spasmed. He quickly downed the rest of the whiskey and slammed it on the bar as if he couldn't get rid of it fast enough. He wiped the wetness from his mouth. Embarrassed, he scanned the bar to see if anyone had noticed his arm flailing like a fish out of water. He pulled his right arm to his chest and covered it with his left—which didn't have the same problem—and attempted to suppress the shaking.

"Can I get you another one?" the bartender asked.

Chase Gray lifted his head so fast he could have snapped it off at the neck. "No, thank you," he replied. As the bartender turned to walk away, Chase stopped him. "Could I get a glass of water?"

"Sure."

The bartender took the empty glass and came back with water. Chase thanked him and gulped it down. His throat was dry. *Of course it is. Alcohol dries you out and makes you thirsty,* he told himself. His arm settled down some, but the nerves in his stomach still popped like jumping beans.

He hadn't seen Oakley in over a year. *Has it been eighteen months? Will she understand why I couldn't see her?* He doubted it. She might not know what had happened. Her mother wouldn't have been inclined to tell her.

He debated ordering a third beverage. The first two hadn't calmed his nerves. *Liquid courage, my ass.*

Chase looked at his watch. Oakley should have arrived by now. Kira, his ex, had agreed to drive down from Boulder to Denver to drop Oakley off. It wasn't anywhere close to meeting halfway, but he'd take it. Kira had set the drop-off at the mall, and Oakley was going to meet him in front of Bath and Body Works. *Why not meet in the parking lot?* he had wondered. *Is she with her new guy?* Chase had arrived early, found a bar across from the store, and entered it.

He looked out the window and saw a lot of people walking. There were all types of folks. Many appeared exhausted, some looked anxious, others were engaged in conversations, but most were oblivious to their surroundings, faces buried in their phones.

Would he recognize her? That would be awful if he couldn't. But Oakley was his daughter. It didn't matter what age or what she'd done to her hair—he would recognize his own flesh and blood.

He saw a young lady in a red shirt and jeans, with a duffel bag strapped to her back and long black hair that hung past her shoulder blades. Her skin was light mahogany, and she was one of those people staring at her phone more than paying attention to where she was walking.

Is that her? She's much too old to be Oakley. Wait. Oh shit, I think it is. He slid off the barstool and approached warily. The closer he got, the more focused on her phone she became.

"Oakley!" he called.

She lifted her head and gave a soft, closed smile that vanished as quickly as it came.

"Hey, sweetie." Chase wrapped his arms around her.

She hugged him like he was a cactus. "Hi."

"How are you doing?"

She shrugged. "All right."

"Here, I'll take your bag." Chase took it off her shoulder and carried it as they walked. "Do you have more?"

"No. This is it." She gestured to her bag.

"You got everything you need in this?"

"Yeah." It came out more like "Duh."

"Okay."

They walked in awkward silence. Chase felt like he'd lost the ability to communicate with his daughter, and he needed to strike up a conversation.

"How is your mother?"

"She's fine."

"How is school going?"

Oakley stopped walking and turned to him. "Is this how it's going to go? 'How is Mom, how is school, how are your friends'? I can answer all those in a single text. I didn't need to come all the way out here to tell you that."

"Why did you come out here, then?"

Oakley huffed and rolled her eyes.

"Let me guess. Mom made you?"

"Pretty much."

"Nice." Anger boiled in his stomach. "You don't want to be with your dad?"

"I've got a lot going on. I'm missing a summer trip with my friends and tons of concerts. It's not like I'm six and you need to have your two weeks because the courts ordered you to."

"That's not what this is. I want to see you. It's been too long."

"That's the whole point." Oakley threw her hands up. "I haven't seen you in, like, two years, and out of the blue, you want to take me on a trip."

"Well, I didn't move my kid three states away. The distance makes getting together a bit difficult."

"So it's Mom's fault?"

"No—I didn't mean that. It's complicated."

"Complicated. That's a word I've heard all my life. I'm fourteen. You don't need to keep things from me anymore. Mom doesn't—she tells me everything."

"So she told you about what happened to me?" Chase asked.

"More like what you did."

Her words dug deep. He swallowed and gazed at the floor. Her face softened as if she realized she'd gone too far.

"Hey, I didn't mean that." She touched his arm, and he lifted his eyes but kept his guard up. "It's vacation time, right? You planned something fun for us?"

A smile crept onto his face. "Oh yeah. We're going to have a blast."

"So, what are we going to do?"

"It'll be a surprise."

Chase merged from I-70 onto I-15 and headed south toward Cedar City. Twenty minutes later, he drove through the city of Beaver. He'd been driving since he picked his daughter up, and it had been a long and quiet trip so far. Only small talk had transpired before Oakley placed an earbud in each ear, turned to the window, and transported herself beyond engagement with her father.

Chase glanced at his daughter and sighed. Oakley had smashed a pillow against the door and curled up into it. She was fourteen going on twenty. Where had the time gone? She was growing into a beautiful young woman. The last time they'd been together was the Christmas before last, when she'd spent three days with him at his home in Phoenix. Conversations were uncomfortable. He had sensed she was biding her time until she could go back home.

Had his divorce cost him his relationship with his daughter? *No*, he told himself quickly. He and Kira would have caused Oakley more damage if they'd stayed in a tumultuous relationship. Their fights had increased to five or six times a week, and the ugly words they threw at each other cut deep. He knew the arguing had taken a toll on their daughter.

They'd attempted marriage counseling, which had ended in disaster once Chase discovered that Kira was seeing another guy. He wondered if Oakley knew about that. It didn't matter, and Chase wouldn't be the one to tell her. News like that could only backfire and turn him into the bad guy. Sometimes he still felt like the bad guy anyway. Who knew what stories Kira fed their daughter?

He glanced at Oakley as she pulled the earbuds out, yawned, and stretched.

"Mornin', sunshine." He grimaced. "Did you have a good nap?"

"My neck was kinked, and I have a massive headache."

"You can play whatever music you want. The truck has Bluetooth."

He was listening to his road trip playlist that consisted of eighties country, classic rock, and the Eagles, a band that was a requirement for road trips the way "Margaritaville" was for beach resorts. "Life in the Fast Lane" was playing.

Damn, I love this song, he thought.

"I don't think you'd like my music." She shook her head with a chuckle.

"Oh, come on. Give me a shot. I like Lady Gaga—some of her songs, anyway. And Pink."

Oakley gave him an incredulous look. "That's not what I listen to."

"It's not that hippety-hop shit, is it? Oh no, it is, isn't it? I'm sorry."

"This is fine." She gestured to the console, which displayed his playlist.

"Well, you did always like the Eagles. Do you remember when we drove to California?"

"Barely. I was six."

"Wow. Has it been that long?"

Chase looked out his window at the open fields and mountains painted a radiant red and spotted with pines. His mind sifted through ways to spark a conversation, but he was at a loss for words. He shifted in his seat and threw her the only question he could think of.

"How about your friends? How is... ah, what was her name?"

"Kelly?"

"Yes, that's it. Is she still your bestie?"

"No."

"Why not?" he asked.

"I don't want to talk about it." She placed the earbuds in and closed her father out.

They drove without speaking.

After a while, he tried again. "So, you didn't tell me what happened to Kelly. You guys were tight."

"It's been over five months since I talked to that bitch."

"Five months? Wow. What did she do?"

She gazed at him and hesitated before answering. "There was this boy. Max. She knew I liked him—I talked about him constantly. But before I could get the nerve to talk to him, she swooped in and snatched him away. She didn't even like him before I did. It was like she hated me and wanted to hurt me in the worst way. Honestly, I don't know what he sees in that two-faced whore."

"Hey, language, young lady."

"Why? Mom lets me talk like that."

"I'm not your mom. I'm your dad."

She shrugged. "Most dads call or visit more often than just on holidays."

Ouch. "Remember, I live three states away, and I couldn't leave the state for months because of the investigation."

"So, they didn't allow you phone calls either?" Oakley scowled.

The hits keep on comin'. "You're right—I haven't been the best at it. I'm going to be better. I'm not with SWAT anymore. I have more freedom now. I'll be there for you more, and I'll call you more often, okay?"

"You don't need to. It's fine, really."

"I get it. I screwed up, Oakley. I don't want it to be like that anymore. That's why we're taking this trip. We are going to have a ton of fun."

"Are you ever going to tell me where we're going?"

"Okay, I guess it's time I reveal the surprise." He took a deep breath and drum rolled on the steering wheel. "Bryce, Zion, and the magnificent Grand Canyon. We are going to hit all the major parks."

Her deadpan expression killed his excitement.

"Come on. It's going to be fun," he said.

"Are there hotels at these places? Is there Wi-Fi?"

"Where we're going, we don't need hotels or Wi-Fi. We're going to camp. I have all the gear with me."

"Fuck."

"Again with the language?"

"Really, Dad?"

"I know—your mother lets you swear. You can if you want to. I just think you're better than that."

"Everyone swears."

"Do you want to be like everyone? You're a beautiful young lady, but when words like that come out, it diminishes some of that."

"And you don't swear?" she asked.

"I do, but I wait until it's the perfect time. So when I do curse, it's more impactful." He spread a grin, and she chuckled. Her laughter tickled him.

"How far away are we?" she asked.

"About forty minutes from Cedar City. I thought we'd stop there for lunch."

"I don't know if I can wait that long. I've gotta use the bath-room."

"Damn, we just passed a rest area. No problem. I'll stop at the next place."

They rode without speaking. The music shifted to John Denver's "Country Roads."

"Hey, do you want any snacks? I made your favorite," he said.

"What's my favorite?" She scrunched her face.

"Gorp. Remember? It's a staple for road trips."

"Is that some kind of trail mix?"

"Peanuts, M&M's, raisins, and sunflower seeds. It's the best. There's a container in the back seat. I have a cooler with Coke and Mountain Dew too."

"I'm all right."

What am I supposed to say? How do I talk to my own daughter? I'm trying too hard. I have to be natural, right? How do I do that?

Oakley was texting someone on her phone, then she turned to him with a pained face. "Is there no cell service out here?"

"I doubt it. Look around—it's mountains and pastures."

"Where the hell are we?"

"Utah."

"Where all the Mormons live?" she grumbled.

"Yes, the Mormons. We are really here to see them," he mocked. "Come on, Southern Utah has some of the most beautiful canyons on the planet."

"Are there any theme parks?"

"I don't think so."

"Disneyland would have been more fun. Or Six Flags or some-thing."

"I'm sure glad I'm dragging you against your will," he said with some bite. *Where did our connection go? Was it only there when she was a child? Will we ever get it back?*

"I don't know. It's just—canyons? Hiking and camping? It's never been my thing," she said.

"That's why we're doing this. Try something new. Get out and be one with nature. Give it a shot. I think you're going to really like it."

"I don't have much choice, do I?"

"No. I've kidnapped you, so you're my hostage for a week. You will do everything I say." He grinned, and Oakley broke into a smile.

Progress, he thought.

They drove for another few miles, absent of conversation. "On the Road Again," a classic Willie Nelson song, played.

"Is there not another rest stop anywhere?" Oakley asked.

"You've gotta go pretty bad?"

She nodded.

"We'll stop in Parowan—it's a small town up ahead. I have to get gas too."

Chase took the exit and drove the road into town. He stopped at the first gas station he saw, parking next to a gas pump, and Oakley jumped out before he could shut the engine off. Chase stepped out and began pumping fuel. His eyes wandered to the station and the parking lot. An older couple ambled into the store, the husband holding the door for his wife.

A Dodge Charger drove onto the lot at a high rate of speed, barely missing the old couple, and squealed to a stop in a parking stall. Two college-aged boys bounced out of the vehicle, engaged in laughter. One of them strode toward the entrance while the driver stayed outside, leaned against the building, and lit a cigarette.

"Pick me up a pack of smokes, Johnny!" he hollered to his friend. "I'm down to my last one."

Chase tensed at the thought of these boys interacting with his daughter. She'd be exiting the bathroom any minute, and these were the type of boys to stare at her with lustful intentions. Throughout his years on the police force—the last ten of them spent on the

SWAT team—he'd learned to pay attention to details and people's behavior.

He looked at the man pumping gas across from him. He was tall and thick, in his mid-fifties. He wore a handlebar mustache and a cowboy hat that looked like it had been run over by a few trucks and pressed into motor oil. Mustache Man turned and caught Chase's gaze. Chase didn't flinch away—he simply gave a friendly nod.

Mustache Man returned the nod then switched his gaze to the driver of the Charger. He seemed to have the same hesitant curiosity about the Charger boy as Chase did. The boy had one foot planted against the wall as he blew out a cloud of smoke. The young man darted his eyes around and halted on Chase's stare. The boy's lip curled in a slight snarl, then he cut his eyes to Mustache Man.

"What the fuck?" the boy mouthed.

Chase's pump clicked off. He withdrew the pump handle and screwed the gas cap back on as Oakley exited the store and jogged toward the truck. Charger Boy's eyes fixed on Oakley, and Chase's blood boiled.

"What's wrong?" Oakley asked Chase.

"What? Nothing."

"You look pissed."

"No, I'm fine." Chase placed the pump handle back in its cradle.

Mustache Man finished pumping his fuel and marched toward Charger Boy.

What the hell's he doing?

The second boy, Johnny, exited the store with a bag of items and met up with his friend at the same time as Mustache Man arrived.

"Hey." Mustache Man's voice was deep. "You ought to be more careful next time you drive into here."

Oakley and Chase turned their attention to the situation. The driver removed his foot from the wall, puffed his chest out, and flicked his cigarette away. "You got a problem?"

"Yeah. You can't drive in here like hell on wheels! You could hit somebody!" Seeming satisfied with having said his piece, Mustache Man turned to walk away.

"I didn't hit nobody," the driver said.

Mustache Man spun back to him. "That's not the point. Slow down." He pointed at the elderly couple now ambling out of the store. "There're people walking in and out across this parking lot. Slow down! Next time, you won't be so lucky." He marched back to his truck.

"Go fuck yourself," Charger Boy said.

Mustache Man halted but didn't turn. His face tensed, and so did his fists.

Don't do it, Chase urged silently.

Instead of fueling the fire, Mustache Man took a deep breath and stepped into his truck.

"What the hell's that all about?" Oakley asked.

"Just a couple of punk kids," Chase said.

CHAPTER TWO
Tocho

Twelve Years Earlier

A dark presence entered Tocho's room and tickled the back of his neck. Tocho's eyes fluttered open when he felt the tingles, and then his bed shook. Its wooden frame banged against the tile floor, rattling for several minutes before it ceased.

He'd left work early because of a migraine—that was what his boss had called it—and lain down for a nap in hopes that he could sleep it off. But the shadow appeared, the fire in his skull remained, and the filthy thing in the corner was laughing. Not a physical laugh—the entity couldn't speak. It projected its thoughts into Tocho's mind, telling him its name was Uncle Willie.

Tocho didn't have an uncle named Willie. At least none that he was aware of.

Uncle Willie reeked of rancid sewage and formaldehyde as if he'd just been dug up from his grave. His stench was so thick Tocho could taste it, and his stomach roiled. This wasn't the first visit from the specter, and the smell always gave him away. He also brought a sense of dread so heavy it thickened the air like gravy.

The shadow darkened a quarter of Tocho's room. The form was human, but its features were indiscernible except for a white smile that flashed occasionally. Several appendages stretched out from its skull, like bare branches from a tree. Or they could have been arms—it was tough to tell.

Uncle Willie pointed at him, and Tocho's migraine flared up like lava boiling over. It was the fire in his head that his father, Micco, had warned him about before he'd died. When Tocho was eight, his father had sat him on a fallen tree near the river where they liked to fish.

Micco had placed his hands on Tocho's shoulders and looked him square in the eye. "The fire has taken my brain, and now it has moved into my soul. The flames have sent dreams to me—a vision of what I must do. One day, you, too, will feel the fire. You will also have a vision, and you must fulfill your destiny."

Tocho's father had taught him their language and all about his Paiute heritage and their history, a broken story filled with blood, violence, and betrayal. Micco also dabbled in a dark magic that differed from what had been passed down by a lengthy line of shamans, and it had gotten him into hot water with his family, so much so that his father had banished him, telling him that the magic Micco was practicing was evil and not approved by the Tribal Council.

"Son." Micco tightened his grip on Tocho's shoulders. "Our people will tell you that the magic I have taught you is wrong, but it is not. They are afraid of it because they have lost their way in life and have been blinded by modern conveniences and technology. But I have seen wonders."

His father had died a few months later, but he'd never told Tocho about having visits from Uncle Willie or any other ominous spirits. Perhaps Uncle Willie was an ancestor. Tocho didn't know, and the thing wouldn't tell him.

The Uncle Willie thing stood motionless, his invisible eyes staring into Tocho. A low, incessant humming exuded from him, a propelling power, and the constant reverberation slid under Tocho's skin and spread like flames throughout his body until his whole being was a raging inferno and his skull was about to explode. He grabbed his cranium and gritted his teeth, but nothing suppressed the pain. And now he was hearing voices he believed to be his Paiute ancestors calling to him. Their chants and songs rang in his head along with the thing's chuckling.

Tocho had received the first headache a week before, when Uncle Willie had first appeared, and the episodes were becoming more frequent and intense. He'd felt it earlier that day while working at the stables, launching an explosion of pain that was overheating his body.

"What's wrong?" Tate, his closest friend, had asked.

"It's happening again—the fire in my head. The time is close. Be ready."

The foul Uncle Willie was impatient. The moment Tocho's father had warned him about was now. He knew what he had to do.

The shadow and its smell slowly dissipated. Tocho rolled out of a bed that was almost too tiny for his six-foot-seven, broad-shouldered frame. His size had always made him stand out, especially in school, but it also intimidated people, which filled him with a sense of power. Tocho ran his fingers through his lengthy black hair and crossed the bedroom floor to the dresser. He opened a jar that contained a colored substance, war paint he'd made using the same method as his ancestors—drying and smashing clay into powder then mixing in berries and adding egg yolks and some of his blood as a binder.

Tocho dipped two fingers into the mixture and began to paint his face with lines spreading from his nose and across his cheeks. He pulled his shirt off and placed a necklace of bear claws around his neck then stuffed his legs into deerskin pants. Moccasins from the closet finished his ensemble.

Tocho grabbed his homemade tomahawk and stuck it into his belt, strapped a quiver of arrows onto his back, and gripped his bow. The inferno in his brain continued to scorch, and he took the pain and made it his strength. He felt the flames glowing within him, empowering him.

He pushed open the door and marched along the hall and into the family room. He stood in front of his foster dad, James, who sat reclined in a chair. *Wheel of Fortune* was playing on the TV. Tocho scowled at the middle-aged man before him. James's pot gut poked out as he stared blankly at Tocho.

James gulped the last of his beer, crushed the can, and flung it across the room. "What the hell are you doin', boy?"

Tocho remained silent. His foster dad's eyes moved to the bow in Tocho's hand—it was loaded with an arrow.

"I asked you a question, Tom," James said, his tone intensified.

"My name is Tocho."

"In case you hadn't heard, Indians haven't been around since the eighteen hundreds. Take that outfit off. It ain't Halloween."

"You are mistaken. Paiutes are still here. My people are alive. They've been sleeping for too long. It's time to wake them up."

"I got news for ya—you ain't a Paiute." He chuckled. "I seen your birth certificate."

Tocho wrinkled his brow as confusion spun his thoughts. He hadn't expected to be hit with this news, and he didn't believe it. James would say anything to piss him off.

"Your mother was white. Hell, she was whiter than me. And your daddy, well, he came from a mixed couple too. Bet you didn't know that. He may have had a little Indian blood in him, but that wouldn't have left much if any in you. Why do you think you're with us? Why aren't you on the reservation? Why didn't your people—your 'tribe'—take you in?"

Tocho loosened his grip on the bow and studied the floor as if a story was written on the carpet. James's words shook him, and doubts about his true ancestry crept in. He'd never known his mother. She'd passed when he was three. He'd seen pictures of her, but it didn't register that she could have been anything but a full-blooded Paiute.

He pressed his thoughts to recall her image. He remembered an old picture of her when she was young. The color of the photo was muted. She had long black hair, a narrow face, and high cheekbones. *Could she be? Maybe.*

It didn't matter. He knew he was Paiute. He *felt* it, and his mission stayed the same.

This new revelation—if it was one—only fueled his hatred toward James, and he shook with rage. He tightened his grip on the bow, and his upper lip curled into a snarl. Nervousness fluttered in James's eyes. Tocho had him at a disadvantage, and James was realizing it. Tocho raised his bow and aimed it at the man in the recliner.

"Come on now, Tom. You don't have to do this. Let's talk. You can be an Indian. Okay? This—this is crazy." James's voice shook.

The bow groaned as Tocho stretched the string.

James's mouth gaped, and his eyes swelled in horror as he scooted his butt, pressing his back against the chair as if he could push himself through it to safety.

The arrow flew. It struck dead center in his chest with a sickening thud. The arrowhead protruded from the backside of the chair. Blood spread through James's T-shirt.

Satisfied, Tocho set his bow down and withdrew his tomahawk. Pat Sajak was explaining to the contestants what the next category was while James choked from the fluids filling up his lungs.

Tocho walked upstairs and entered his foster mother's room. She squealed, as he'd known she would. His first scalping was easier than he'd expected. He strode out of the bedroom, carrying a piece of her dripping scalp. He smashed it against the face of James—who was still in his death throes—and left it there.

He stepped out of the duplex and onto the road. It was empty and shrouded by the darkness of night. A refreshing breeze wafted, but it didn't chill the fire and rage inside.

The night was quiet as Tocho walked the neighborhood. A car passed him without a glance from the driver, which confirmed to him that people ignored Paiutes—even one displaying a full-blown tribal outfit and carrying a bow. He arrived at the trailer park two blocks north and on his right. He knocked on his friend's door, and Tate answered.

"What's up?" Tate scrunched his face, then his eyes widened as he looked at Tocho's blood-spattered chest.

"It's time. Is everyone in place?" Tocho said.

"I'll call them," Tate said. A young woman peered over his shoulder. He nodded to her. "Chenoa is coming with us." Chenoa was Tate's sixteen-year-old girlfriend. "Is Stone coming?"

"Why wouldn't he be?" Tocho asked.

"He seems off lately, you know?"

"I'll get Stone. Get the others, and meet me on Main next to the drugstore in twenty minutes."

Tate nodded. "Do you need a towel or something?" He pointed at the blood.

"No." Tocho turned and tramped away.

Stone's house was a few minutes' walk from Tate's, and all the lights were out. Tocho crossed the yard to a window near the rear and rapped on the glass.

A moment passed before footsteps approached and the window slid open. Stone stuck his head out. His slitted eyes flew open at the sight of his visitor.

"Tocho? What the hell?"

"It's time. The Brotherhood is gathering on Main Street."

Stone's eyes dropped. "I can't go with you."

"That's your grandfather talking. He's poisoned your mind."

"You were caught practicing dark magic. Just like your dad. And you've been talking about human sacrifice again. Is that something you're really going through with?"

"I had a vision, Stone. It's what needs to be done."

"Paiutes do not sacrifice humans, and they never have. That's why your dad was banished. And now you."

"It's all lies. The Council is as brainwashed as our people. They've lost their way. They need to be reminded."

"Listen," Stone urged. "I know your life has sucked. You lost your parents, and you've bounced from one hellhole to another and had some really shitty foster assholes. I get it. But doing this—it's wrong. There are other ways we can honor our bloodlines."

Tocho pursed his lips and looked away. "It's too late. I am leaving this place."

Stone gasped as he caught sight of the blood on Tocho's body. "Oh my hell, Tocho. You didn't."

"Go back to scraping up scraps from the white man's table like your grandpa," Tocho fumed and sprinted away.

Tocho arrived in front of the store on Main Street in under ten minutes. Parowan Drugstore was closed, as were its neighbors. Tocho stood on the sidewalk, panting. His heart thumped like the pounding of a drum, sending shockwaves of pain with each beat.

A vehicle approached from behind, crunching gravel beneath its tires. The engine shut off, the car door opened, and footsteps advanced. The wind blew against Tocho and sifted through his hair. He closed his eyes and inhaled.

"Tom?" a gruff voice spoke. "This is Sheriff Gunther. Son, I need you to stay put and raise your hands slowly."

Tocho lifted his hands halfway and turned to confront the sheriff. Gunther was a large man dressed in a two-tone tan uniform and Stetson hat. His right hand rested on the butt of the gun holstered on his hip. The lights on top of his patrol car splashed his body with color.

Sheriff Gunther's eyes searched Tocho, sizing him up. "Raise your hands above your head, son."

"Am I under arrest?"

"I need you to follow orders. Put your hands behind your head and get down."

Tocho stood steadfast and stared at the sheriff.

"Now!" Gunther shouted.

Another vehicle approached from behind Tocho. He recognized the rhythmic knock of its engine. It was Wovoka's truck—his friends had arrived. Gunther bounced a glance their way then back to Tocho and swallowed hard.

"Cavalry is here." Tocho smirked.

Sheriff Gunther flipped the leather snap above his gun with his thumb. "You don't want to do this, son. I need you to follow my instructions."

Having melded his pain into strength and feeling the ghosts of his ancestors, Tocho straightened his posture and grimaced. "I am Paiute! Son of Micco! His fire lives in me!" he yelled in the Paiute language.

Tocho's hand moved quickly, grabbing the tomahawk in his belt. Sheriff Gunther drew his gun and aimed. The tomahawk flew.

Gunther fired a shot. The blade stuck in his forehead, the blow snapped his head back, and he crumpled. The sheriff's bullet exploded in Tocho's chest, right above his heart and below his shoulder. The round exited his back.

"Tocho!" a woman's voice cried.

Footsteps clamored, and his friends soon surrounded him. Tocho turned to them. Wovoka was there, and so was Honi, wearing a top hat. Encircling it was a band of turquoise jewelry, black leather, and silver.

Jaci, Tocho's girlfriend, grasped him. "Are you okay?"

"I am fine. I don't feel a thing." He pushed her away. "My fire has come, and I've made peace with it."

He walked to where Sheriff Gunther lay. Gunther squirmed, half in and out of consciousness. The blade was buried deep in his skull. Tocho yanked it out. Blood ran and painted the sheriff's face. Tocho lifted the weapon and brought it down on the sheriff—hacking at him two more times until he was satisfied. Tocho wiped the blade clean on the sheriff's uniform and stuck it back in his belt.

Tocho faced his band of cohorts. Tate, Wovoka, Shilah, and Honi were his warriors, and Jaci and Chenoa were the only girls. They were all full-blooded Paiutes.

Wovoka tore his shirt off and quickly pressed it against Tocho's wound. "You're hurt, brother. We need to get you help. Shilah! Put your shirt against the wound on his back!"

"Jaci..." Tocho turned to his girlfriend. "My moon. Can you sew?"

She nodded.

"You will sew up my wounds. We will use Honi's medicine. I will heal. But we must leave. Our enemies will arrive soon."

Wovoka wrapped the bullet hole with one of their shirts and tied the sleeves together under Tocho's arm while Jaci wiped splashes of his victims' blood from his upper body. Then Wovoka helped Tocho to the bed of his pickup, where he rolled out a blanket. Tocho lay on it. Jaci sat next to him.

Honi and Chenoa hopped in Tate's Jeep while the rest piled into Wovoka's truck. They shot out of there with a screech of tires. Tocho lifted himself to a sitting position.

Jaci motioned to him. "You should stay down."

Tocho cut his eyes to her, and she backed away. Resting his elbow on the edge of the bed, he watched the stores rush by.

"Where is Stone?" Jaci asked.

"Stone's not coming." Tocho's face hardened as he turned to her with a condemning look.

Main Street was empty except for an occasional car and a handful of pedestrians. Tocho breathed in heavily as he scanned the town. A distant scream broke the silence. Someone had found Sheriff Gunther.

He glanced at Jaci, who was staring at him in horror. She pressed her back against the opposite side, as far away from him as possible.

"Do you believe in my vision?" he asked.

She hesitated then nodded.

"It is my destiny. It is all our destiny. We are going to take back what is ours."

She nodded again.

He looked at the roads they passed by then quickly slammed his palm against the window so hard Shilah jumped. He stared at Tocho with egg-white eyes.

"Turn here! At this next road!" Tocho pointed ahead, and Shilah directed the driver to turn.

Wovoka turned so sharply the tires screamed, and Jaci dropped into Tocho's lap. She gawked at him.

"Everything is going to be all right," he said.

"You were shot. You need a doctor." Jaci's speech was shaky.

"Honi is my doctor, and you are my nurse. We will be fine."

Tate's Jeep careened and followed.

Wovoka rolled his window down and called to Tocho. "Where are we going, Chief?"

"There's one more thing we need."

Tocho hadn't moved his gaze from Jaci's. They stared at each other as if trying to read each other's thoughts. Tocho gently brushed Jaci's bangs back from her eyes. He pushed past her to the opposite side of the pickup and, perched on his knees, began scanning the neighborhood they drove through. They passed a young boy on a bike, who glanced at Tocho and quickly looked away.

It was a Friday night, and even though it was late, Tocho knew there would be older kids still out. The teens always liked to wander the streets—there was nothing much to do in this town. But they reached the end of the street without seeing anyone else.

"Go down the next road!" he called to Wovoka.

"We gotta take off before the state police show up."

"Am I not your chief? Am I not your shaman?"

"Yes."

"Have faith. All of this is for nothing if we don't do this."

"What are we looking for?" Jaci asked.

Tocho didn't answer.

They got lucky on the next street. Two young women walked side by side, and as they approached, Tocho hit the window. "Pull up to them."

Wovoka slowed to the pace of the girls. Tate followed at the same speed. Tocho snatched up the blanket he'd been lying on and wrapped it around his torso.

Jaci leaned in and wiped a couple of blood drops from his brow that she had missed.

The girls turned their attention to Tocho's grinning face.

"Hi, ladies."

They each mumbled a return greeting but kept their eyes ahead. One was blond and the other brunette. They looked to be around fifteen.

"What are you girls up to?"

"Nothin.'" The blonde shrugged.

"Tenley, is that you?"

The blonde pushed her hair back behind her ear and turned with a smile. "Yes."

"You go to my school. We have English together—you helped me with my essay."

"I didn't do much."

"Yes, you did. A lot."

She shrugged.

"We're going to a party up in the canyon. Everybody will be there," Tocho said.

A sly grin slid up Tenley's face. "I don't know if we should go," she said playfully.

"We've got beer and pot. Do you smoke?"

"I did once."

"Tenley," her friend murmured, "we gotta get home." She threw Tocho a distasteful look.

Then Jaci's head popped up. "Come on—it will be fun. You'll be with me."

"Kelly?" Tenley scrunched her face.

"It's Jaci now."

"I thought you didn't like me."

"Whatever gave you that impression?" Jaci asked.

Tenley shrugged.

Tocho grinned. Jaci had chosen—she was helping him.

"Don't do this." Her companion tugged at Tenley's shirt.

"You two are sophomores, right?" Jaci continued.

The girls nodded.

"It's a chance to hang out with the cool seniors. We'll be friends."

Sirens wailed in the distance, and Jaci's smile dropped.

"Come with me," Tenley begged her friend, but she shook her head.

"Don't do this," the friend said, on the verge of tears.

"Don't be such a chickenshit. I'm going," Tenley said resolutely.

Her friend pleaded with her eyes.

"Just don't tell my mom, okay?" Tenley asked.

"Fine," the other one grumbled.

"Hop up in here." Tocho lowered a hand.

Tenley gripped it and climbed into the bed of the truck.

"Wovoka, to the promised land!" Tocho called.

With the revving of his engine, Wovoka sped out of the neighborhood, and Tate peeled out after him. Tenley's friend stood alone on the sidewalk and watched them drive away. They turned to the south and headed toward the mountains.

Present

Tocho leaned against a tree and observed the valley below him. Standing on the bluff gave him a view of the canyon and parts of the town of Parowan in the distance. Six of his men sat around a fire thirty feet behind him, painting themselves and filling their bellies with their morning kill. They were the best of his warriors, and Tocho had ordered them to eat before they hiked down the incline to the vehicles waiting below.

He breathed in the air. A putrid scent reached his senses, and he gagged. The foul stench was unmistakable, carrying an aroma of rotten eggs and garbage on a sweltering day.

Tocho's gut twisted like a taffy machine. Uncle Willie had never left him. The wraith had become his spiritual guide of sorts, and Tocho had to come to terms with the specter's visits, although they crept under his skin. The weight of Uncle Willie's words sat on Tocho's shoulders like a heavy demon digging his nails in.

For the past twelve years, Uncle Willie had visited him at least twice a year—sometimes more—and each time, he would bring a new instruction. With each new order given, the specter guaranteed a reward. Tocho had received them, but there was still one giant promise looming, and his patience was running thin.

The low humming increased and rattled his bones. "I'm doing it," he told the thing as if it had asked a question.

"Doing what?" Tate asked, approaching and eating an apple. He gripped a shotgun in his other hand.

"Are the men ready?"

"Yes. Shilah has the list. Are you sure we have to do it? Again?" There was reservation in Tate's tone.

"You doubt my vision?"

"No—it's just..."

"Have you not witnessed miracles? Have we not quadrupled our numbers, our family, our children? Our army?" Tocho pressed his face close to Tate's and broke him down with his steely gaze. "Do you no longer have faith in your chief and shaman?"

Tate stepped back and shifted his eyes. "Of course I have faith. You are still my chief and shaman. But it's been twelve years and..."

"We have been tested, I'll give you that. But this is it—the time is so close."

"Are we going to find *the one*? Are you sure she'll be there?"

Tocho moved his eyes to the shadow resting back in the trees. "The prophecy promises it."

"And if she's not there? If this doesn't fulfill it? What then?"

Tate was right. Tocho felt the same discouragement. But if he showed any sign of weakness, lack of belief, or absence of loyalty, the promise would be withheld.

"Patience and faith, my friend. That is how we are being tested."

CHAPTER THREE

Chase drove slowly along the Main Street of Parowan, glancing at the historic buildings with their brickwork of another age and an old-fashioned drugstore pulled straight out of the fifties. A handful of people walked in and out of shops, and giant maples filled the empty spaces.

They passed the city building. Farther in, Chase reveled at a historic edifice called the Old Rock Church—a small, cozy structure with a tall steeple overlooking the town as a monument of faith and sanctuary. It had been transformed into a museum. He felt the urge to visit it but knew Oakley would dispute with attitude.

As Chase turned right onto another street, he saw a quaint grocery store and parked in front of it. "I've gotta get a few things. Do you want anything?"

Oakley shrugged.

"Go pick out something fun—snacks or a souvenir."

"A souvenir?" she asked incredulously.

They exited the truck and entered the store.

"I need an energy drink."

"It looks like they're in that last aisle. Grab a couple of extra ones for me too. I'm going to grab the other stuff, and I'll meet you back up front."

Oakley went one direction, and Chase went the other. He grabbed a cart and wandered the aisles until he found paper plates and cups—he'd forgotten to buy any when he prepped for the trip. He'd been on campouts without them before and knew that eating a steak and potatoes out of your lap wasn't fun. He also grabbed plastic silverware and napkins.

Leaving the aisle, he ran into a section of local souvenirs that sat close to the front of the store. Chase perused the rack of tourist guides with pictures of famous red rock formations and petroglyphs. He picked up one titled *The Parowan Gap* and studied it as he made his way to the checkout, realizing how close the location was. He wanted to check it out and wondered if he could convince Oakley to go.

Maybe this trip was wrong, he thought. *Should I have planned a trip to a theme park like she mentioned?* But he wanted to go to a place where they could talk and bond. A theme park seemed too loud and distracting.

He shifted from the magazine rack to a tree of ball caps. He could use a new one. He saw several Parowan hats, and there were some good ones. He liked warm colors and simple logos, and as long as it looked good on his head, he'd buy it. One cap read, Ride the Gap, with a design of a Kokopelli riding a bike. There were hats with slogans of Moab and Brian Head, and then he stopped at one that made him laugh: I like Beaver. Underneath the statement was Beaver, UT.

If that isn't redneck enough...

A loud crash rattled his nerves, followed by a woman's shriek. The hairs along his arms and neck stood at attention, and he twisted to see the source.

A shopping cart had toppled on its side, and groceries had spilled onto the floor. A couple of cans of chili and three apples rolled a few feet before stopping, and a middle-aged woman collapsed to her knees.

A man marched to her, yanked the purse from her hands, and shoved it under his armpit, between his ribs and arm. He was short and stocky and wore a blue flannel shirt. Long black hair draped from beneath a top hat rimmed with silver and turquoise, and he carried a shotgun in one hand.

Adrenaline and fear shot through Chase. *Where is Oakley?*

"Sarah!" A man—probably the woman's husband—ran and slid to his knees next to her. He jerked his gaze to the shotgun man with a mixture of rage and confusion. "What the hell are you doing?"

The top hat man pounded the stock of his shotgun into the man's face, knocking him to the ground. The man moaned, holding his face in his hands. Top Hat rummaged through the purse, hauled out a handful of cash, and then tossed the handbag.

Chaos erupted as more racks crashed to the floor and a mix of murmuring voices—griping with anger—thickened the air with tension. Top Hat was not the only perpetrator. Several men were running through the cash register lines, pushing patrons out of the way and throwing others to the floor.

A hand holding a pistol rose above the crowd and fired a shot. It cracked with an echoing blast, eliciting more screams.

"What do you want?" a male voice demanded. It was answered by a skin-on-skin slap like knuckles hitting a cheekbone.

Chase stood at the far end. In a crouching pose, he crept carefully to a short stand that held tourist trinkets and peered around the edge. *Oakley, where are you? Please be safe. I wish I was packing.* He had weapons in his truck but wasn't carrying one because he'd felt it would make Oakley uncomfortable. At least, that was what he had told himself. He hadn't carried one since he left the force—not since the incident.

He pulled his phone out and texted Oakley: *Find a safe spot and hide. The store is under attack.*

He waited for a response but didn't get one. He looked through the crowd of panicked faces, but he couldn't locate her. He hoped she was far from it.

Chase texted again. *Where are you? Are you close to a back exit or a restroom? Take either of them if you can.*

He turned his phone to silent mode and waited. Finally, his phone vibrated. It was her. She sent a thumbs-up emoji. Relief settled his heart a little. He peeked around the corner as another man emerged, holding a woman against his chest with one arm while his other hand held a gun to her head. *Is he wearing a deerskin shirt and a headband like a Native American from an age ago?* Judging by their features, they were Native Americans, but he had never seen anyone wear the old, traditional garb, except at a powwow he had attended years before. The Native's pants were contemporary, constructed of black leather, and he wore cowboy boots.

But that wasn't the strangest part. His face was marked with red and yellow paint, and his eyes were wild. His long black hair whipped around as he jerked his head. He was a giant of a man, standing well over six feet and built like a tight end.

He threw the lady to the ground and raised his arms to the ceiling. "We are Paiute! This is our land. This is our store. We're grabbing supplies from our store. We will let you live if you cooperate. If you don't want bloodshed, no one better call the cops!"

Three of his men emerged from the crowd with shopping carts.

The man in charge turned to them. "Find her."

They took off, dispersing into the store and running along aisles. Two men corralled the remaining patrons against the far wall. They waved their guns at the group of men and women. Most of the people were middle-aged, two women were between seventy and eighty, and one young lady—who couldn't be a day past twenty-five—pressed two toddlers against her bosom.

"Shit." As Chase watched the men race through the store, he realized Oakley's chances of being hurt had just increased. *Find her? What does that mean? Find who? Is this personal?*

Chase wanted to get closer to them. The man with the top hat and shotgun was nearest to him by twenty feet, making Top Hat far enough from his buddies that Chase could take him out without being noticed. The husband and wife remained on the floor, holding each other. The husband's face was smeared with blood.

Chase bided his time. Keeping low, he darted around the stand, quickstepped to the next register, and hid behind a fridge stocked with drinks. He peered around the corner.

The war-painted man had tossed his hostage away and picked up a candy bar. He tore through the wrapping and bit into it with a growl, flipping his hair back and raising his chin in an overconfident grimace. He stalked the people huddling in fear and stared each one of them in the eye with a menacing look. Uncontrolled sobs and sniffling increased as the patrons either followed him with their eyes or looked away, probably wondering what the man was going to do next.

Top Hat's back faced Chase. Chase had to move quietly and quickly.

Top Hat checked his shotgun and then glanced at the couple on the floor. "Get up," he demanded, pointing the gun in the direction of the crowd. "Over there. With them."

Crouching, Chase shuffled around the corner and hid behind the next stand. His heart drummed, and his entire body tensed, at full alert. He was now six feet from the man. Chase glanced at the shopping aisle across from him, where one of the raiders pushed a cart and threw boxes of cereal into it. His heart dropped. If the man turned, he would see Chase. Fortunately, the perp was too distracted. But if Chase made his move now, he'd catch the man's attention, thus thwarting his plan.

He waited several excruciating seconds for the thief to move to another aisle, praying he wouldn't be seen. Finally, the cart man turned and moved out of sight.

After careful consideration, Chase chose not to attack. He couldn't take them all out, and removing one of them from the equation could turn the place into a violent frenzy. So far, this was a robbery. Let the men get what they wanted. Hopefully, no one would get hurt.

Boots clicked against hard tile. There was barely a shadow of the man approaching Chase, and it was growing in size. Top Hat was coming.

If he sees me, I have to take him out. Chase did this for a living. This was what he was good at. *Follow your gut and instincts.*

The man crossed in front of him, but his attention was on something in the opposite direction. Chase hadn't been seen. He sat crouched, wound up like a spring ready to pounce.

Go for the barrel first. Fast and efficient.

Top Hat rotated his head Chase's way, his eyes widening and his body jerking in surprise. Chase sprang, grabbed the shotgun barrel in both hands, and pushed it away from Top Hat as he shot a low kick to the man's knee. It buckled, the grip on the gun lightened, and Chase pushed the gun with a harsh force, pounding it into the man's gut. Chase snatched the gun away and swung the shotgun like a bat for the man's head.

His enemy blocked the blow with one arm, the shotgun whacking against it with a loud crack. Top Hat smacked Chase's ear with a fist. It stung, and Chase saw stars. Then Top Hat pushed against Chase, and the fray was on. Chase crashed to the floor and slid into the counter, smacking his head. The gun clattered to the tile and skated out of range. Top Hat wrapped his hands around Chase's throat like a vise. Chase pounded against his arms, but they didn't release their grip. They grappled for what felt like minutes, his assailant trying to crush the life out of him and Chase prying back his fingers.

Top Hat released one hand to grab something from the back of his pants. Chase crunched the man's remaining hand in his grip then pounded his other fist against his radial nerve, releasing his ene-my's clutch. Chase shot knuckles into the man's throat as the attacker swung a knife. Chase followed up by snapping a palm punch to the underside of his nose. The top hat flew off his head.

Blood ran on impact. The man's eyes watered, and he grabbed his nose. Chase quickly slammed both open palms against the man's ears, incapacitating him. Chase threw the man's body off.

Seizing the gun, Chase jumped to his feet, spun, and sent a final kick to Top Hat's head. The perp's eyes rolled, and he crumpled like an empty bag. The man was unconscious, and Chase was armed.

He quickly peered around the stand to witness more yelling and chaos that covered any sound their fight had made. The war-paint-ed man was kicking an attendant curled up on the floor, pound-ing his foot against the worker's ribs. People watched the scene with shocked faces. Some screamed, and some yelled for the man to stop.

Chase ached to text Oakley again but feared it would draw dan-gerous attention to her. He moved to the exit of the register lane, staying low, and shifted to the next lane. No one was in his vicinity, making it easy for Chase to move freely unseen.

"What part of 'don't call the police' did you not understand?" War Paint hollered as he continued kicking the attendant.

"Please. Please don't kill me. I have family," the man pleaded.

The police. Shit. I hope they don't show, Chase thought. The minute police officers arrived, this would turn into a hostage situa-tion. *Get your shit and get out of here. What's taking them so long?*

"If you wanted to live, you shouldn't have called the police. That's not my fault. You killed yourself." The tormentor's tone was noncha-lant.

"Please, I'll do anything. Just let me go. I have kids."

A man in a shirt and tie stepped forward. He wore a name tag, and Chase guessed him to be the manager. He also appeared to be Native American.

"You are not Paiute!" He stabbed a finger at the gang leader. "You are a disgrace!"

"And who are you, old man? Wearing the white man's clothes and working for the white man and turning your back on your heritage." The leader approached him.

"You're nothing but a thief and a bully. Now, please, let this poor man go."

"Why did you bow down and let them take our land? Let them beat and abuse us while you're bent over, kissing their feet?"

"You are a confused, twisted, sick individual. You are no Paiute."

The leader sent an uppercut to the manager's gut so powerful it lifted him off his feet. The man doubled over, gasping for air. "I should cut you, but I won't. I want you to live long enough to watch as I take back what is rightfully ours."

Dread sank to the bottom of Chase's stomach and churned. He had dealt with deranged men like this who lived in different, chaotic worlds of their own, and their moves were hard to predict. They were the most dangerous type of criminal.

War Paint turned back to the attendant he'd been kicking and racked the slide on his pistol. The man curled into himself in terror.

The blast from the gun shook Chase as it echoed throughout the store, triggering shrieks and cries from the crowd. Bloodcurdling screams electrified the air. Chase snuck forward and peeked out. The attendant was unmoving, and a spray of blood crowned his head.

This is beyond a robbery. What the hell is their agenda? Where is Oakley? Please be safe, he prayed.

The rattling of shopping carts raced to a stop.

"We got everything," one of the men said.

Several people were still crying, hyperventilating, and complaining, but the muffled whimpering of a young female stood out.

"You found her," the deep voice of War Paint said.

"She's a hellcat." Another voice laughed, and a shiver ran through Chase's body as realization sank to the bottom of his gut like an anchor.

"You see, Tate! Where is your faith now?" War Paint howled.

"Honi!" another voice cried out. "What the hell happened to Honi? You okay, brother?"

Damn. Someone noticed Top Hat. Chase gripped the gun, checked the chamber for a round, and squatted, at the ready. A tall, broad-shouldered man popped out from the lane where Chase had left the unconscious man, and the man's eyes locked with Chase's. The man raised a pistol, but Chase's barrel was already aimed.

The shotgun spat with a bang, and the impact knocked the man off his feet. Chase's enemy squirmed on the floor, fighting for breath, his white shirt turning red. Chase jumped to his feet as War Paint appeared three lanes away, a mix of rage and insanity on his face. War Paint aimed his gun. Chase twisted and fired a shot at the man, who shifted, and the shotgun blast missed. The rack of candy and chips behind War Paint exploded.

Chase dove behind a register for cover.

"Who are you, white man?" War Paint hollered. "Your blood is mine! The spirits will see to that!"

"Just take your stuff and leave! I don't want to harm anyone!" Chase yelled.

He peeked around the corner. War Paint scanned the area as if contemplating his next move.

"We gotta go," one of his men said, pushing a cart out the front door.

War Paint hollered, "Move out!"

The rest of his men scurried to the exit with two more carts and armfuls of items. One of the perps dragged a young woman behind him, and War Paint snatched her away and pressed her back to his chest. He raised his gun and—pressing it underneath her chin—turned to face Chase.

"White man!"

Chase cautiously rose, pointing his gun. Oakley was in War Paint's arms.

Chase's world fell apart. A million memories flew by in a millisecond. He saw himself holding his baby minutes after her birth and a Christmas morning as a pajama-clad four-year-old Oakley ran to her presents, their trip to Disneyland when she was six, and how she'd rolled her eyes and given a giant smile after Chase told her one of his favorite dad jokes. His knees weakened as his thoughts swam.

Hold it together, he told himself as he watched the massive barbarian back out the door with his daughter.

Oakley's tear-filled eyes locked with Chase's as if to say, *Save me, please.*

Chase took a deep breath, pursed his lips, and gave her a look of undying determination, willing his thoughts to her and hoping she would receive the message that he was going to get her back.

"I am taking what is mine. I won't hesitate to kill her, white man."

Sirens wailed in the distance, increasing as they approached. The terrorists jumped into their vehicles. One was a Jeep, and the other was a Dodge truck.

Chase felt the customers gawking at him, but he didn't avert his eyes from the vehicle that held his daughter. Tires squealed as the thieves tore out of the parking lot, and Chase bolted out of the store. He crossed the asphalt to his truck as two sheriff cruisers sped in. He didn't pay them any attention—he was inside his vehicle and tearing out of the lot in a matter of seconds, hot on their tail.

CHAPTER FOUR

Chase pursued the vehicles through town, turning sharp corners and rocketing to a four-way stop. As he entered the intersection, a driver slammed on her brakes as Chase's truck came barreling toward her. He jerked the wheel, barely missing her, then straightened it back. The tailgate of the kidnappers' truck was fifty feet ahead of him, and he pushed his vehicle's speed.

The Jeep in the lead took another corner without slowing then leaped over a curb and onto the front lawn of a house. The vehicle cut across it, digging up sod, and shot over a sidewalk, just missing a couple walking a dog.

Chase saw the flashing lights in the rearview mirror. The police car was far behind.

One of the men popped up from the bed of the truck Chase was following. The man rested a rifle on the edge of the tailgate and took aim. Chase yanked the wheel as the gun fired. The bullet missed Chase, who jolted the wheel the opposite way to avoid an oncoming car.

Heading for a sidewalk, Chase bumped over the curb, yanked his wheel, and hit a streetlight. The clash of metal against metal rang out, broken pieces of glass exploded from his headlight, and his truck ricocheted off the pole and back onto the road. The light pole, rocking back and forth like a pendulum, bent forward but didn't fall.

Chase punched the pedal to the metal—engine roaring—and was back on the truck's tail. He backed off about two car lengths to keep his distance. He glanced at his iPhone, mounted on his dashboard.

"Hey, Siri. Call Miles."

"Calling Miles Horn," the robotic voice answered.

Miles was a good friend and an FBI agent in Salt Lake City. They'd served together in Afghanistan and for a time on the Phoenix police force until Miles followed his passion for the FBI and Chase had moved to SWAT.

"Miles," his friend answered.

"Miles, it's Chase. I've got trouble."

"Chase, how're—wait. What's wrong?" Miles said.

"They took my daughter."

"What? Who?"

"We were in a store in Parowan. Some guys robbed the place, and they took her hostage. Miles, they have my Oakley."

"They took Oakley?"

"They killed a man. I killed one of theirs and knocked one out."

"Shit. Do you know where they went?"

"I'm following them right now. I won't let them leave my sight."

"Chase, don't antagonize them. You don't know what they'll do. They might hurt Oakley. Back off, and let me get down there. What are they driving? What's the license plate?"

"They don't have one. It's an old Jeep CJ-5 and a Dodge truck, midnight blue, four-door. There are five guys. Used to be seven."

"I'm getting in my truck right now. I'll make some calls and get a team together. Be careful."

"I'm going to kill them." Chase shook as adrenaline shot through his body like a lit fuse and tears ran from his eyes. "I'm gonna bash their skulls in."

"Take a deep breath. Keep cool. Nothing good can come from losing your temper, remember?"

Chase took in a deep breath and blew it out. "Cool as a cucumber."

"That's my friend. Stay safe, and I'll be down in a jiff." Miles ended the call.

Chase continued following the two vehicles as they headed into the mountains. They left town and followed Highway 143 East into the canyon. The road wound through the mountains. Red cliffs and pines passed in a blur in his peripheral vision as he drove eighty miles per hour, which meant the terrorists were going at least eighty-five per hour or more—much too fast for the curvy road. His tires squealed on turns, but the car handled it well. The rearview mirror reflected the lights of the police officer still in the distance.

The gunman popped up again with his rifle and took aim. Chase swerved left and then right, attempting to make himself a tough target. On this road, he could lose control and roll. He turned the wheel to his left, and the man fired. He heard a thud on the right side of the back door, followed by a metallic ricochet.

He straightened his vehicle again. The man held onto the side of the truck as they took a tight turn off the highway and onto a dirt road. His truck vibrated on the rough terrain. A river ran alongside the road like a blue snake. The shooter took aim again.

Chase bided his time, attempting to read the man's movements and judging when he would fire. Chase made the truck weave again. The man fired, and a round exploded at the far edge of Chase's windshield with a loud crack, leaving a spider web of fractures. That was too close.

He had an idea. Flooring his vehicle, Chase approached the truck at a rapid speed. The shooter prepped to fire again until he realized what Chase was doing. He dropped his rifle onto the bed and gripped the sides of the truck as Chase's grill rammed the back bumper. The gunman toppled but stayed inside the bed. He disappeared for a moment.

Chase squinted, peering through the back window of the truck, trying to make out his daughter, but all he could see were dark forms. Nothing was clear.

The shooter stood and pressed his back against the cab. He lifted his rifle to aim, and Chase sped again to ram. The rifle was pointed lower. Chase realized too late what the man was aiming for. The gun fired.

There was a loud explosion on the driver's side front as his tire blew. The steering wheel pulled and shuddered as he fought to steady the vehicle. His truck tipped forward and to the side. He fishtailed, and at his high speed, he couldn't pull himself out of it. The truck thumped, rattled, spun out of control, and flipped.

Chase's world spiraled. Flashes of colors and objects blurred by. His teeth crashed together, his body lifted, twisted—the seatbelt cutting—then his body slammed up and down. The windshield busted. The roof pushed in. A sharp triangle of metal pressed toward him. Chase white-knuckled the steering wheel, turning it—as if that would do anything.

His vehicle tipped off the side of the road and rolled down the embankment. He hit the river and rolled two more times before coming to a stop. The crashing of metal and glass continued to ring in his head long after. His vision blurred, and his senses darkened.

CHAPTER FIVE

The frigid water against his skin woke Chase up. It gripped his ankles like cold hands. His thoughts became hazy, and it took him a moment to pull his wits together. He couldn't see through the mangled windshield, and his truck was tilted. The sound of rushing water surrounded him, and a strip of pain and tightness ran from his hip and across his chest to his left shoulder. He was still strapped into his seatbelt. He hit the button and released it.

The water rose to his knees and splashed up under his butt. He twisted to the back seat, but the crunched-in roof made it impossible to get through. Anything back there, he would have to get by going in through the side door, and there wasn't much he needed.

His door took several pushes and a hard kick to open, and he hopped out only to fall into the water. The river came up to his thighs. He moved to the toolbox mounted in his pickup, opened it with his key, and withdrew his rifle case and pistol.

"You all right, mister?" a man's voice called from behind.

Chase turned to see a young deputy at the top of the embankment. He was bent forward with his hands on his knees and squinting from the sun.

"Let me help ya." The officer stepped down the rocks to Chase's side. He was barely over twenty, with brown hair beneath the cowboy hat and a smile from ear to ear that Chase guessed never faded. His Western-accented voice was friendly. "That was a hell of a crash. I hate to see a Ford in such shape."

They both looked at Chase's truck. The front end was lifted to the sky due to the boulder beneath it. The driver's-side tire hung from the mangled rim like remnants of flesh, and the grill was smashed in. Smoke curled up from the hood, and the roof looked like Bigfoot had run over it.

"I feel like it looks," Chase said.

"You need to be checked out, sir. That's a big cut on the side of your head."

Chase felt wetness along his temple, and his fingers came back red. Now he felt the ache.

His attention snapped to the deputy as if he had suddenly woken up. "Where did they go?"

"The robbers? Hell, they're long gone by now, I suppose. I pulled over to help you."

"Why? You idiot! You're supposed to be following them—they have my daughter."

"A kidnapping?" His smile disappeared, and blood drained from his face. "I-I'm sorry. I was just following protocol—"

"Don't give me that protocol shit." Chase stumbled through the rocky stream to the embankment and rushed to the police officer's car. Pain screamed at him from several places throughout his body, and his legs were numb from the icy water. "We've gotta move fast. Come on!"

The deputy ran after him. Chase opened the driver's side door of the squad car and pushed his rifle to the back seat.

"Hold on there, mister—I can't let you drive."

"Then you'd better fly like hell."

Chase took the passenger's side, and the young man took the wheel. Tires spat gravel as they shot forward along the dirt road.

"There ain't nowhere to go up here. It dead ends."

"That's good news. We'll catch them there." Chase removed the .50 caliber Desert Eagle from its case and checked the ammo in the clip.

"Good Lord. What do you hunt with that hog leg?" the officer asked.

"Anything that moves."

"Seems excessive."

Chase leaned into the back seat and opened the case to his M1A SOCOM 16 rifle.

"Kenny Lloyd," the deputy said. "That's my name—Kenny. What's yours?"

"Chase Gray."

"Nice to meetcha, Chase Gray."

"Do you know who these guys are?"

Instead of answering, Kenny's face shifted suspiciously, and he gulped.

"Who are they, Kenny?"

"I don't know. Not really. Just heard they're a tribe you don't want to mess with."

"I'm the one they shouldn't have messed with."

Kenny's eyes were as big as eggs. Chase sensed his nervousness.

"How long have you been with the sheriff's department?" Chase asked.

"A year this October."

Shit. Kenny looked much too young and green to have fired a weapon in combat. "I'm a cop, too, from a SWAT team in Phoenix. When we reach them, you stay back, okay?"

"I can provide backup."

"The backup I need is for you to stay on the horn. Let them know where we're at. Got it?"

Kenny nodded.

"They only used her to get away. They'll let her go when they get to the dead end." *I hope,* he thought.

The pain in his head pounded in rhythm with his heart, and more blood ran from his wound down the side of his face. He reached into the pocket of his jeans and withdrew a crumpled tissue, which he dabbed the cut with. The tissue came back soaked. Dizziness blurred his vision. He tried to shake it off.

They followed the road, passing aspens and mountain brush on either side. The path curved, and when it straightened, Chase saw the vehicles ahead. They were parked at the dead end, which led into a rocky hillside. Kenny slowed and crept to within twenty feet of the truck and Jeep. It was unclear whether people were inside.

"She's not here." Chase swallowed.

He gave Kenny a nod and exited the vehicle. He strapped the rifle to his back. Holding the pistol in both hands, Chase cautiously approached the truck.

Kenny exited the patrol car and, keeping his distance, kept a hand on the butt of his gun ready to back Chase up.

Chase stepped on the back bumper, hoisted himself up, and pointed into the bed, preparing to shoot the rifleman. The shooter was gone. He quickly cleared the truck and then the Jeep. There was no sign of his daughter. *They still have her.*

He inspected the ground, which was filled with scuffled and pushed dirt from several shoes. He followed the tracks that led into the hillside. A tiny trail snaked its way through the mountain grass and up the incline. There was nothing beyond but mountains, large rocks, and pines.

A breeze whispered through the trees and blew against his face. Under normal circumstances, the gentle wind would have been a welcome reprieve, but there was no solace for the pain he felt. His heart ached with emptiness and rested on tension and fear.

Chase turned and saw Kenny approaching the hill, keeping an eye on him. Chase slid the pistol into the holster on his hip and unstrapped the rifle. He crouched, rested the barrel on a giant boulder, and inspected the hillside through the mounted scope. He saw nothing. He moved his vision past trees and rocks and along the trail. Beyond the pines, he saw a cloud of dirt—more like a puff—that rolled with the wind. It was them.

"Oakley! Oakley!" he hollered, and his voice echoed through the canyon. "Let her go!" He pointed the rifle to the sky and fired a shot that cracked the silence.

His vision swam. The vertiginous head wound overwhelmed him. His arms lost strength, and his legs turned to spaghetti. The thumping of the ache and heartbeat pounded in his ears. He gulped in deep breaths and let them out. He turned to step down from the rocks, but his legs wouldn't obey his commands, and he crumpled.

Before Chase hit the ground, Kenny caught him. "I got you, buddy." Kenny laid Chase carefully on the dirt.

Chase's eyes rolled, and he almost lost consciousness, and then he gripped Kenny's elbow and through a dry, cracked voice said, "My daughter."

"I know. We'll get her. I promise."

CHAPTER SIX

Oakley followed her captors along the steep trail into the mountains—the man in charge pulled her behind by a rope. She had a good six feet of slack, and the other end was wrapped around her wrists. Several men in the back of the line dragged giant black tarps they had wrapped all their groceries and stolen goods in. The man who led her was a hulk of a guy, and she thought it odd that he wore a quiver of arrows and a bow strapped to his back.

She felt the cool breeze blow against her face and through her hair. The scent of pines and dirt greeted her, but she couldn't appreciate it. Her mind spun in a surreal tornado. Her thoughts couldn't land on anything rational.

"Oakley! Oakley!"

The far-off cry caused the men to stop in their tracks. A cloud of dust covered her. She felt it caking her face.

"Let her go!"

The thundering crack of a rifle shot followed. The leader twisted his head to Oakley. A single tear ran down her cheek.

"Oakley?" The man smiled. "Your daddy's come to get you."

"Can you just let me go?"

The sneer vanished from his lips, and darkness crossed his eyes.

"Just leave me here, and I'll make my way down. I won't tell anyone about you or where you went. I don't even know where I am. We just want to be left alone and go about our day."

"You don't want to be with me?" her captor asked. "You're mine. You were always meant to be mine. You'll be among gods. You will be at one with them." He tugged at her rope, turned, and continued to hike.

"He's going to come after me, and he'll kill you. He'll kill all of you." The moment the words left her lips, she knew it had been a stupid thing to say, but it didn't matter. The declaration gave her strength, even if she had to fake it, and a little hope too.

"I'm planning on it," the leader said without turning or stopping. "But it won't turn out the way you think. If you want your father to live, you will call to him and tell him not to follow."

Images of her dad being cut down by this horde of men flashed through her brain. The man had a point. Her dad—as good as he might be—didn't stand a chance against this many.

The leader halted and turned. "Go ahead. Call to him."

Oakley locked eyes with the man. A breeze blew his bangs across his face, but it didn't break his stare. A few seconds dragged by. Oakley shook her head.

Resolute, the man turned and recommenced hiking.

CHAPTER SEVEN

Chase sat on the edge of an exam bed in an emergency room as the doctor finished stitching the cut above his temple. The doctor inspected his work and then stepped back.

"It only took ten stitches. In a few weeks, they'll dissolve, but you'll be in some pain for a while. I'll prescribe some ibuprofen and anti-nausea for you to take as needed."

"Thanks."

"You suffered a concussion, so the best thing is to get some rest. Refrain from any activity that could enflame it."

Chase nodded, knowing he would not follow instructions. There would be no rest until he got his daughter back.

"Parowan Drugstore is on Main Street—I'll have the prescriptions sent there." The doctor's eyes softened. "I'm sorry about what happened. I'm sure they'll get your daughter back."

Chase pulled a half smile and nodded. The doctor patted him on the thigh and exited the room. As Chase hopped off the bed, Deputy Kenny Lloyd leaned into the doorframe.

"They get you all stitched up, pardner?"

Kenny's innocent smile was comforting under the circumstances.

"Yes. I'm fine now. Do you have any leads?"

"No. I mean, we're pretty sure who took her, and we're setting up a team to track them down. The feds are going to be here soon, and they'll take over."

"I'm going with them."

"That'll be up to the sheriff—or the FBI."

Chase gave him a firm look.

"But I'm sure there'll be no stopping you, will there?" Kenny said.

"No."

Kenny drove Chase to the grocery store where hell and nightmares had erupted. A surreal feeling crawled along his skin at the sight of the scene of his daughter's kidnapping. The image of that man pressing the gun to her throat—the same weapon he'd used to kill a man just minutes before—slid into his mind.

Yellow tape and cones marked off the area. Crowds of people gathered in the parking lot among two sheriff cars, four state troopers, two ambulances, and a fire truck. Several reporters were setting up cameras in a spot where the sheriff's department prepared to give a statement.

"We've still got several witnesses to interview. We'll need to get a statement from you as well," Kenny told Chase.

"Every minute we spend wasting time, they get farther with my Oakley. We need to go now."

"I get it. I do." Kenny parked the car and turned to him with a serious look. "I'm gonna do everything I can to get your daughter back, sir. Night or day, I won't sleep until she's with you again."

There was a sincerity in his voice, confirming that he meant what he said.

"Where's the man who was knocked out?"

"Who?" Kenny's eyebrows creased.

"I fought off a man in there. I left him unconscious. I also shot and killed another."

"There weren't nobody left in the store. There was blood, a lot of it, but none of their group was found."

"How can that be?"

Kenny shrugged.

"Someone had to see what happened," Chase said.

"We can ask the witnesses."

"I want to see the security footage."

"The sheriff is not going to let you."

"Why do you say that?"

"Because that's what he told me," Kenny said.

Heat boiled inside Chase. He wondered where Miles was and how soon he'd get there. He withdrew his iPhone and was preparing to call Miles when a thought came to him: *I can track Oakley's phone.* She was on his account. Oakley's mother, Kira, had insisted that Chase buy her a phone and pay for the service. He'd have to call and tell Kira what had happened at some point. He hoped to find Oakley before needing to make that call.

"Do you know how I can track my daughter's phone with my phone?" he asked Kenny.

"There should be an app called Find My on your phone." Kenny took the phone from Chase's hand and shifted through the apps quickly then clicked on one. "Here." He handed the phone back to Chase.

Chase found his daughter's name and selected it. A map appeared with a flashing pin marking her location. Excitement shot through him, but it was short-lived—it showed the device being close. Her phone was inside the store.

"Shit. It's in there," Chase said.

"Let's go get it."

Chase followed Kenny, passing the news conference being held by the sheriff, and headed for the taped-off entrance. The sheriff, who was tall and bearing a beer gut that hung over his belt, addressed the crowd.

"At approximately one thirty this afternoon, a group of men entered the store and held it up." The sheriff talked into several microphones mounted on a stand. "They were armed, they terrorized the patrons inside, several were injured, and it's believed that one of the employees has been killed. In addition to robbing the store of several items, the group took a hostage as they escaped. Their whereabouts are unknown at this time." His eyes shifted to Kenny and Chase as they passed him, and a scowl crossed his face.

"What is the name of the hostage?" a lady reporter asked.

"I cannot release her identity at this time, but she is fourteen years old."

"Is there a ransom demand?" she asked.

"Not at this moment."

"Do you know who these men are?" a different reporter asked.

"No. We do have our suspicions as to their identity, but it has not been confirmed." The sheriff turned back to the crowd. "We're still collecting evidence and interviewing witnesses. We'll have more details to report later."

Another deputy stopped Kenny and Chase. "Sheriff said no one enters until the feds show up."

"It's okay, Dean—he's a cop. These shitheads kidnapped his daughter. We won't touch nothin'. She left something inside that could give us clues pertinent to the case."

"All right." He nodded and lifted the tape, which they ducked under. "I didn't let you in. Make it quick, and don't touch anything, or I'll get my ass chewed."

"Thanks, Dean."

Chase saw the smear of blood on the floor where he'd dropped the man with the shotgun. He quickly walked past the aisle, and just like Kenny had said, both men were gone. Chase and Kenny rushed to the back of the store, where Chase believed Oakley had been, and crossed three aisles up and down until he found her phone on the floor. It rested against the far wall. His heart sank. He picked it up, picturing her being grabbed by a man and the captor tossing the phone. He touched the screen, and an image of the Cranberries appeared. He swiped through to her home screen. Fortunately, she didn't have a security lock. *Thank you, God, for that.* Chase glanced across her apps. He didn't know what he was looking for or expected to see.

He saw the app for photos and opened it. "Holy shit."

Kenny turned the corner and approached. "You find it?"

"Yeah. She took a picture of him."

"No shit?" Kenny leaned his head in and looked at the photo.

She'd taken three shots of the perp. The first one was of his back as he walked up the aisle, pushing a cart. He was tall, muscular, and had long black hair hanging to the middle of his back. The next picture showed half of his face as he had turned, his eyes boring right through the camera. The last photo was a close-up of his face, wrinkled in rage. He was gritting his teeth. His arms were stretched out as if to grab the person holding the camera. Oakley.

CHAPTER EIGHT

Sheriff Jerry Reese charged through the front door of the police station. His eyes swept across the room until they landed on Chase. Face reddening with rage, ready to explode, he marched to him.

"Just who in the hell do you think you are?"

Chase sat in front of Kenny's desk as the officer was in the middle of taking his official statement. Kenny held both palms out to calm Reese.

"Sheriff, this is Officer Chase Gray of the Phoenix Police Department. He's the father of the victim who was taken." Kenny emphasized the word *officer* as if hoping that would settle his enraged boss.

"I don't give a damn who he is. I said for no one to step into my crime scene. Was I not clear?"

Kenny nodded.

Reese turned to Chase. "I'm sorry about your daughter. But you can't go stompin' into my crime scene and messing with all sorts of evidence. This is my investigation. And what in God's name got into your head to go chasing them through my town and into the hills? You're like a coyote jumpin' into a hen house and scarin' them off in every which way. Officer Lloyd says you're an officer from Arizona. Well, my town is not in your jurisdiction, is it?"

Spittle flew from his lips, and beneath wrinkles of skin were two dots for eyes that were cracked red, either from the stress of the situation or a rough night of drinking. Chase believed it was the latter, since he'd caught a hint of whiskey on his breath.

"It's now under my jurisdiction," a calm voice said from across the room.

Reese, Chase, and Kenny turned their heads. Miles entered with two other men. He wore a white button-down shirt, jeans, and cowboy boots, and his steel gaze cut through the room. He carried an air of authority.

Miles sent Chase a friendly nod before turning back to the sheriff. "Sheriff Reese? I'm Agent Miles Horn, and this is Agent Carl Benson and Agent Abraham Ike." He hooked a thumb over his shoulder toward his men. Miles stuck his hand out, and Reese shook it hesitantly. "I'm here to help you, and I'm sure I'll have your full cooperation."

After a beat, Reese nodded. "Of course. My men are at your disposal. You can have this awful mess of a case. You can deal with the press too. Don't much like doin' that shit."

"I got it."

Reese looked as if he was going to spout something else, but Miles dismissed him by turning to Chase, who stood. They embraced and patted each other on the shoulder. Reese headed toward the door, cursing under his breath.

"How've you been, Miles?"

"Better than you. You've had one hell of a year, and then this."

"I know. They got my little girl." Chase's bottom lip trembled.

"It's okay, buddy. We're going to get her back. Tell me everything."

Chase walked him through the whole story, filling him in on how many perpetrators there were, what they looked like, what he'd heard them saying, and where he'd lost them. Miles ordered his men to retrieve the security footage, then they turned their attention to Kenny.

"Miles, this is Officer Kenny Lloyd. Kenny, this is Agent Miles," Chase said.

They shook hands.

"Kenny, do you know who these men are?" Miles asked.

"Yeah, sort of. They've always run together since they were kids. Kind of a gang. Tom was their leader, but I think he goes by Tocho now. They got into trouble all the time, but mostly petty theft and fistfights. They used to live here a number of years ago."

"Where do they live now?" Chase asked.

"Somewhere in the mountains, but no one knows where exactly."

"Sheriff Jerry Reese?" a man called in a meek tone as he entered the station. He was balding and in his fifties, with stubble on his chin and a lost look in his eyes. He held a piece of paper at his side.

Reese had his hand on the doorknob but halted. He sighed. His shoulders sank, and he turned to greet the man. "What can I do for ya, Hank?"

Hank's eyes bounced from Chase to Miles then back to Reese. "It was them, wasn't it?"

"Not now, Hank. I've got a shitload to deal with. Let me do my job—"

"Your job!" Hank's stern voice shook the room. "It's been twelve years, Jerry. Your job was to find my daughter." He lifted the piece of paper. It was a flyer with the picture of a young girl.

Reese's eyes turned up with empathy. "I know, Hank. I have exhausted every resource, but I have never given up on finding her."

"My Tenley is still alive. She is with those men. I know it."

"Come with me." Reese led Hank into his office.

Miles and Chase turned back to Kenny, whose eyes shifted downward as he pursed his lips.

"What's the story there?" Miles asked.

Kenny took a deep breath. "Tenley Baker was taken twelve years ago. She lived just down the road from me." He glanced at Chase and then away again as if tempted to hold back information. As his tale went on, Chase knew why he'd hesitated. "There was a witness. Tenley's best friend saw her jump into the back of a truck filled with a couple of guys and a lady. A Jeep was with them too. It was... it was the same men that raided that store today. We believe. There's been no sign of Tenley since."

The hairs on Chase's neck prickled.

"She's not been the only girl who has gone missin'. Two others have disappeared since."

"And now my Oakley."

"You said they live in the mountains?" Miles pointed at Kenny.

"Sort of. I think. It's just—I don't know all the facts."

"Just tell us what you do know."

"Growin' up I always heard tales about them. How they'd run to the mountains and began living like the Native Americans of the old days. Tepees, bows and arrows, and such. Then the stories got even crazier. You know, like urban legends. Kids would tell stories to scare other kids. I was a scout, and whenever we went on a campout, me and my friends competed on who could tell the scariest story. I heard things like how they used black magic to turn into demons and suck away souls. And how they sneak through windows at night and steal children, and then there's a place they take you to in the mountains to meet the devil. That kind of stuff."

"Skin-walkers?" Chase asked.

"Yeah. They can turn into any animal they want, and they can curse you."

Miles rolled his eyes. "Let's get out of Harry Potter world for a minute."

"It's not that I believed that stuff, but when people go missing—especially young girls—it tends to haunt the town. You start wonderin' what's true and what's not."

"Were all the missing girls from here?" Chase leaned in.

"Two from Parowan and one from Cedar City. Tenley was from Parowan."

"And none were ever found?"

"There was one that got away. But it wasn't one of the girls that went missing. She had once been a part of the tribe. She was a mess. All strung out and crazy like. It was before I was on the force. Dean told me the story about how she wandered into town. The FBI questioned her for hours and hours. She gave up some information that corroborated parts of what we knew, but most of what she said didn't make any sense. The feds finally convinced her to lead them to her tribe. She got lost—she couldn't remember where the gang's camp was. Then she broke away and ran to a cliff and took a swan dive."

"She killed herself?" Chase said.

Kenny nodded.

"Let's start from the beginning," Miles said. "Go back to when this gang lived here. Why did they leave? What have they done?"

"They killed my friend." Sheriff Reese's words dropped like a brick. He and Hank had returned and were standing at the door. After ushering Hank softly out the front door, Reese approached the desk with a somber look on his face. "Gunther was the sheriff, at the time, and my friend. I was his deputy, and I was off duty that night. I was supposed to be working, but it was my birthday, and Gunther told me to go home and celebrate. Tom—the leader of them Indians—shot his foster daddy with an arrow and then scalped his foster mommy. Just like an old-time savage. Gunther stopped him out on Main Street. He had him dead to rights. There was an altercation. The sheriff shot Tom, and Gunther never missed. Tom's blood was there on the sidewalk. A good amount of it too. But somehow that bastard buried a tomahawk into my friend's skull."

"A tomahawk?" Miles asked incredulously.

"Yes, and then he hacked him to bits with it. Couldn't even recognize him. We had to have a closed casket."

Kenny took his hat off and buried his head in his hands.

Reese continued. "This town ain't been the same since. It's like it's been cursed. And them devils pop in every so often—raidin' and stealin,' kidnappin' and whatever else. They act like they own this town."

A cold chill ran down Chase's spine as he thought about Oakley and her fate.

Miles gripped Chase's shoulder and gave him a firm look. "She's all right. He took her for a purpose, which means they're keeping her alive. We'll get her back."

Benson and Ike returned with the security footage, and they all watched it together. Chase gripped his fists until his knuckles turned white, and as badly as he wanted to look away from the screen, he held fast. He had to. If there were clues in the video, he needed them. Miles studied the film like a college student and scratched notes on a pad.

Several minutes after Chase had run out of the store after the group, two men had entered from the back of the store and dragged their dead friend away. The other one—who was knocked unconscious—stood on wobbly legs and followed them out.

"That's what happened to those guys," Kenny said to Chase.

Chase turned to Reese. "Where were you and your men?"

"What do you mean?"

"When I left that parking lot, you guys were just arriving. Yet it still took another five minutes before these men showed up to take away their friends. Why weren't you or your men inside the store already?"

"I was outside dispatching men to chase your ass down and them Indians!"

"You didn't have a spare man to check on the injured patrons?"

"I don't know if you've noticed, but I don't have a big city department. We barely run a skeleton crew here." Reese stood with a huff.

"You need anything else, you've got my number. I'll be in my office."
The sheriff shut his door and closed all the blinds.

To take some shots of the whiskey in his drawer, Chase thought.

"We have to find out why they took her," Miles said.

"I don't want to know why," Chase said.

"I know, buddy, but finding out will tell us whether she's still alive or not and how to get her back. I know that's tough to hear, but we've got to find out more about this gang. Kenny, what more do you know about them?"

"I don't know much other than what Sheriff Reese just said. I know they were young— like, teenagers—when it all happened."

"Who else knows these people?"

"Probably Stone Cannon. Story is that he used to run with them back in the day."

CHAPTER NINE

"Stone Cannon?" Miles asked the man who opened the door.

Chase, Miles, and Kenny stood on the porch of a small white house, and a man stared at them through the screen door. He was less than six feet tall—close to Chase's height, thin, and wiry but with muscle. Black hair stuck out of his cowboy hat and dangled above his shoulders. He was Native American.

"I am," he answered.

"I'm Agent Miles Horn with the FBI, and this is Officer Kenny Lloyd and Officer Chase Gray." He hooked his thumb at them. "Can we ask you some questions?"

Stone glanced from Chase to Miles. "What is this about?"

"Tom Henson and his gang and the grocery store holdup. I'm sure you've heard the news."

"It travels fast here."

"We were told that you knew Tom when he used to live here. Is that right?" Chase asked.

"Yes. Are you the father of the girl they took?"

Chase nodded.

"Who is it?" a gravelly voice called from inside the house.

"It's the FBI, Grandpa."

"What the hell do they want?"

"They want to know about Tocho."

There was a moment of silence, and the air thickened with tension.

"Can we come in?" Miles asked.

The screen door cried as Stone pushed it open, and they entered. The front room was dark and cloudy, and the scent of marijuana hit Chase immediately. In the far corner of the room sat a short old man smoking an e-cigarette. A worn straw cowboy hat sat atop his head, and beneath it was an aged face with deep wrinkles and dark, kind eyes. A crimson throw with black, white, and yellow designs draped his lap. From beneath the blanket poked two cowboy boots. Chase sat on a couch covered by a similar blanket, and the seat sank to the boards.

"Do you have a medical prescription for that?" Miles pointed at the e-cigarette, and the old man huffed and turned his eyes away.

Miles didn't press the point. The issue was not their priority. He sat next to Chase, and Kenny and Stone took wooden chairs.

"This is my grandfather, Larry Mayo."

"What does the FBI want to know about Tocho?" Mayo asked.

"Tom—I assume that's who you're referring to—robbed a grocery store this afternoon with several other men, and they kidnapped a young girl," Miles said.

"My daughter, Oakley. She's only fourteen."

Mayo's stoic expression didn't change.

"They also killed a man, and several others were injured," Miles stated.

"Tocho is *atsa*. He was born *asaakwasi*."

"He is evil and was born the devil," Stone translated.

"Tocho is the son of my cousin Micco. Tocho believed he was a great-great-grandson of Wovoka, a great medicine man who brought the Ghost Dance. But I don't believe he is any relation."

"The Ghost Dance was said to reunite the living with the spirits of the dead, and the dead would fight on our behalf and make the white colonists leave. It was meant to bring unity and prosperity back to our people," Stone explained.

Mayo took another hit from his e-cigarette, set it down, and broke into a number of coughs. "Micco thought he was a shaman, but he was bad medicine. He practiced dark magic that was evil and forbidden. He was told many times to stop, but he wouldn't listen, and he was banished from his family and from our Paiute tribe. When Micco spoke to the spirits of the dead, the dead brought demons with them. He listened to these demons, and he believed they were our ancestors, but they were of the dark, and they cursed Micco with the Fire. Micco passed the Fire on to Tocho, and now the Fire has taken him over. Now Tocho sits with the demons, and they have promised him power. But this power comes with great sacrifices." Larry turned his eyes to Chase. "Your daughter."

Chase's mind spun, and the words curdled in his stomach. "What do you mean?"

Stone turned to him. "Tocho plans to sacrifice your daughter on the eve of the blood moon while performing the Ghost Dance."

"I didn't think Indians did that," Miles said.

"They don't," Mayo said emphatically.

"When is this blood moon happening?" Chase asked.

"On Monday."

"That's in three days. If I'm counting Monday as one of them."

"Tocho lives like his father," Mayo said. "They are of the old ways. They speak our native tongue. They dress like our ancestors, and they live off the land. They dreamed of a day when all of our tribes would unite and become one with nature and take back the land that is ours. But this is all a lie. The demons they worship want nothing more than their souls."

"If they live off the land, why did they steal food and supplies from the grocery store?" Miles said.

"I don't know." Stone shrugged. "My guess is that Tocho realized they can't live completely off the land, and he would say the spirits allowed certain conveniences. He is nothing more than a cult leader, and he has brainwashed his people into following everything he says. He is very convincing."

"Like the gun he used to kill that man. I'm pretty sure semiauto pistols weren't around in the eighteen hundreds," Chase said.

"That's Tocho," Mayo said. "He is a contradiction unto himself. But make no mistake—he is more deadly with a bow than you would be with your rifle. And at close range, he is also dangerous with the knife and tomahawk."

"I heard that you used to run with this gang," Miles said to Stone.

"When I was a teenager, I wanted to be like Tocho. I admired his strength and his confidence. Yes, I would spend time with him and his friends, and they tried to recruit me."

"But you didn't go?"

Stone shook his head and pulled a sly smile.

"I tied him to that chair." Mayo pointed at the chair Stone sat in. "Stone desired to honor our people, and he believed that Tocho was the one chosen to do that. Until I sat him down and told him exactly who Tocho really was. I also explained to him about Tocho's real agenda—which was the same as Micco's—and his pact with *asaakwasi.*"

"I wasn't easily convinced," Stone said sheepishly. "But I'm glad that my grandfather did that for me. As time went on, Tocho was talking about doing some awful things."

"What kind of things?" Miles asked.

"He was talking about human sacrifice and pacts with the spirits. That's completely against anything we believe—against the law and any rational moral code. And there was an evil aura around him. I could just feel it. Something wasn't right. The night Tocho killed his foster parents, he came to my house and tried to convince me to go with them. Fortunately, I had already made my decision before then."

"Do you believe in taking back your land, like Tocho? Reuniting the tribes and bringing back your heritage?" Miles looked at Mayo, who smiled.

"My heritage is here." He pounded his heart with his hand. "And here." He touched his head. "And in my tongue. In how I treat my fellow man. In how I treat the land and the beasts, the water and the wind. My heritage is not determined by other men or by what land I stand on or what has happened in the past."

There was silence as Mayo's words sank in. Then Stone turned to Miles and Chase. "He has stolen other girls and sacrificed them. This is not the first."

A chill startled the hairs up and down Chase's arms.

"There was a blood moon in 2015. I believe he did it then too. A young woman from Cedar City went missing around that time and was never found," Stone said. "I think there were two others. I'm not sure of those dates."

"Those were the girls I told you about," Kenny chimed in.

"Tocho's power was strengthened by this sacrifice," Mayo said. "He has discovered the ways of the skin-walker. I came upon him in the woods one evening. I was by my campfire, alone, talking with nature and God. I was praying, and when I opened my eyes, I was not alone. A beast stood near my fire. A demon. The flames were reflected in his eyes as he stared into my soul. He stood like a man but had the features of a wolf. It was Tocho. He was angry with me. He believes that I defy our ancestors. He is blind to the truth. He wanted to rip my heart from my chest and eat it. Then my power would be his. This I know. My only protection was God and my prayer."

Miles gave Chase an incredulous look. Disregarding Mayo's comments, he directed his questions to Stone. "Do you know where they've gone? Where they are now?"

"They are deep in the mountains, but I know those areas like my own backyard. I can track them, and I can find them. It won't be easy, and we cannot take vehicles where they went. Horseback is the only way."

"Horses?" Miles asked.

"Yes. Jessie's ranch is close to here, and they have the best mountain horses. I'm sure they would oblige."

"Tocho's power may be fading now. That's why he needs the blood moon. But he is still strong. He has the strength of ten men." Mayo's eyes drove into Miles as if he knew the doubt that lingered in the FBI agent's heart, and Miles looked away.

CHAPTER TEN

Oakley stepped on a large rock, and her foot twisted and slipped. She landed on the hard dirt in a cloud of dust. The palms of her hands stung from the impact, and her kneecaps ached from taking a hit. Being tied to the end of that man's rope prevented her from catching her balance.

The big asshole—as she referred to him in her mind—turned and glowered at her.

"A little help, please?" It was more of a sarcastic statement than a plea.

"Shhh," he said, putting his finger to his lips.

The entire group froze and listened. Oakley didn't hear a thing at first, and then distant laughter rose. It sounded far off and below them. They were on a hill, so she pictured the chuckling coming from someone at the bottom of the incline.

Her captor dropped her rope, parted the branches of scrub oak, and carefully stepped into the brush next to their trail. Another man followed him. They crouched on the ledge and peered over.

Oakley heard male voices, two or maybe three men—it was hard to tell, and their conversation was too far away to make out their words. Two men chortled at whatever the third man said.

The men behind Oakley murmured. "What are men doing this far? How did they enter our territory?" one asked.

"I don't know. I thought it was protected by magic. That's what he told us."

"I guess it's not that protected."

"Tocho is going to kill them."

Tocho? Is that the big asshole's name? she wondered.

Ahead of Oakley, the trail peaked and then sloped. Being on the ground already, she decided to crawl to the edge. She was worming her way through the dirt and over rocks when one of the men whispered at her in a harsh tone.

"Hey! Where are you going? Stop!"

She disregarded the demand. She was already at the ledge and was able to look down the slope and see the group of men. There were three guys, all unarmed, and they appeared to be on a hike. She could hear their voices better.

"So, where the hell are we, Rex? Are we lost?" one of them said.

"We shouldn't have passed through that arch. I told you it looked creepy. We're probably on private property. I've got a weird feeling."

Tocho stood on the ledge and armed his bow. He pulled back the bowstring and aimed. Oakley wanted to warn them, but her mouth was dry, and her words were caught in her throat.

The first arrow hit the center man in the chest, knocking him back. The man wore a confused look. A second arrow flew and struck him in the head, and he fell back.

It took a few seconds for his friends to realize what was going on.

"Mark?" one of them called out, then he quickly ducked and looked left to right in a panic.

"Hey," the other one said. "Hey! Who did that? You shot my friend!" His voice shook.

Spinning their heads and backing up, they searched for their enemy. Tocho hopped down from the ledge and stood on the slope facing them.

"Holy shit!" The man in the blue shirt stumbled back.

"You are on our land. How did you find our land?" Tocho demanded.

"I—I don't know. We took a wrong turn. Honest. We'll leave."

"We don't mean any harm," the other one said.

Tocho slowly armed his bow.

"Please. You don't have to do this." The blue-shirt man dropped to his knees and pleaded with his palms out to Tocho as if to show that he wasn't armed. "Please. I'll give you anything." He was on the verge of sobs.

Tocho pulled back the bowstring and let it fly. It struck between the pleading man's eyes. His head jerked, and his hat popped off.

"Fucker!" the other man hollered, turning and running in the opposite direction.

Tocho didn't act with urgency. He slowly and carefully armed his bow again. The running man was a good distance away. Oakley could barely see him. Tocho aimed for what felt like minutes before firing. He released the arrow, and it flew straight and fast. The man fell face down in the dirt, with a shaft sticking out of his back. A few seconds later, his arms moved slightly.

Tocho turned back to his men. "Shilah! Go send this man into the next world. Bring me his scalp."

Oakley's mind spun. She trembled with a new fear, and she pleaded with God to give her strength.

Oakley sat against a large boulder, watching her captors cook a couple of rabbits—minus the fur—on a spit over flames. The darkness had finally shrouded the sun, and the night brought a cold chill. Some of the fire's heat touched her, and the smoke blew in her direction, making her eyes water.

The men talked to each other in their native tongue, which was as alien to Oakley as Chinese. Two men laughed at whatever topic they discussed, and Oakley thought about the violence that had taken place in the supermarket and on the hill. *How can they laugh af-*

ter doing something like that? She was pretty sure she had seen a dead man being dragged past the checkout stands. He'd been lying, unmoving, in a pool of blood. Fortunately, someone had laid a jacket over the deceased's head. And then, after watching the murder of three innocent hikers, she had a sick feeling in her gut that didn't go away.

And what about Dad? Is he okay? When she'd seen his truck roll into the river, she nearly vomited. She would have been all right to spew all over these men. Hope sprang when she'd heard his voice calling to her from the valley below. *He is alive.*

Pebbles poked her buttocks, and she shifted her rear as the leader approached. Tocho— she was positive of his name now—wore feathers in his headband, his face looked carved out of stone, and his eyes were fierce. He held a piece of meat, which was stuck on a stick, which he offered to her. Oakley emphatically shook her head.

"You need to eat. We have a long walk tomorrow," he said.

"Where are you taking me and why?"

"Eat," Tocho demanded.

Oakley's gaze dropped. She wouldn't get answers from Tocho. At first, she'd believed Tocho was using her as a shield, but he'd put a huge distance between them and the police. *Why haven't they let me go? Am I being held for ransom?* She had seen enough movies where that was the case, but her gut sensed something more sinister than that. Her stomach roiled. She might be discarded like that man in the store—like those men on the hill. She shivered at the thought.

Tocho studied her for a minute, his eyes running over her. "Cheyenne?"

She shook her head. "Cherokee. My mom's side."

"You are Paiute now."

"No."

"You will see. Eat."

Impatient, he set the meat in her lap and walked away. She waited five minutes before finally digging into the meat with her fingers and eating some. She had no appetite. Her stomach was busy somersaulting, but she knew she needed protein and energy. The meat was bland but moist and edible.

A man wearing a short top hat sat down near the fire and began to eat. His face was bruised as if he had been pummeled by a boxer. He chawed at a leg while staring into the fire. He shifted his butt and then cut his eyes to Oakley. There was white fabric underneath his hat that appeared to be a bandage, and a thin line of blood leaked below it. He was squinting. She didn't think it was from the fire smoke but rather from the pain he was in. The man scowled and burned a glare at Oakley.

Several feet beyond the fire, two people attended to a body on the ground. She watched as they stripped the form of all its clothes. The body remained still. Dead. One of the men brought a bucket. They dipped rags into it and washed the body. The water ran with blood. Oakley saw the crimson liquid streak down the body's sides and mix with the dirt. They treated this body with reverence. They mumbled indiscernible words while washing him, and there was rhythm to the words—like chanting.

"Niyol was a great warrior. Niyol means wind."

The voice snapped her out of a trance, and she jumped as she turned to see Tocho standing behind her. She hadn't heard or seen him approach.

"He leaves a woman and child behind. Your father took him from them. Took him from me. Now I take you. You are now mine."

"If my dad killed him, then he did it in self-defense. You guys attacked first."

"No!" His voice shook. The people around the camp froze and turned.

Oakley looked into his eyes. She'd struck a nerve, and his gaze told her how serious it was.

"White man attacked first," Tocho said.

The man had turned to walk away when Oakley stopped him. "Wait. What's your name? You know mine already." She knew his name, but she wanted him to tell her. Anything she could do to build a good rapport with him could make it more difficult for Tocho to hurt her.

His head slowly turned to her. "Tocho."

CHAPTER ELEVEN

Chase entered his motel room, kicked off his boots, and threw a shot of whiskey down his throat. He poured another one, staring out the window at the neon sign of the motel, which shimmered in the dark. He withdrew his phone, found the contact he needed, and stared at it with trepidation. He'd been dreading this all day. The contact's name read *MY EX Kira*. As if he needed to be reminded of their status.

How am I going to tell her? He'd gone back and forth, trying to arrange the correct words, but there weren't any. He just had to leap into the cold lake and flail about like a drowning man and pray that he didn't sink by the end of the call.

He touched the call button. *Oh shit. It's ringing.*

She picked up on the third. "Hello?"

"Hi, Kira."

"Hey, Chase. Did you guys finally make it? How is Oakley doing? She hasn't returned any of my texts."

Chase didn't answer. He couldn't.

"Chase, is she okay?"

"That's the thing. She's okay, but something happened."

Kira gasped halfway through his sentence. "What do you mean, she's okay? Where is she? Let me talk to her."

"I can't. She's been taken."

"Taken?"

Chase could swear he heard a ton of wheels spinning in her head. The surreal, strangling moment when you heard the dreaded news of a missing daughter—or any loved one—was like standing in the middle of a tornado, watching a million images blur past you but unable to grab any of them. As hard as it was, he told her everything.

"What will they do to her?" Kira's voice cracked, and Chase could hear that she was on the verge of losing it. Her mind must have been imagining all the worst, just like his was.

"They're not going to harm her. In any way. They need her." He couldn't bring himself to tell her why.

Sniffles and whimpers came across the phone.

"What for?"

"To bargain with us," he lied. "We have three days to get her back before we think they'll do anything."

"I shouldn't have let her go. She didn't want to, you know." Kira's words stabbed his heart. "I convinced her. I'm always trying to keep her relationship with you, despite what you might think."

"What's that supposed to mean—despite what I might think?"

"You act like I'm the enemy and am trying to keep her from you."

I'm not the one who moved her three states away, he thought but bit his lip. "I don't think that. It's just been difficult to see her in the past couple of years. I was used to seeing her every week until you moved, and it's been a hard adjustment for me."

"It's been hard on me too. And her. But you need to call her."

"I do call her," he said. She was right, dammit, but he didn't want to admit that.

"Call her more, then."

"I know."

"I'm coming out there," she said.

"If you do, stay in town. Don't try going after us. The media will hound you. Only talk to reputable ones, and get our story out to the world. The more attention, the better our odds that someone will find her."

"I can do that."

"You've got this, Kira. Stay strong."

"Chase, just promise me you'll get her back."

"I will bring her back."

She needed the promise, and if he failed, that would mean he was dead. Death was the only thing that would stop him.

They ended the call amicably. They were parents first, and now they were partners who could work toward the same goal. He set the phone down, took in a deep breath, and chased it with another shot of whisky. He promised himself not to get wasted. He needed his wits about him at all times. He just wanted to drink to numb his nerves and silence his mind enough to get some sleep.

CHAPTER TWELVE

Chase arrived at the ranch early, and the morning chill bit into him. The sun outlined the mountain ridge with fire, and the world around Chase was gaining light. Stone guided a horse toward him and introduced him as Roman, a mahogany Rocky Mountain horse with a sandy-blond mane. When the sun caught his body just right, it shimmered red.

"Good morning, Roman. You're going to help me find my daughter, aren't ya?" Chase stroked his neck.

Roman's left eye looked at him, and he gave a snort.

"You know these mountains? I'm counting on you."

Stone took the reins from Chase and led Roman into the horse trailer with the rest of them. "That was the last one. We're ready to go if you are."

"I was ready yesterday," Chase said.

"We'll drive to the area where you last saw them, and we'll take horses from there."

"Are you sure we can catch up with them in time? We're so far behind."

"They're not on horseback, and they left their vehicles behind. That gives us some advantage."

Chase nodded and hopped into Miles's truck. Benson and Ike sat in the back, and Kenny, being the smallest, squeezed between them. Stone and a couple of other ranch hands, Jon and Dillon, took their places in Stone's truck—which hauled the trailer—and drove out of the ranch. Miles followed.

"Those two guys with Stone volunteered to go with us," Miles said.

"The more, the better," Chase said.

"They know these mountains well. How about you, Ken? You said you're pretty familiar with where we're going."

"Oh yeah. I grew up here. I do a lot of camping and fishing in Kolob, and during the winter I snowboard at Brian Head. I like to hike, too, and there are some great trails."

"Good, 'cause we're fish out of water here."

As they drove through the canyon along the path that Chase had followed the previous day, he was viewing it through a different lens. The vehicle chase seemed like days ago yet also not. He shivered as they passed his truck, which still sat tilted in the creek, and his stomach dropped when they reached the dead end where he had passed out. He had been so close. *Will we be able to catch up and save Oakley in time?* He pushed those thoughts away as best he could. *I will bring her back*, he kept telling himself.

Within fifteen minutes, they were on their horses and riding on a trail through trees. They were making suitable time. The trail took an upturn, and they climbed higher. The scent of pines was strong, and the air was heavy with morning dew. The sun had popped its head above the horizon and spread its rays across the valley, which was now below them. They reached the top of the ridge, and the canyon opened up to a breathtaking view. A wide span of trees lay below them, intermixed with boulders and rock, the sun glinting off the granite. The canyon walls were fire red and orange with accents of greenery and shades of brown. It was a spectacular view of nature, but it held the secret of a dark tragedy. He wondered what other murky secrets lay hidden within these mountains.

His phone vibrated with a new text. It was Kira. She had texted him several times through the night.

Any news?

He texted a response. *Not yet. We just headed out and are on their trail now. We see their tracks.*

Tracks? Do you see hers?

I do. There are shoeprints that fit her size.

The small size they saw wouldn't fit any of those giant barbarians who'd taken her.

Keep me updated, please. Anything at all.

I will. I'll probably lose signal. Just know that, he texted.

Thank you.

He stuffed his phone back into his pocket and took a swig of water. Then he clicked his teeth and gave a gentle heel kick to start his horse. The sun kept rising and radiating heat. An occasional breeze was the only reprieve from the hot temperature. About two hours in, their trail led them down a green hillside and into a forest of pines at the valley floor.

Miles rode alongside Chase. "So, how did Kira take it?"

"About like you'd think. She's driving to Parowan now."

"I'm sorry to hear that. This divorce has been tough enough on you without adding this. Not to mention what happened in Phoenix. How are you dealing with that?"

"A day at a time. I took an innocent life. There's no getting past that," Chase said.

"It was an accident. It happens to the best of us."

Chase clenched his jaw and looked away. "My therapist keeps telling me the same thing. She's giving me some tools to help cope with it, but in all honesty, I shouldn't have taken the shot."

"That man would have killed her. Someone had to take the shot."

"It doesn't make it any easier."

Miles nodded, staying silent.

"Parents lost a daughter that day, and a child is left motherless. How do you apologize for that? They grieve every day, and I'm haunted by their images."

Out of nowhere, Chase's right hand spasmed and began trembling while he held his reins. It shook so badly his arm quaked. Miles's eyes shifted to Chase's hand.

"You okay?" he asked.

"Fine." Chase shook his arm as if he could wiggle the convulsions out of it and then cradled it against his stomach.

They rode in silence for a while, and breaking from the trees, they climbed a slight incline and descended a rocky slope. A small lake rested at the base of what Stone told them was Sugarloaf Mountain. They rested their horses and let them drink.

"So, you're doing security now?" Miles asked.

The words stung. Chase shifted in his saddle and dropped his eyes. "Yes, for the moment. I haven't decided exactly what I'll do." That part was true. He didn't have a clue. "I have a friend in the bail bonds business. I might do something with him or start my own PI firm." He didn't have any desire to bounty hunt or become a private investigator, but he felt he had to tell his friend something.

"There's some good money in both of those. I have friends who do really well as PIs. Ninety percent of it is catching cheating spouses, but it pays well, and there's no shooting involved. Rarely."

Great. Now he thinks I'm incapable of using firearms. Chase sauntered over to the rest of the group, who congregated near the horses and water.

Agent Benson took a piece of jerky out of his saddlebag and tore off a bite with his teeth. He turned to Stone. "Beautiful lake. Any fish in it?"

"I'm sure there is, but I've never fished in it."

Chase stared at the green water as a breeze rippled its surface. The area was so quiet and vast that it scared him. He wondered how he would ever find his daughter among all this. She was a needle in a haystack.

"So, where are they headed exactly?" Chase asked.

Stone hesitated as if holding back information.

"You said they plan to use my daughter... as a... something to gain power. Where do they do that?" He couldn't muster the word *sacrifice*.

"It's a place called Angel's Landing. Also known as the Temple of Aeolus. It's in Zion at the top peak of a mountain."

Miles jumped into the conversation. "Why don't we take a team to Angel's Landing and catch them there?"

"We need to track them this way. It's the only way," Stone said.

"That doesn't make any sense," Miles said.

Chase eyed Stone, who kept shifting his eyes left to right. The man was definitely hiding something, perhaps relating to what he had just said—that they wouldn't be able to find Tocho, his people, and the other world unless Stone tracked him this way. Hopefully, there wasn't something else he was hiding.

"It's better this way," Chase said. "We can catch them before they get to Angel's Landing. I don't want them to ever reach that place. Besides, if they get spooked and change courses, we can still track them."

Miles nodded. "We'll stay the course. I'm going to call and have a second team stake out Angel's Landing just in case."

"That's a great idea," Chase said.

They mounted their horses and took a path around the lake. Arriving on the other side, Stone halted, dismounted, and crouched to inspect something. Chase rode up alongside him and hopped off.

"What is it?"

Stone tugged something from a prickly bush and held it up. It was a torn piece of red cotton. Chase trotted over to Stone and snatched it out of his hand.

"This is Oakley's. It's the color of her shirt. They've been this way." Adrenaline surged through him. He stared at the cloth as if he'd just discovered gold. It was hope, and he needed that.

Stone patted him on the shoulder and shared a warm smile. "From the frayed edges, it looks like she tore it off herself and dropped it into that bush. She's helping us. We'll find her."

Twenty minutes later, the group entered a strange area alien to anything they'd been through previously. The pines had broken away to an open land of red sand with the appearance of an aftermath of a forest fire. The red desert was spotted with leafless black-and-gray trees, and very few had patches of short green needles. Their trunks were twisted, and several branches jutted out like jagged, broken teeth at the ends of tentacles. It was as if a bomb had exploded inside an octopus, leaving the creature to petrify.

"What the hell are these?" Ike asked.

"This is called Twisted Forest," Dillon, one of the ranch hands, answered. "It's a tourist spot. A lot of hikers come up here."

"Yeah, but what's up with these trees?"

"They're bristlecone pines. They are some of the oldest trees on the planet. Many of them are as much as sixteen hundred years old."

"Holy shit," Ike said.

Stone stepped down, approached a tree, and ran a hand over its trunk. "We call them wind timber. There are limited nutrients and water for these trees, and some of the tree dies off, but not all of it. They will hold on to their nutrients instead of using them up in order to live longer. Their needles don't shed. They're survivors. Despite what tries to kill them, they choose to live. You either live with the land or die from it. We respect these trees. My ancestors were given very little. They lived on what resources they had. They were killed, raped, enslaved, stolen from, and eventually removed from their lands. But we live on. We survive."

The group was silent as Stone's words sank in. Chase and Miles crossed the plain to an edge that dropped off into an open valley—a canyon of white and red sand and rock cut out of the green earth, not unlike the view of the Grand Canyon. They dismounted and stood together, taking in the view. The cliff under their feet was sheer and ran vertical to the valley below.

"I didn't mean to offend you back there. If it was something I said..." Miles rested a soft hand on Chase's shoulder.

"No, you didn't. It's just that my head is a bowl of spaghetti. And when they took my daughter, it was like someone picked up that bowl and smashed it against the wall." Chase turned to look at the massive valley surrounded by monstrous mountains. "She could be anywhere out there. She could be right below us, and I wouldn't know it."

"I know your mind is spinning right now. Just hold on to faith. We'll find her. I've got a team headed for the rendezvous spot, I've got surveillance in the sky, and the media is all over this. They're not getting away. Oakley is lucky to have you as a dad. If I were her, I'd want you to be the one to rescue me. You were always good at that. You're a natural leader and the best sniper I've ever been with. Hell, I wish I had you up in Salt Lake with me."

"Thanks, Miles."

"Now, come on. Let's go find your daughter."

An hour later, Chase recognized the heavy silence that crept under his skin with an unnerving sensation. They had come across several critters on their trek, such as rabbits, squirrels, coyotes, mountain goats, and hundreds of species of birds. But in the last thirty minutes or so, he hadn't seen or heard any animals. During a hike, it was unusual not to at least see a raven or a squirrel darting across the path.

Chase turned to Dillon, who was closest to him. "Do you hear that?"

"Hear what?"

"Exactly."

Dillon scrunched his face. "I don't get it."

"Ever since we started this journey, I've been hearing crickets and birds chirping. Now there's nothing. I don't even see a chipmunk."

"We're not on a nature hike. I don't know how many times I've gone through Yellowstone and not seen any animals."

"That's not what I'm saying."

Kenny twisted in his saddle to join the conversation. "What are you getting at?"

"I get a really strange feeling—like we're being watched, and whatever is spying on us has scared away all the animals." Chase scanned the area with wary eyes.

Kenny's mouth hung open, and the blood drained from his face.

"It ain't nothin.'" Dillon shrugged. "I've been through here a hundred times. Sometimes it's just quiet."

"I feel it too." Kenny shivered. "It's creepy."

"He's just getting into your head," Dillon said.

"I'm being aware," Chase countered.

Dillon cocked his head at Chase. "You thinkin' ambush?"

"Maybe."

"I think it's something else. There's not even a breeze. It's as if everything is completely still—frozen. Like all time has stopped." Kenny shivered again.

Dillon shook his head.

Stone halted, and so did the rest of them. He closed his eyes and seemed to meditate for a couple of minutes before dismounting. He crouched and inspected the ground and surrounding brush then

stood up with his hands on his hips and ran his eyes over the land before them.

"What is it?" Miles approached.

"I don't see their tracks. I haven't for a while now. They disappeared about an hour ago. I thought we'd pick it up at some point,
but now I'm not so sure."

Chase cringed, and his stomach tied itself up in knots. "Why
didn't we stop back where you lost them?"

Stone didn't answer for a moment. Then he turned to Chase. "At
the point where I lost their tracks, there was nowhere else they could
have gone. There were footprints and drag marks and then nothing.
It was as if they disappeared."

"Let's spread out and look," Dillon said. "I've done my fair share
of tracking. I can find them."

"Good idea." Kenny nodded as he dismounted.

Instead of leading the group, Stone headed away from them.
Chase followed. Stone's demeanor was indifferent—almost absent
from the present—and Chase wondered where his mind had gone.
Stone stuck his arms out to his sides, opening his fingers as if to feel
the air. Perhaps the answers were in the wind.

He stopped and turned to Chase. "Wait here. I'm going on a
search. I will pick up the trail."

Chase had no choice but to trust him. Stone was their guide.
Chase nodded and sauntered back to the group.

Two hours had passed. The sun began to descend in the west,
and there was still no sign of Stone. Miles was attached to his
satellite phone, giving orders and receiving information. Kenny sat in
the dirt, flipping small rocks to pass the time, while Ike and Benson
gossiped about work-related issues. Jon and Dillon were playing a

game with their knives. They stood across from each other, and on each turn, one person would throw their knife at the ground to the side of their opponent's foot. If it stuck in the ground, that person would have to stretch their foot to that spot and retrieve the knife. They would continue until one person couldn't stretch their legs far enough before losing balance.

They had spent a lot of time searching for signs or clues as to where the captors had gone, but they had come up empty. A cloud drifted over the sun, shading them for a moment.

"Where do you think he went?" Kenny asked Chase.

"I don't know. I'm losing my patience, though. I think we should head back to where we lost their tracks."

"Stone will find them. He's good at it. He won't let us down."

"I hope so. We can't sit and wait here any longer." Chase could only imagine what Stone was doing to find the tracks. Maybe the man had some tricks up his sleeve or a strong gut instinct he was following.

A few minutes later, Chase caught sight of Stone in the distance. A cloud of dirt followed him as he jogged back to the group. Chase trotted to meet him. Stone was out of breath. He stopped, and Chase fed him some water from his canteen.

After wiping the wetness from his lips, Stone said, "I found their trail. I picked it up that way." He pointed to the southwest.

"Are you sure it's theirs?"

"Positive. Your daughter has distinctive tennis shoes."

Relief washed over Chase as they quickly mounted their horses and followed Stone. It took another hour before they reached a dirt trail that carved its way through rabbit brush, and Chase saw the footprints and marks similar to the ones they had been following. The trail bent around a large crop of boulders and descended into a valley of trees. When they broke into a clearing, they came to a stop. A chill ran through Chase's body.

A man-made arch built out of tree branches sat over their trail, like a giant mouth ready to swallow them whole. Lined along the shafts—from the ground up—were a number of human skulls. Most of them were bleached white, but a handful were still in decomposition and covered with a dark, dingy yellowish color. In the center of the arch—hanging over the trail—hung the skull of an elk. Sticking out of each of its temples was a giant rack of antlers. Eagle and hawk feathers tied to straps of leather adorned the skulls, along with beads and metal trinkets.

"What the hell is that?" Miles grumbled.

"I don't know," Stone said. "But it is something they made. The elk is a deity of sorts. It represents the god he always described."

"This is Tocho's? Are we close?" Chase asked.

Stone shook his head. "No. But I fear that this is where they mark the entrance to their territory."

"So if we go through it, are we desecrating an ancient burial ground or something, like in that movie *Jeremiah Johnson*? Did you ever see that?" Kenny's voice shook.

No one answered him.

"I count fifteen skulls. All human except for that beastly one." Miles pointed at it with a nod of his head.

"Any of them a child's skull?" Ike asked.

Miles shot him a stern look as if to say, "Zip it."

It was too late. Chase felt dizzy, and his stomach wanted to vomit. He thought of Tenley. *Is one of those skulls hers?*

"You think they killed all these folks?" Kenny asked Stone.

Stone looked at him but didn't answer.

"That's a hell of a lot more than three missing people," Kenny said.

"Sick fucking bastards." Jon spat tobacco that splattered on a rock.

"That's the reason we don't hear any animals," Chase said, staring at the grisly display.

"I wanna get the hell out of here," Kenny said.

"Come. They've gone this way." Stone gave his horse a gentle kick, and his steed led him through the gate.

Chase and Kenny were the last to go through. "I don't like this," Kenny said.

"Me either. But my daughter went this way. If you and I are this scared, imagine how terrified she is. And she's all alone."

Once the posse crossed through the archway, a strong gust of wind blew against their backs, and the metal trinkets chimed. The chimes continued to ring as if signaling the group's trespassing, and the sound went on for several minutes until the gate was a tiny dot behind them.

The wind died down to nothing again. The tips of the scrub brush lining the trail were blackened, and some grew as tall as a man. Chase stared at one bush that stood like a cactus—or a man. It leaned forward with two lengths of branches shaped like arms. He was reminded of Dorothy walking through the forest in *The Wizard of Oz* and how those trees were shaped like angry, scary men.

The sun hid behind clouds, dimming the world around them ominously. Trees spotted the area, but like the shrubs, they were blackened, leafless, and dead. Many of their trunks and arms were twisted and appeared humanlike but in severe agony.

Of course they would be, Chase thought. *I would be if something twisted me like that.*

They turned a corner and headed past a cluster of giant boulders, which were all nearly covered with the same spotty blackness, as though Jon had been sitting above them, showering them with spits of his black tobacco for days. Chase led his horse alongside one of them to inspect the dark growth and touched it. It was fuzzy and thick like felt matting.

"There's something on the road ahead," Kenny said.

"It's a body," Miles said.

Chase snapped his head around. He trotted his horse alongside Miles, who had already withdrawn his binoculars and was looking through them. He handed them to Chase.

"It's a man. He's got an arrow sticking out of him. He appears to be dead," Miles said.

The men quickly armed themselves and warily trotted their horses to the man. Chase scanned the trees and high grounds for any possible sniper. The dead man was lying face down in the dirt with the top of his scalp torn away. The red gore beneath it—half-covered with dirt that had blown in—faced them like a sore eye. Tufts of his hair blew with a breeze. The shaft of an arrow stood erect from between his shoulders. The dead man, the silence, and the weird shrubs and trees added to the cloud of dread in the air.

Miles bent down to inspect him. "He looks like just a regular hiker."

"There's two more." Kenny pointed at Stone, who was heading farther down the trail toward a couple of clothed lumps.

"Good hell." Jon spat more tobacco. "What did we get ourselves into?"

It took about thirty minutes to drag the bodies off the route and onto an opening, where the seven of them laid the deceased together. The men circled the bodies, staring at them. The grisly sight of corpses roiled Chase's stomach. The lips were peeled back from one of the men as if he were still screaming, and dirt stuck to the blood that smeared his body. His eyes were frozen in a stare, and when Kenny tried to close them, they shot back open like shades.

Kenny shrieked and jumped back. "Why won't they stay closed?"

"Rigor mortis has set in," Miles said.

"But in the movies, they—"

"The movies are wrong."

"Do we bury them?" Dillon asked.

"We're losing daylight. I hate to say it, but we are falling behind. We need to leave them," Chase said.

"That don't seem right," Dillon said.

"I know. None of this is right. We can circle back once we have my daughter and bury them then. The authorities will come back and bring them home to their families."

"By then, the coyotes will have eaten most of them, and the buzzards will snack on the rest."

"I think I'm going to be sick." Kenny clutched his stomach.

"Do it over there." Miles pointed away.

"Jon and I will stay back. We'll build a shallow grave and cover it with rocks. At least enough to keep animals away. We can catch up. It won't take us long."

Chase nodded. It was the right thing to do.

CHAPTER THIRTEEN

Crouching on a ledge, Tocho peered down into the valley. He sniffed the air as if he could smell danger. He saw a cloud of dust rise in the distance. As he expected, they were being followed. He didn't know how many, but from the dust they kicked up, it couldn't be more than a handful of men.

Shilah approached. "We're being followed."

Tocho slowly turned to him with a scowl.

"They're on horses," Shilah pointed out.

"They have passed the barrier into our territory." Tocho's tone was low, with a tinge of anger.

"I thought it was protected. The barrier should hide us."

"It did until yesterday. Those three men found the entrance. They passed through the gate, and now it is tainted. The barrier is broken and can now be seen by anyone."

"Shit." Shilah rubbed his upper lip. "Call upon the gods. They should curse them. Make them lose their way."

"No. We must do it ourselves." Tocho turned and marched back to the group. "Tate!" he called, and his right-hand man ran to greet him.

Oakley was at the opposite end of the troop, and she popped her head up.

Tocho disregarded her curious eyes and spoke to Tate. "Take two men with you. We have followers. Make them pay for their transgressions. They killed one of ours. Put the fear of the snake into them. I want them to shake in their boots and piss down their pants with the sheer terror of the power we possess."

Oakley's mind raced through possible scenarios as horror ran shivers through her body. They had commenced their trek, and she was following Tocho up a hill with the rest of the men at her back when she contemplated escape. She had to warn her dad. Tocho had ordered three men to attack them. They were going to kill him.

She took in her surroundings. A red crag towered over them on her right, but on her left was a treacherous slope dotted with scrub oak. She didn't have time to think. On instinct, she jumped.

Her feet hit dirt, and gravity pushed her forward so fast she was going to fall if she didn't catch herself. She sped up, her arms careening to steady her balance, but it wasn't enough. She toppled head over heels and rolled for twenty feet before her back slammed into the trunk of a tree. Air escaped her lungs, and she took a second to regain her wits.

Two men chased down the hill after her. Oakley jumped to her feet and ran. Pumping her legs like pistons, she quickly navigated her course, jumping over rocks and small shrubs. She worried if the men were gaining, but she didn't look back for fear of losing focus.

The ground sloped ahead, and she leaped onto it without realizing that it was steeper than the last one. She leaned back and put her right foot out as if sliding into home base and skidded through loose gravel for several feet until the ground leveled out.

Where am I heading? I don't even know where I'm at. Am I moving in the right direction to find Dad? She didn't think so. She was simply going downward from where she had started.

She saw a rocky trail on her left that she believed was heading the right way, and she took it. She steered around trees and a couple of big boulders and then stopped to catch her breath. Her lungs were on fire, and with hands on her knees, she bent over to suck in more air. She straightened herself and twisted to look behind her. The two chasers were stumbling down the gravel slope.

Oakley tore off like a gunshot and increased her speed in hopes of distancing herself from them. She couldn't outrun them forever. They would eventually close the gap. If she ran far enough to get out of sight, then she could find a good spot to hide and hold out until the bad men had moved on.

Why do I matter to them, anyway? She couldn't understand it.

She ran for another thousand feet until her body started to give out from exhaustion. Despite her wishes, she was slowing down. She turned a corner around a rocky hill and froze. She didn't know if it was the growl she heard first or the sight of the beast that stopped her, but she nearly lost control of her bladder. Her heart leaped into her throat, catching the scream she wanted to release.

Not ten feet away stood an enormous animal. It had been feeding on what looked like a dead deer when Oakley had startled it. The creature's coat was golden but with tinges of black, and it appeared to be a mountain lion, but based on Oakley's knowledge, it was three times the size of any cougar she had seen in magazines or movies. It was more like a Bengal tiger disguised as a mountain lion.

The lion jerked away from its meal at Oakley's approach. The animal growled at her with a blood-smeared face. Its eyes were wild and fierce, and it raised a clawed paw twice the size of her hand. The beast tensed as if ready to pounce on her.

A shadow clouded her, a hand clasped over her mouth, and an arm wrapped around her waist.

"Shhh," the male voice said.

She let out the breath she was holding inside and tried to calm herself.

He removed his hand from her mouth and held it out toward the creature. "Chira," he called, and to Oakley's amazement, the lion thing closed its mouth and lowered its head, locking eyes with the man. "She is not yours. Go back to your dinner."

The animal grunted as if in protest but complied anyway.

Her body was convulsing uncontrollably, and she felt ill enough to vomit. Her legs gave out, and she collapsed in the man's arms. She lifted her head and saw that it was Tocho.

Oakley fell in and out of consciousness as Tocho lifted her in his arms and carried her back up the hill. She closed her eyes, and after a while she felt ground beneath her as he laid her down. Another man leaned over her and splashed water onto her face until her eyes flew open wide.

Tocho then lifted her head and brought a canteen to her lips. She gulped water until her stomach hurt. Tocho ran a wet cloth across her forehead.

"Do you have the run out of you now?" he asked.

Oakley gave him a quizzical look.

"Are you going to run again?"

"Are you going to kill my dad?"

He didn't answer. Surrendering after a minute, she shook her head. He gave her a couple more minutes to regain her strength, and then they continued their journey. Her thoughts drifted back to her father. She wished she could have warned him and wondered if this was her curse for being so mean to him. She'd barely spoken three words to him, and now she wished she could run into his arms and get the hell away from these people.

She thought of the short conversations they'd had, turning over every word she'd said in hopes she could somehow change them. But she didn't know how to talk to her dad anymore. They'd lost something in the past couple of years, but it had started even before that.

What is so wrong with him? She knew he was a victim of her mom's choice to move away. He'd been very much against it. And visiting him in his apartment in Phoenix was... well, sad. It had been bare of furniture, and the fridge and cabinets were just as empty. He was suddenly a different dad, and it was an odd adjustment.

But as altered as he had been during that first visit, it didn't come close to the change she'd seen when she met him at the mall. His beard and hair carried streaks of gray, and crow's feet stretched out from his eyes. He appeared to have aged ten years instead of two. But that wasn't the worst of it. His eyes were somber and lost. It was as if he'd dropped something and couldn't find it but had continued looking.

Her thighs burned as she trekked up the incline, and her right foot slipped on a large rock. She caught herself, and the rock tumbled away.

"Keep up," Tocho griped without turning around.

Fuck you. Her dad would scold her for using that word. She pictured him jumping out from behind a tree—stabbing his finger at her—and saying, "That's not the language of a young lady." She couldn't help but chuckle at the thought. She would welcome that response from him now.

She wondered if her dad had found the piece of shirt she had torn off and dropped into the bush. None of her captors seemed to notice. But she also got the feeling that they didn't care. She stomped every so often to leave a good foot impression, and sometimes she'd kick dirt or step on a dry branch sticking out, breaking it off. She did whatever she could to leave a trail, and none of them batted an eye. It was unnerving. *What do they know that I don't? What are they hiding that makes them not worried about being tracked?*

They had to know that they were now the subject of big news. Even worldwide attention. There would be hundreds of people searching—helicopters, vehicles, and people on foot. She'd seen it dozens of times when a child went missing. Unfortunately, she hadn't noticed any planes, helicopters, or people. The trek had been silent but for the occasional wind that whistled through the trees.

They reached the top of a ridge, and she couldn't believe her eyes. In the valley below—tucked against a mountain—was a village with twenty or more huts. Smoke rose from fires, and people bustled about. She was too far to distinguish more than just shapes, but as they neared, she observed that the majority of them were women and children. The tepees were not made of buffalo hide or deer hide, like she'd seen in movies, but the frames were made of willow and then covered with grasses and sagebrush. They were shaped like domes instead of triangles.

Most of the women and children were garbed in deer hide and moccasins and adorned with beads and feathers. Some wore jeans and a leather jerkin or a regular shirt and deer-hide pants. Oakley wondered if it was a requirement to dress in traditional tribal clothes, at least partially. As she was led through the village, most of the women made eye contact with her but then quickly averted their gazes. A small boy—two or three years old—stood next to a woman weaving a basket. He stared at Oakley for a long time.

"Chenoa!" Tocho called out, and a woman in her late twenties turned and jogged to meet him. "Take her and feed her. She will stay with you until it's time."

Until it's time for what?

"After you have given her food, come see me."

Chenoa nodded and turned back to Oakley. The woman studied Oakley without expression then motioned for her to follow her. Chenoa moved fast, and Oakley had to pick up her pace. As they neared one of the huts, a young girl about Oakley's age, with long black hair and brown skin, knelt next to a firepit, stuffing dry grass beneath a pile of sticks, preparing to build a fire. She locked eyes with Oakley, and her jaw dropped. Before following Chenoa into the hut, Oakley thought she saw tears in her eyes.

It was dark inside, and Chenoa motioned toward a pile of blankets. "Sit here. I will get you some food and water."

"Thank you." Oakley plopped down. "My name is—"

Chenoa disregarded her and swiftly exited the tent.

"Nice to meet you too," Oakley grumbled.

CHAPTER FOURTEEN
Tocho

Sunlight illuminated the dark, smoky interior of Tocho's hut as Chenoa opened the door. Darkness fell back into place as the door closed behind her. Chenoa's eyes shifted to Tate, who was sitting in front of Tocho, and Tate returned her glance. The chief took a toke from his pipe and offered it to Chenoa. She shook her head and sat down.

Tocho sat with his legs crossed and rested his elbows on his knees. He looked from Chenoa to Tate with a devilish smirk. "It is no secret that you two have not been able to make a child. Is this correct?"

Tate nodded emphatically. "We have tried several times. We haven't stopped. She got pregnant once, but we lost the baby in a miscarriage."

Chenoa kept her gaze down.

"This makes you sad?" Tocho asked her.

"Yes," she said, nodding. "We want to start a family. So many of my friends have kids running around, and I want that for us too. But for some reason, I cannot have a child. Sometimes it's not meant to be." She gave Tate a firm look, and he returned it. "But our love is strong, and I can be a second mother to the children of the tribe. That makes me happy."

"But you desire a child of your own. It is the purpose of every woman to bring life into this world. For our people to have a future and continue to grow strong, we must fortify this tribe with children. Is that not so?"

Tobacco smoke—not having much escape but the small opening in the ceiling—circled about the room and thickened the air. Chenoa let out a cough.

"What would you have us do? We can't have children. I mean, we'll keep trying." Tate gave a pleading shrug.

Tocho eyeballed Tate. "Clearly, the gods have chosen for your seed not to go on. You have done something to anger them. Your lineage ends with you."

Tate's eyes upturned in pain, and Tocho regarded Chenoa. "But you are fertile. You will stop being fertile in a few years. I have seen this. The gods have spoken to me in a dream."

Tate's eyes dropped, and he fiddled with his fingers nervously.

"You are to be my wife," Tocho said.

Tate's eyes shot up, and Chenoa placed a hand against her chest as if to catch her breath. "But you already have a wife. You're married to Jaci." Chenoa's brows wrinkled.

"I am to take a second wife. Jaci's faith in the gods and in her chief are strong, and so must yours be."

"I am married to Tate." Chenoa's tone was resolute, and she sat up straight with pride.

"I will find other uses for Tate, but the gods have stricken him, and he is useless as a father. I do not wish to break up your love for each other. We are all one tribe, one people, one love. We three must hold strong and do this for our tribe."

Chenoa pursed her lips and balled her hands into fists.

"It is not my will," Tocho continued. "But thine will be done. You do not agree with this? You do not love your chief? You do not wish to be my wife?"

Chenoa's body tensed, and Tate slid next to her and placed an arm over her shoulders. "Chenoa is my wife." Tate stabbed him with a look.

Tocho glared without a word for several seconds. "To go against the gods is to curse this tribe. You do know what happens to those who bring a curse."

"When is this to happen?" Tate asked.

"Not now. After the blood moon. I need Chenoa to stay with the Cherokee girl and prepare her, and I need you to stop the men who follow us. Leave now, and meet up with Delsin and Shilah."

Chenoa closed her eyes, took a deep breath, and reopened them. "I will be your wife."

Tate shot her a look.

A grin pulled across Tocho's face. "You are the dove and a daughter of the gods. I knew you would see the truth in this. Tate, you are my friend and a good warrior. Think on these things, and you, too, will see that this is the way. Dig deep into your heart and find out why the gods have lost their trust in you. Ask them for forgiveness, and I will help you."

Tate nodded, but his body language said the opposite of submission.

CHAPTER FIFTEEN

A cold chill ran through Chase, and his head spun. He looked around as if he could discover the source of the disruptive feeling of dread and darkness. The air was charged with it, and he wondered if anyone else felt it.

The group had stopped to make camp for the night as the sunlight was nearly gone. Chase figured they had another thirty minutes before it went completely dark, but all the tents were up, and Stone was building a fire. Jon and Dillon were trotting into camp after burying the bodies on the trail.

Chase crossed the camp to Miles, who stood next to a crop of boulders and was talking on his satellite phone. He finished his call as Chase approached.

"Any word?" Chase asked.

Miles shook his head.

"Did they get some copters over the area?"

"Yes. Two of them, in fact, and a number of drones. We've spread the word to Brian Head and all of the visitors' spots and campgrounds, and we have hundreds of volunteers searching for them, but there's not been one sighting."

"How can that be?" Chase saw his own doubt and fear in Miles's eyes. "I haven't seen any helicopters, planes, cars, trucks, or ATVs. I haven't heard any either. And not one soul is in sight anywhere. Why is that?"

"I don't know. I can't explain it. I talked to the pilot myself. He covered this area right above us several times, yet he hasn't spotted us. And like you, I haven't seen or heard anything."

"It doesn't make any sense. Something's not right," Chase said.

"What are you getting at?"

"I don't know. I get an unsettled feeling. The air is heavy with it. As if we're constantly being watched and…"

"What?"

"And something unseen is with us. Always. It's not like anything I've ever felt before."

Miles paused and then said, "What you're feeling is normal. I'm anxious to find her too. And we will."

"It's not anxiety."

"What, then? You're not buying into the supernatural story that old man was selling us, are you?"

Chase shrugged, turning his eyes to Stone, who sat next to the fire about thirty feet away, watching them. Chase felt a chill again. "I've got to talk to Stone. He knows something we don't."

"Want me to go with you?" Miles asked.

"No."

As Chase approached Stone, Kenny stepped to the fire, holding a pot. He crouched and found a section of hot coals to place the pot on. "My mom made some stew and gave me a bunch before we left." Kenny spread a cheesy grin.

Stone glanced inside the pot. "That looks delicious."

"That's real thoughtful of her." Chase stopped short of Stone.

Jon approached. "How's Roman treating you?"

"Roman's a fine horse," Chase said. "No problems at all. It's been so long since I've ridden—I thought he might be jumpy, but he's great."

"Roman is one of my best. I delivered him and have trained him since he was a colt."

The rest of the group ambled to the fire and started up small conversations. Chase chose to hold off speaking with Stone until he had a moment alone. It didn't take long for the stew to warm up, and

Jon spooned portions into each of their mess kit bowls. Stone handed out pieces of bread, which worked great for dipping into the stew. Chase didn't think he was hungry until he took his first bite and then found himself devouring his portion and asking for more.

Kenny struck up conversations with everyone as if he had a constant need to learn about each person. It didn't seem to come out of insecurity but genuine interest. Chase found it an endearing quality.

Kenny turned to Benson. "So, where are you from?"

"I'm out of Salt Lake, but I grew up in Georgia."

"I thought I caught a hint of an accent. What part of Georgia?"

"Right in the heart of Atlanta. My dad changed careers and moved us to Utah when I was fifteen."

"You like it out here?"

"Yeah. Nice people. It didn't take long to fall in love with the mountains. I finally tried skiing a couple of years ago."

Kenny perked up. "Really? You like skiing?"

"I'm not good at it, but I got the bug."

"Do you snowboard?"

"No." Benson shook his head emphatically. "I have two feet that need two skis."

"I'll have to take you sometime. It's not hard to pick up, but it is the shit."

Benson nodded and smiled.

"You like the FBI?" Kenny asked.

"Yes. It wasn't my first choice. I was going into criminal law. Thought I'd be a lawyer. But life has a funny way of turning directions."

"I get that."

"What about you?" Benson inquired.

"Law is in my blood. I always knew I'd be a cop. Like my dad."

"Have you ever thought about joining the FBI?"

"I have from time to time. But there's just somethin' about this place that keeps me here. I don't know if I can wear a suit every day."

Benson chuckled.

Two hours later, most of the men had retired to their tents. Jon checked on the horses, and Ike stepped away to have a smoke. Chase found himself alone with Stone next to the fire. It crackled, popped, and flickered its fiery glow across Stone's face.

"What is it with this place?" Chase asked, and Stone turned to him, squinting. "Something isn't right. I can feel it."

"What is it that you feel?"

"I can't explain it other than it creeps under my skin. Like when you're walking through a haunted house or you just saw a ghost."

"Have you seen a ghost?"

Chase paused. "One time I did. Or at least, I think I did. I was sixteen. A friend of mine coaxed me and some others to go to this cemetery. It was said to be frequented by ghosts. It was a tiny, re-mote graveyard tucked away in the hills, and we had to hike to it. The cemetery only held ten or fifteen graves, bordered by a small wrought iron fence. It was next to the burnt remnants of a house. A fami-ly who had been killed in a house fire were buried there. The house dates back to the eighteen hundreds. The father of the family went mad, tied up his family, and burned them alive in their home. And now they haunt the cemetery."

"Did you see the ghosts?"

"I saw something." Chase shrugged. "Shadows maybe, crossing back and forth among the trees. But the air was electrified with... I hate to say it because it sounds corny, but it felt evil. The atmosphere was thick—you know, smothering. And I feel it now. Ever since we crossed that lake. As if we walked into somewhere else."

Stone held a mug of coffee and took a sip.

"Your grandpa told us some wild tales about who Tocho is and what he does. It's too crazy to expect any of us to believe them. I can't buy into them either."

"You mean you don't want to," Stone stated.

Chase smiled nervously and shook his head. "Ghosts, demons, and skin-walkers—I mean, come on. It's like Miles told me. I'm in so much distress because of my daughter that my mind is buying into the crazy. I don't even know why I brought this up." Chase picked up a stick and fidgeted with it before snapping it in two and tossing the pieces into the fire. "Do you believe in it?"

Stone sucked in air and let it out. "I've been brought up to believe in the ways of our ancestors. We believe in God, whether He's the traditional God that most people believe in or something else. We believe that all objects have a life and a soul. The wind, the sun, the earth, rocks, trees, and so on. I believe there is good and bad in all those things. And where there is good, it is always balanced with the bad. There is evil in man, just as there is good in man."

"But what about the supernatural—other worlds?" Chase urged.

"If there is a God and you believe in God, is that not believing in the supernatural?"

"And if there is a God then there's the devil too?"

"It may not be the devil, and I'm not sure that I believe in all of it. But I am open to it. We live in this world. It is unlikely that this is the only world. We are vain to think it would be. My grandpa talked about other worlds, other gods, other species. When I ran with Tocho as a young teen, Tocho talked about it constantly. He was obsessed with it. He was as equally obsessed with bringing back the old ways."

"Tell me more about Tocho. I need to know everything."

CHAPTER SIXTEEN

Stone took another sip and nodded. "He lost his mother at three, I think, and his father died when he was seven or eight, but Tocho was not so young that his father didn't instill all of his beliefs and goals in him. The system bounced him from foster home to foster home, and from what he told me, many of them were abusive. Most of them were white families, and they confirmed the hate he'd been told your race held for people like him. I knew him all my life, or at least since I started grade school. He was quiet and kept to himself. He always looked sad to me. I would always try talking to him, but he kept his eyes down and barely said anything in return.

"This changed in the fourth grade. There were a couple of bullies. They were always taunting me on the playground. One of the kids bragged about his father and how he would go out on the weekends—once a month—to the reservation and roll an Indian."

"Roll an Indian?" Chase asked.

"Beat him up and take his money. They'd wait until our people got paid their monthly government checks, watch for the ones who were getting drunk, and roll one or two."

"That's awful."

Stone nodded. "These bullies continued day after day, making fun of me—and a few others like me—but they never bothered Tocho. They were scared of him. One day, Tocho came to school with a black eye. Later, I learned it was from a beating from his foster dad. I could see the change in his eyes. It was a dark rage I'd never seen before. Later, on the playground, those bullies decided that they wanted to roll an Indian like their daddies did. They were pushing me around and calling me ugly names until Rod—he's the biggest one—punched me in the gut and threw me to the ground.

"Tocho came out of nowhere and clocked Rod with a haymaker. That boy soared like a rocket before hitting the ground. Then Tocho turned and pummeled the next guy and picked him up and threw him like a sack of potatoes. Tocho was big already, but he was also fueled by years of abuse. He jumped on Rod while he was still squirming on the ground and began chipping away at his face. He wasn't just hitting Rod. He was picturing his foster dad and everyone who had abused him over the years. He took it all out on that boy.

"Rod was unconscious after the third punch. Tocho was hitting a rag doll at that point. I was afraid for Rod's life. Tocho would have killed him if no one had stopped him. It took three teachers to pull him off. As they dragged him away, he kept yelling at Rod and telling him that if he didn't leave us alone, he was going to scalp him. He meant it too. Those boys were scared. I saw the wet patch spread on one of the kids' pants. Tocho had scared the piss right out of him.

"Rod never returned. He spent a week in the hospital. Our teacher had the class create a giant card that we all signed, and she delivered it. Then I heard that he was transferred to a different school. His two friends were still at our school, but they were so embarrassed that they distanced themselves from everyone."

Stone picked up a log, threw it onto the fire, and stirred the flames with a stick. "We were solid friends after that. There were five Paiute boys and two girls in that class, and we all gravitated to Tocho. He was changed. He became the cool kid, and he'd be disruptive in class—boisterous and loud—and spend as much time in the principal's office as he did in class. We made our own little Paiute tribe on the schoolyard. Suddenly, this quiet boy couldn't stop talking, and he could really be charismatic when he wanted to. He shared his dad's stories and talked about the history of our people and what they'd gone through. His intelligence blew me away.

"He told us how the Spanish came to America and started a violent slave trade, and because Paiutes didn't adopt horses as a way of travel, we were frequently raided. The new Mexicans continued with the Spanish tradition of abuse, and so did the American white man. But it wasn't just the white man or Spaniards who transgressed against us but all men, including other tribes. Killing, raping, stealing, and warring. And disease came with the Mormon settlers, too, killing ninety percent of our people. Are you familiar with the Mountain Meadows Massacre?"

Chase shook his head.

"It happened near here. In 1857, there were rumors about these immigrants, and war hysteria was already running rampant amongst the Mormons. So the Mormon militia disguised themselves as Paiute Indians and attacked a wagon train, killing more than one hundred innocent people. They killed men and women, and what children were left, they brought back as orphans. For years, they blamed that massacre on the Paiutes. Some folks still believe that was who did it. But this is not true, and Tocho brought this story up many times. It enraged him like no other."

Chase's features fell slack, and he shook his head. "I am so sorry."

"Those were only the actions of a few. I don't look for blame. I don't feed the future on what happened in the past. I live in the present and do what I can for the future. But Tocho lives in the past—even though it wasn't his past—and he takes on that rage."

"What is his purpose—his ultimate goal?"

"Every chance he got, he talked about decimating white men and enslaving those who are left. And not just the white man but all races who are not our race."

"He's insane. I can't believe people follow him," Chase said.

"He preys on the weak and the lost. Like I said before, he is very convincing."

"We've got to find them fast, Stone."

"I vow to do my best. I am ashamed of what Tocho represents our people to be. The Paiutes are not Tocho. You save your daughter, and I will take out Tocho. My grandfather talked to me after you left our house. I made a pact to take the head off of the snake. To kill Tocho."

"Is he really powerful, like your grandpa said?"

"Yes. I have seen some of it. Evil encircles him like a dark aura. If Tocho is successful, he will bring into this world the Destroyer. My grandfather has seen this in his dreams. We will need God on our side because this thing—this creature—will destroy us all."

Stone withdrew a flask from his jacket, took a swig, and offered it to Chase, who lifted the flask to his lips and took a hefty swallow. He clenched his facial muscles as the whiskey burned his throat. He quickly took a second swig, wiped his lips, and handed it back to Stone.

"Can you answer me this?" Chase asked. "It's been bugging me from day one. You said that we have to track them through the mountains on horse even though we could have saved a lot of time by driving to many of these places. We could have driven close to that Twisted Forest place and started from there."

"I said that I'm not sure I believe in all the supernatural, but I am open to it. My grandfather believes it so much that he also made me promise to track Tocho this way. He didn't tell me why, but he said it was extremely important. It may have something to do with an alternate world that Tocho believes in. My grandfather is convinced it's somewhere in this mountain. I do not know where it is, but if it is real, we must follow his trail exactly so that we don't miss it. If we went any other way, we would not find your daughter. We could miss our window completely."

"This other world is... around us right now," Chase said. "That's why this air, this place, feels the way it does. Why we don't see any other people or aircraft. I think we entered that world the minute we crossed through the arch."

"Are you turning into a believer?"

"Let's just say that I'm like you. I'm not superstitious, but I don't want to take any chances, just in case it's real."

Stone pulled a grin.

CHAPTER SEVENTEEN

The sound of drums and chanting woke Oakley from a deep sleep. She'd drifted off after eating dinner. Chenoa had brought her a plate of chicken, bread, and vegetable mash. Oakley's stomach churned from anxiety and fear, and food was the last thing on her mind, but she forced herself to eat, knowing how important it was to keep up her strength and keep her wits about her. She didn't like the mash but made sure she ate all of the chicken for protein.

Glints of firelight found their way through the cracks in the hut she rested in. She stood and crossed to the door. She pushed it open. No one was there. She half expected a guard or at least a lock on the door, but once again, nothing was set in place to keep her from running, not even wrist restraints.

The chanting and firelight came from fifty feet away, which she guessed was the center of their village, and several figures danced and marched around the bonfire. Many of them wore headdresses and Native American garb. A rain dance—which was all she was familiar with when it came to Native dancing—came to mind, although she had a feeling this dance wasn't for rain. The rest of the village appeared empty, meaning that they had all gathered at this event. Oakley had not been invited.

This was a good chance for escape.

She glanced around. The glow from the fire only spread so far, and the world beyond was black. The full moon shone like a spotlight, and she hoped that it would help guide her. She crept to the back of the hut and traipsed past the neighboring shelters until she entered some tall brush and dove into it. Sharp branches scratched her arms and entangled themselves in her hair as she pushed her way through it in the opposite direction of the village. The ground inclined, and she carefully felt her way around large boulders and rocks, but as the light was giving out, the terrain became more difficult to navigate.

Oakley looked down at the village and now had a good overview of the non–rain dance, as she thought of it. She rotated back to the night ahead of her, blind to everything but the outline of mountains and trees. She pressed on for another fifteen minutes, nearly twisting an ankle, and stopped short of a fifteen-foot drop. She caught her breath and sat down on a rock. The boulder's points pressed sorely into her buttocks.

What am I going to do? I could kill myself trying to get away. It didn't matter. She wasn't going back. To stay captive was to give up and die. Especially when her time came. Whatever that meant. *Dad, where are you? I'd give anything to see you. Or Mom. Come down and save me. Anyone, please save me.*

"Where's the damn search party, for hell's sake?" she said aloud.

"They won't find you."

The girl's voice came out of nowhere, and Oakley jumped so badly she nearly fell off the rock. She spun toward the voice and saw a girl in the dim light of the moon. The stranger stood ten feet away. She then climbed a few rocks to get to Oakley's spot. She looked familiar. She was dressed in a tanned animal-hide tunic and jeans, had long black hair, and wore a leather headband. Oakley finally placed her. She had locked eyes with her just before she'd entered the hut earlier that day. The girl had been making a fire.

"My name's Inola."

"You're from the village. I saw you today."

"Yes. What do you think you're doing?" She pointed at the cliff Oakley had nearly stepped off.

"If you're here to take me back, I'm not going." Oakley clenched her fists and tensed her muscles.

Inola chuckled. "You're a fighter. I like that. I'm not here to take you back. But you should go back. You'll die out here."

"What do you know?"

"I know these mountains a lot better than you, and I'm not stupid enough to walk out here at night."

"You should be. Those people are insane murderers. They killed a guy back at that town, stole me and then killed three innocent hikers. God knows what they're going to do."

"I know. I'm sorry about that. But if you want to live, you have to go back."

"They're going to kill me, aren't they?"

She didn't answer.

"Look, Eloa? Is that right?"

"Inola."

"Inola. You might be right. I can't walk through this at night. I'll just sleep here and move at first light. And if you're smart, you'll come with me."

"I wish I could."

"You do?" Oakley was surprised.

"I've run away more times than I can count." Inola's pitch softened, and her mouth turned down.

"Come with me, then. You know these mountains. We can do it."

"I wish I could, but every time that I've tried, I've failed and have been caught."

"What happens to you when you get caught?" Oakley asked.

"They punish me. Every time."

"Punish? How?"

Inola's eyes watered as she recalled, and with a somber tone, she said, "Tocho whips me. I got five lashes the first time. I think I'm up to ten now, and he's made me the village slave. They work me constantly. Cooking, sewing, cleaning—you name it, I do it."

"What about your mom? Your dad?"

"They're not around anymore." Inola's bottom lip trembled. "My dad left when I was too young to remember him, and my mom was... well, she was killed."

"Oh my gosh, I'm sorry."

"Me too."

"How did she die? Who killed her? If you don't mind me asking."

"Tocho killed her. You see, my mom and I tried to escape. That was my first attempt. My mom didn't like what was going on at the village and the way Tocho was running things. There's some *reckoning* he kept talking about, and it really scared my mom. She wouldn't tell me what it was, but I have a pretty good idea."

Oakley's heart sank for her. Inola was completely alone in this world. "What was your mother's name?"

"Mai."

"That's a pretty name. I'm sorry."

Inola dropped her eyes.

"You don't have anyone who can help you? Other friends in the village?" Oakley asked.

"No. Everybody shuns me. Tocho's orders. If anyone's caught talking to me, they'll be punished."

"That's awful. This Tocho guy is eviler than I thought."

"I'm trying to help you. You can't run away. Not yet. You'll die out there."

"But my dad is out there looking for me. I know he'll come. I left a trail that even the dumbest of guys could follow."

"They won't find you here," Inola said. "We're not... exactly anywhere. Not where they or you might think."

"What do you mean we're not anywhere?"

"It's hard to explain, but trust me. They could be standing right in front of you and still not see you. Tocho is magic. He's a sorcerer. He's got ways of hiding all of us and this place."

Oakley's shoulders sank, and she let out a gasp. "But I've gotta get out of here somehow." Tears welled up, and as hard as she tried to keep them in, one escaped and ran down her cheek.

"I understand. I do. Come back with me. We'll think of something, but this isn't it."

Oakley nodded.

Inola held out her hand, and Oakley took it.

"Follow my steps exactly and don't let go."

"Okay." Oakley stood up. "Hey, Inola. When we get back to the village, you have a friend. I'll talk to you."

"I'm not sure you want to do that."

"Why? I've got nothing to lose."

Inola smiled.

CHAPTER EIGHTEEN

A sheer drop greeted Chase on both sides of the narrow mesa he inched along. The moon and stars blurred with an ominous glare, and in the distance, Native American chanting chilled his blood. A stone altar sat thirty feet ahead of him—where the mesa ended—and a green light licked at the darkness from below.

He knew he was dreaming, but it felt so real. His body was heavy and slow. His throat was dry, and his saliva didn't quench it. A figure appeared on the altar—a young female. It was Oakley.

"Oooakley!" he tried to call, but his words came out like molasses. She didn't respond. *Why isn't she moving off of the altar?* She wasn't struggling against any restraints. "Oooak..." He couldn't get the rest of her name out.

A figure rose from behind the altar and loomed over her. He was tall and broad shouldered, and his features were shrouded by darkness except for his blazing eyes. It was Tocho. He stood like a giant, and in his right hand, he gripped a tomahawk.

"Nnnooo." Chase's voice dragged. He felt the weight of a gun in his hand, and he lifted it. It was his rifle.

Tocho raised the tomahawk above his head. The chanting increased and surrounded him, yet Chase couldn't see the source of it. The green light flickered and brightened.

Chase could stop this. He had the rifle in his hands. As close as he was, he could hit his target without much aim. He lifted the rifle, but it shook. His damned arm. He tried steadying it with the support of his left, but it was no use. The barrel vibrated out of control.

The gun aimed at everything but his target. It moved around Tocho and bounced down to Oakley.

This can't be happening! Suddenly the dream was real, and his daughter's life hung in the balance with only seconds left. The blade was coming down.

Squeeze the trigger, he commanded himself, but he couldn't do it. He couldn't lock onto the target. His arm shook so fast it blurred. It had never shaken that badly before.

Trust yourself. Shoot! Shoot! The tomahawk was close to her throat. It was now or never. He fired. The gunshot cracked and split the night like an explosion.

He screamed and shot up in his sleeping bag. He hadn't seen where his bullet had hit, and he didn't want to. He was sure he'd hit Oakley accidentally. It was his curse. As he wiped sweat from his face, he heard a second gunshot. His heart leapt.

"Chase." Miles's voice was quiet but direct, and he touched Chase's arm.

Chase turned toward him. Miles was holding a flashlight. The dream slowly drifted away as he awakened to reality.

"What?" Chase asked.

"Don't move. Look." Miles pointed the light at the foot of Chase's sleeping bag.

A snake was coiling inches from him. *A rattlesnake.* Its rattle filled the tent. Chase froze.

Miles moved the light to his own feet to expose the snake crawling up the end of his bag, and there were more than the two. Another one was curled up against the entrance flap. A piece of the tent flopped open from a breeze—its edges were jagged. Someone had cut a slash in their tent and placed snakes inside.

"Do you have your gun?" Miles asked.

Chase nodded. Keeping the rest of his body still, he slowly reached with his left hand to search, hoping there wasn't another serpent waiting to strike his hand. He patted the floor. It wasn't there. *Where is it?* He kept blindly searching with his hand until it hit the stock of his rifle. Relieved, he picked it up and carefully began to strategize his next move.

Miles kept the beam on the snakes. The serpent at Chase's feet was coiled and set to attack. His feet were in range of it. The creature on Miles's bag was still crawling but not in danger of biting yet. It had to be still in order to bite, Chase believed, but it was halfway up his body. Sweat dripped down his temple as Miles kept statue still.

As slowly and carefully as he could, Chase slid his feet backward. The snake flinched, and Chase stiffened, heart hammering. He took a deep breath and continued to slide his feet away from the snake until his knees were hugging his chest. He was temporarily safe from the snake if it chose to lash out.

"Put the light on your snake," Chase said.

Using just the tips of his fingers, Miles moved the flashlight. The snake was between his legs, and it lifted its head above his belly. "Oh Lord," Miles whispered.

Chase moved the barrel of his rifle to the snake and slid it underneath its body, just below its head. He yanked the snake off of Miles and flung it against the entrance. Miles drew his knees to his chest in a flash. The coiled snake attacked and bit Chase's bag but only got fabric. Miles moved the light to the attacking snake. Chase aimed and fired. The gunshot cracked and rang in their ears like a note struck in a belfry.

The round obliterated the snake—entrails flipping through the air—and Chase dispatched the other two while Miles simultaneously illuminated the targets. The two men hopped to their feet.

Miles frantically cleared the rest of the tent with his beam of light. The entrance was clear except for smoking pieces of snake, and so was the area behind them. They each let out a sigh of relief.

Chase suddenly remembered hearing two gunshots. They hadn't been the only victims. More than likely, the others were dealing with snakes too.

They made their way out of the tent, guns in hand and clearing their path with light. A series of rapid gunshots rang out. Chase and Miles turned their heads.

Jon leapt from his tent, hollering and firing at the ground with a pistol. "Fucking hell!" Two snakes exploded.

"Jon? You okay?" Miles asked.

Jon only stared at them with wild eyes, and his mouth twisted like it was scribbled onto his face.

Stone was at Ike and Benson's tent, lifting snakes with a long stick and flinging them several feet away. Kenny was next to him with a lantern, and he crossed to where the serpents landed and blew them away with his handgun. Stone opened the tent and poked his head in. In a shuffled blur, he tossed two more snakes from the tent, and Kenny spun like an experienced gunfighter and blew them apart.

Stone disappeared into the tent. "Kenny! Lantern! Quick!"

Stone's urgency alarmed Chase, and he ran to the tent as Kenny entered while Miles stayed back and disposed of more snakes with his handgun. Chase opened the flaps to Benson's tent and tied them back. Kenny set the lantern next to Stone, who was crouched next to Benson and tearing his pants leg in half with his knife.

"Is he okay?" Chase asked, knowing it was already a dumb question.

"He is bit." Stone turned to Kenny. "Get my bag."

Kenny sprinted to fetch it. Stone leaned closer to the wound and inspected it.

"The damn thing bit me! It bit me! Oh fuck!" Benson cried.

"It bit him, like, two or three times. The snake was on him before I knew anything. Is he gonna be okay?" Ike asked.

Stone didn't answer. "Try not to panic," he warned. "I need you to sit up. Ike, prop up your pillows behind his back." He ran his eyes over Benson's arms and hands. "Take off your ring and your watch."

Benson obliged without question.

"Why?" Ike scrunched his face.

"They can act like a tourniquet. It will make it worse. Do you have a marker or a pen?"

"No," Ike said.

"In my bag." Benson gritted his teeth, and Ike quickly rummaged through the bag until he brought out a pen. He handed it to Stone.

"What time is it?" Stone asked.

Ike glanced at his watch. "Four thirty-seven."

The pen didn't work so well at writing on skin, but after several scribbles back and forth, it created a line. Stone circled the bites and wrote the time next to them.

"For the doctors?" Ike asked, and Stone nodded.

Kenny entered with Stone's bag. Chase kept out of the way. Stone rummaged through his satchel and withdrew a small jar. It contained a cream of some sort, which he smeared onto the wound.

"This will help slow the poison," Stone said.

"Do you need a bandage?" Kenny asked.

"No. Keep the wound open."

"Looks like you've done this before."

"A time or two."

"Oh fuck—it hurts. Am I gonna die?"

Stone softly patted his leg and pulled a slight smile. "You'll be okay. But we must get you off the mountain and to a hospital."

The sun was starting to stretch its arms but hadn't cleared the peaks yet, giving their world a blueish glow. Miles, Jon, and Dillon made their way to the tent.

"Everything okay?" Jon asked, and Chase filled them in.

"I got a snakebite kit," Dillon offered.

"No." Stone was firm. "I have seen those make things worse. He needs to get off the mountain and to a hospital as soon as possible."

"I'll take him down," Jon said.

Jon was the right one to go. He was a local and knew the mountains as well as anyone. He and Benson quickly prepped their horses and gear.

"Can you ride?" Ike asked.

Benson nodded. His face was pasty, and his eyes swam like he was ready to vomit.

"When you get to a clearing, call Darin Barnes," Miles told Jon. "Benson has his number in the phone. He will get a copter to you and airlift him out."

Jon nodded, and they rode out as the sun began to peek over the mountains.

CHAPTER NINETEEN

Inola's tone was somber. Her body language, the trauma in her eyes—everything about her read despair. Oakley couldn't blame her. She couldn't wrap her brain around the stories Inola had told her. Images of Tocho whipping Inola and forcing her to work and her being shunned by the tribe unsettled her.

And then there was Inola's mother. Oakley wondered how Tocho had killed her. *Was it just for trying to leave the village? Are they all forced to live here, and to leave means death?*

Oakley sat outside the hut, watching the tribe as they went about their daily duties. Several women were busy sewing clothes or making blankets, two were skinning an animal, and three were busy cutting up vegetables. Inola was around for the first hour. Alone, she cleaned up the mess left by the previous night's dancing ritual. Then she picked up a large basket and disappeared into the brush, perhaps to gather food or more wood for the fire.

Tocho and five of his men wandered the village for a while, barking at the women, until they entered a hut at the south end that was larger than the others. Oakley guessed it was Tocho's. He was carrying a long tobacco pipe. Soon after entering the hut, smoke rose from several cracks throughout the shack.

So the men get to go smoke dope while their women do all the work? Typical.

Oakley contemplated sneaking out again now that it was daylight, but Inola had warned her not to and said that it was just as dangerous as nighttime.

"They have eyes everywhere," she'd said. "And this place isn't what it seems. I can't explain it, but... we're not exactly in the same world you came from."

She was right about one thing—Oakley had no idea what that meant. As she recalled their conversations, Inola's intentions began to lose validity. *Should I trust Inola? Really?* They could be using Inola to instill fear in Oakley. It could all be a setup to keep her from running. If it was, the plan was being executed convincingly. Inola was easy to trust. She carried a sense of reliability that made it easy for Oakley to believe whatever she said.

Inola's story about how the community was shunning her rang true. All morning, not one soul spoke to her or even glanced her way. She was a ghost in this village, and that tugged at Oakley's heart.

Oakley rose to her feet and walked north toward the firepit. She wanted to test her leash and see how far she could go before someone pulled her back. *Where's the harm in that?*

Several women—if not all of them—lifted their eyes to watch her. They talked and murmured among themselves, but she couldn't make out any of their words. Two boys, about seven or eight, ran in front of her. They were playing tag, and they couldn't stop giggling.

Oakley stopped short of the firepit. Embers still burned and emitted smoke. She scanned the area. Beyond occasional glances, no one paid any attention to her. *Would anyone care if I took off?* She was afraid to give it a try, but she had to. There wasn't much time left for her, and she might not get another chance.

"Never leave with your captors," was what she had always been told. Stranger danger. She had learned these warnings at school. If you left with them, the chances were slim that you'd make it out alive. "Fight, scratch, scream, and do whatever it takes to get away."

She had to attempt it again. How could she not?

Oakley nonchalantly walked between two huts and headed for the hillside she had climbed the night before. She entered the tall brush and began her hike. She scaled the slope at an angle and continued to glance behind her. Nobody was following. The sun was out, and the sky was blue, and only two white clouds drifted by. The weather gave her a false sense of hope. She continued forward and kept herself hidden by the trees and boulders as best as she could. The ground was uneven and treacherous at times, with unstable shale rock. She slipped but caught herself, and eventually, she passed by the cliff she had almost tumbled off.

Okay, I'm already farther than I got last night.

She surveyed her surroundings again. No one was pursuing her, and Inola hadn't popped up out of nowhere. Oakley cared for Inola and didn't want to abandon her, but she had to look out for herself. Once Oakley was safe, the police would come and save Inola. They'd have to. These people had broken the law.

She hiked over more rocks, careened around a giant boulder, and twenty feet below, found a thin dirt trail that led through the brush. A path that could lead her out of this place—her heart leapt with excitement. She followed it for twenty minutes and saw that it led into a copse of trees. She could use the cover. The village was getting smaller and smaller behind her.

As she neared the trees, she lost the sun—at least some of it. She looked up to see if there were clouds causing the shade, but none were present. The sun was blazing as always, yet the air had darkened. She couldn't figure it out. She was only a few feet from the forest, which was black as night, its darkness seeming to leak out and spread. The thick canopy sealed off any light.

A cold chill shot through her, and she shivered. She rubbed her arms. The temperature had dropped twenty degrees or more. She warily entered the trees, pondering a thousand tales about haunted forests. Ten minutes in, she was so deep in the woods she couldn't see the exit at either end. She halted and surveyed the area.

The place didn't feel right. It was dead silent. Not even a breeze ruffled the leaves.

A twig snapped, and she jumped, her heart in her throat. The sound had come from her left. A rustling of leaves came from her right, and she caught a glimpse of movement. The dark object blurred because of its speed, so she couldn't make it out. The woods closed in on her. The trees seemed alive and sinister.

"Inola. Is that you?" she called, but her words were swallowed by the thick silence.

She didn't want to be that tropey victim in a hundred slasher movies, calling out to her friends when she heard a sound that was clearly the psycho stalking her. *Why did my mind have to go there?*

Footsteps crunched over leaves and twigs to her left. It sounded like more than two people. She didn't know how much farther the end of this forest was. The trees went on forever. She turned to head back the way she had come, but now it looked just as endless as the other direction. Her heart raced, and her mind clouded over, and in her confusion, she forgot which way she had come. She was lost.

As she stared at the trees ahead, a shadow grew, darkening all that was in its path. Her body spasmed from a chill, and small rocks and sticks began shuddering as if from an earthquake. The darkness formed arms and legs, and she thought she caught the flash of a white smile. A low humming emanated from the specter, and it reeked of raw sewage. Her stomach heaved, but she kept the food in. Her legs melted like butter, and everything turned blurry.

A name appeared in her thoughts as if projected from this being. Uncle Willie. The evil that expanded through the forest over-whelmed her and froze her in her spot as if concrete had hardened around her ankles.

Glancing around, she determined—with her best guess—which direction she had come from and urged her feet to move. They oblig-ed, and she quick-stepped away from the entity. The footfalls followed. She picked up her pace, and so did they. She ran, and the footsteps ran with her, bounding and leaping like lions. Or was that just her imagination?

Oakley heard low grunts, and every nerve was on high alert. The grunts turned into growls. She halted, and so did the sounds. But now there was a new noise—the low, rhythmic panting of a beast. It snarled, and she heard a slurp as if it licked its chops.

What the shit? Inola, where are you? I should have listened. What was that you said? "We're not in the real world anymore." What does that mean? Am I in another dimension?

She commenced walking, one slow step at a time. Whatever they were, their size bent branches as they moved through the trees. Their bulky forms showed between the trunks. They were black as the air around them and thick with bristled hair. Oakley heard scraping, as if they were sharpening their nails on bark.

She swallowed and felt an urge to pee. Her entire body shivered. *What am I going to do?*

She looked down. The dirt trail was gone. The ground was hidden beneath mountain grass and plant cover. The trail wasn't in front of her or behind anymore. Frantically, she explored the surrounding area, but it was as if the trail had vanished into thin air. She pressed forward, but trees were in her way as if the forest had planted a dozen more when she wasn't looking.

The crunching footfalls neared, closing in on her. She tore off, winding her way in and out of trees and hopping over small rocks and bushes. The forest had come to life and swallowed her up. The creatures gained speed, and within seconds, they would have her.

"Help! Help!" she yelled.

She didn't care who heard her. At this point, she'd welcome anyone stepping in—even Tocho. Branches broke against her body and whipped at her arms and head. She shielded her face with her hands.

Suddenly, one of the beasts leapt in front of her, and she couldn't stop fast enough. She ran into what she guessed was its chest. It loomed over her at a height of at least eight feet. The black hair that covered the creature was coarse and poked her bare arms when she hit it. She craned her neck to look at its face. She only caught a glimpse of its yellow eyes, mouth of sharp teeth, and ears pointing to the sky before something smashed into the side of her head, and her lights went out.

"Oakley? Are you okay?"

She thought it was a question from her subconscious until her eyes focused on Inola sitting over her. Her head pounded with pain. Oakley touched something that was dripping down her temple, and her fingers came back with blood. Warm blankets cradled her while she lay on the ground. She recognized the interior of the hut.

Visions of the monster danced through her head. *How did I make it back here? Shouldn't I be sitting inside the belly of the demon, being slowly digested?* Someone had saved her.

"Oakley?"

"Inola. What happened?"

Inola rolled her eyes and shook her head. "You ran away like I told you not to."

"You didn't tell me the forests have werewolves."

"Lycans. Well, skin-walkers. We're not in the same world you came from, remember?"

Oakley propped herself on her elbows. "You keep talking about where I came from. Isn't that where you come from too?"

"Sort of. I guess I was born in your world, but my mom moved us here when I was two. So this place is all I know."

"You've never been in the real world? Where I come from?"

"No. I've heard stories of it, and my mom would talk about movies and stuff." Inola's eyes went as wide as her smile. "I'd really like to see one of those."

"You've never seen a movie?" Oakley pulled a face.

Inola shook her head. "My mom used to read books to me. She had to hide them, though. We're not allowed to have objects from your world."

"No TV either?"

"If you haven't noticed, there is no electricity here or modern conveniences."

"So you all really live like Native Americans from a hundred years ago?" Oakley asked.

"Yes, as much as possible."

"At least you have jeans. I've seen other people wear clothes from our world. And those men stole a bunch of food and items from that store."

"I should say, some things are acceptable. Only if they are a food source or something that is much needed."

"Another rule of Tocho's?"

Inola nodded. "That's why my mom tried to leave. Too many rules and bad stuff. She would say that there is so much evil going on. She would never tell me what exactly. She wanted to take me back to your world. But when we tried to leave, Tocho accused her of stealing me from him and his tribe."

"What an asshole." Oakley scowled.

"Yes." Inola broke into laughter. "That's what she used to call him."

"Why does Tocho make everyone live this way? What is he doing?"

"He's found a place of magic in these mountains. He's become a powerful shaman—or sorcerer. He says that he has visions from his father and from his great-great-grandpa, Wovoka. A shaman from the old days. He believes that all tribes, not just the Paiutes, should live like our ancestors did—off the land. He feels that when we take back the land—the water and its creatures—the gods will run the white man off and return the land to us."

"Where do I come in? Why did they take me?"

"They took you for that reason. Tocho plans to use you on the night of the blood moon, when he will be granted those powers."

Oakley swallowed and felt an anchor drop in her stomach. She was sure she knew the answer, but asked anyway. "So... what exactly happens to me?"

Inola pursed her lips and dropped her eyes.

"Inola?"

"I'd better let them know you're awake. Tocho wants to know the very minute."

"Inola." Oakley grabbed her arm. "What happens to me?"

She took in a breath, closed her eyes, and reopened them. "We just have to get you out of here."

"That's what I've been trying to do."

"We can't do it that way."

"How, then?" Oakley urged.

"I'm still thinking."

"You need to come with me. You know these mountains. You can lead us out of here. We can do it if we go together."

"No. I can't."

"Your mother wanted it. My world is yours too," Oakley said.

"There are the sentinels. The beasts you ran into."

"Do you have horses? I can ride."

"No. Tocho doesn't use horses."

"He uses trucks," Oakley said sarcastically.

"When they're needed to get supplies."

"But 'live off the land,' he says."

"You're right. He's a walking contradiction. My mother used to say that too."

"Your mom sounds pretty amazing."

Inola relaxed from leaning toward the door and plopped down next to Oakley. "She was. She taught me everything I know. Including English. When no one was around and we were alone at night, my mom would teach me scholastic lessons like math, English, and history. She was so smart." Inola smiled. "And we talked about pop culture. She would tell me all about movies and music—what musicians were her favorite—and she'd even sing some of their songs for me. Do you know who the Beatles are? And Billy Joel?"

"Are you kidding? Everybody knows them."

"My mom loved their music. She also liked Bob Dylan, the Beach Boys, and the Eagles."

"My dad loves the Eagles."

"Are they great?" Inola leaned forward with earnest excitement.

"Yeah. Sure. They're kind of old. There is so much better stuff now. I need to introduce you to a whole new world of music."

"They were old even for my mom. She said that she didn't care for the current pop music. She called herself an old soul. At nights—when the nightmares would come—she'd sing 'Hotel California.' It was the only thing that soothed me."

"Do you get a lot of bad dreams?"

Inola nodded. "Every night. There is this recurring one. Sometimes things change, like where it takes place, but the story is always the same. It's filled with monsters and demons who are chasing me. I'm running through the woods to get away from these creatures. They're hairy and have these long snouts and antlers, like they're part elk or something, but they have arms and legs like humans, and they carry these dull, rusty knives. They want to carve me up with them and swallow my soul. Then I reach this cliff with nowhere to go. I turn around, and this other thing—or guy—is there. He's tall and so dark that I can't see him. He's like a shadow, and he really stinks something awful. He calls himself Uncle Willie."

Oakley gasped as her heart leapt into her throat. "I saw him too. In the forest. Who is he?"

"I don't know." Inola shook her head. "He is like the devil, and I think he's from there—the other world—and some of that world leaks out and spreads into ours. That's what surrounds us. That's why no one can find us. People have been looking for their lost ones for years, but this place... it's becoming part of that world. It keeps us hidden."

"They're never going to find me." The realization sank to the bottom of Oakley's gut. She hoped for words from Inola to give her some hope, even if it was false, but Inola was silent. "So, what ends up happening in your dream after that?"

"The devil—the Uncle Willie thing—keeps trying to make me do things. One time, he told me that my mother was just a few steps away and had come to visit. He was so convincing. 'She's just right down there,' he said. I turned to where he was pointing and found myself standing on the edge of a cliff. 'Just jump,' he told me. 'She's waiting for you down there.' And then I heard her voice calling to me from below and echoing through the canyon. 'Come to me, Inola. I've been waiting for you. We all have been waiting for you.'"

A chill wiggled its way down Oakley's spine.

"I didn't jump, of course. It wasn't her. It sounded like her, and I was almost convinced, but I knew my mom. She would never tell me to do that. Actually, she told me my whole life, 'If your friends tell you to jump off a cliff, would you?'"

They both chuckled.

"My mom always said that too. I think it's a requirement for all parents to say that to their children," Oakley said.

"After I refuse to do whatever he says, he begins to laugh, and that's when I wake up."

"That's awful."

"It's not my mother down there. I know it. It's just another trick of his. To get rid of me. To eat my soul."

"It isn't your mom. She's in heaven. That much I'm sure."

Inola smiled. "I think you're right. I always feel her watching me, like my own guardian angel. And sometimes she visits me."

"She visits you?"

"Yes. When she was alive, we would go to a meadow that's close by. Spring was the best time to go because we would search for butterflies. Monarchs were my mom's favorite. Their colors are so beautiful. A few weeks after she passed, I was gathering wood for the fire, and a monarch butterfly—orange and black—landed on my hand. It stayed for the longest time. It wasn't even scared. And it wasn't even spring. We shouldn't have been seeing them for a few more months."

"It was your mom."

Tears filled Inola's eyes as she nodded. "It was my mom. That's happened two other times since. She gives me so much strength, and it tells me that she is with me. I just miss her at night. Nothing takes away the nightmares."

Oakley's eyes softened, and she leaned over and wrapped Inola in a tight hug. Inola wiped the tears away.

"You said your mom liked movies. What was her favorite?" Oakley asked.

"*Forrest Gump*. She saw it fifteen times or so. And she'd recite it like a story, word for word. If I got out, the first thing I'd do is watch that movie."

"What do you mean if? You're coming with me."

"I used to want to. Obviously. But I wouldn't fit in. I'm too different."

"No. That's him talking."

"Where would I go? What would I do?" Inola asked

"Do you have any family? Uncles, aunts, cousins, or a grandma or grandpa?"

"My mom talked about her sister. But I don't even know where she lives." Inola shrugged.

"We can find her. On the internet."

"On the what?"

It hadn't dawned on Oakley that Inola wouldn't know what the internet was. But how could she? Her mom hadn't been in the world for at least thirteen or fourteen years. It was possible she hadn't been versed in computer technology or, if she was, hadn't bothered to mention it to Inola.

"It's a device that helps you find things. Never mind. We both have to get out of here. I won't leave without you, and you can come live with us—for a while, until you get on your feet. My mom won't mind once I explain it to her."

"So, you have a mom and dad?" Inola asked.

"Yes, but they're split up."

"What does that mean?"

"It means they hate the shit out of each other." Oakley's voice took a snarky turn. "They chose not to live together anymore. I went with my mom, and we left him... alone."

"So you don't see your dad?"

"Not as much anymore. At first, I'd see him all the time. Then it turned into twice a year. Three times if I was lucky. But now... this is the first time I've seen him in, like, two years." Tears welled and threatened to spill, and Oakley tried to suck them back in. She hadn't expected to weep. She hadn't thought those words would cause waterworks, but they had. She really was sad that she hadn't seen her dad.

"But your dad is here, looking for you."

Oakley nodded, wiping away tears that defied her. "He is."

"He will find you."

"That's not what you said last night or even a few minutes ago. Because we're in a parallel world or some shit."

"I'm sorry. I can be pessimistic. But if my mom can come down from heaven and find me in the form of a butterfly, that means miracles are possible, right? And as much as he loves you—yeah, I believe he will."

"Does he love me?" She shrugged, and her voice came out nasally as her sinuses swelled. "Why didn't he come see me? Or even pick up the phone and call?"

Oakley's heart thumped rapidly, and she tried to hold back sobs, but they came between her words as she began to feel the gravity of the situation. She might not come out of this alive. She might never see her dad again or her mom. This could be the last conversation she had about them.

"I'd better go. I'm sure Tocho is getting impatient, and we don't want that," Inola said.

"What's he gonna do? Will he whip me for running?" Oakley asked.

"No. I don't think so. He needs you pure."

The term made her skin crawl.

CHAPTER TWENTY
Tocho

The sun was slowly rising when Tate and Delsin sauntered into the village. Tocho sat on a log, stoking the fire. He cut his gaze to the two of them as they approached.

"You look defeated." Tocho nodded to Tate.

"No. We did good. We planted the snakes. We took out two of the men. One man is bit in several places and has to leave the mountain, and another guy went with him."

"The white man still comes?"

"Her father? Of course. You have his daughter."

Anger boiled inside Tocho. He wanted to tear Tate apart. "Then you have failed."

Tate rolled his eyes. "Stone is with them."

Tocho stiffened.

"He leads them," Tate said.

Tocho locked his jaw and stared into the fire. "Leave me."

Tate and Delsin walked away, leaving their chief to brood alone.

Tocho's childhood rushed through his mind. He was a child again on the playground, defending Stone. They had become best friends that afternoon and began walking home together after school. On one occasion, since his foster dad was supposed to be away, Tocho felt comfortable taking Stone to his house. It was a small white home with peeling paint, a sunken roof, and a broken-down SS Chevy Nova sitting on cinderblocks in the front lawn. It was rusted out and missing its tires. There had been another vehicle parked in the carport, a blue one. He didn't know the make, but it still had its tires. The hood was open, and the clanking of metal against metal rang out.

"Shit," a man's voice said.

Tocho froze then turned to Stone. "On second thought, let's go catch water snakes at the creek."

"Why?" Stone scrunched his face. "We're here. We might as well go in. Show me your room."

Tocho hesitated, staring at the legs poking out from beneath the car. "Okay. Just don't bother him. Henry Walters is on another bender, so we'd better steer clear."

"Is he your dad?"

"No," Tocho was quick to answer. "I live in a foster home. This is my third and definitely the worst."

They walked around the Nova and entered through the front door. Tocho led Stone to the back of the house and into his bedroom. It wasn't much bigger than a closet. A single mattress sat on the floor, draped with a rumpled blanket and a pillow. In the far corner was a meager dresser, and that was it. Tocho reached into his closet and withdrew two homemade hatchets. He handed one to Stone. The handle was a solid piece of wood that had been whittled and sanded smooth, and the metal blade was attached by leather straps.

"Did you make these yourself?" Stone asked.

"Yep. Just like our ancestors used to. My dad taught me how. My *real* dad."

"What happened to your dad?"

"He died when I was eight. I wish he was still here. He believed in the old ways. He wanted to bring back our traditions, and he showed me how to live off the land."

Suddenly, a door inside the house slammed as if someone had kicked it open. The sound of a screen door bouncing back followed.

"Tom!" a male voice hollered.

Tocho froze. He didn't say a word. His eyes were wide.

"Tom!"

He still paused before answering. "Yeah!"

"Where in the hell is my socket set?"

Gripping the sides of the doorframe, Henry Walters pushed his head and chest in. His bloodshot eyes sat in deep rings, and spittle hung from his bottom lip. His black bangs hung over his eyes, his fingers were dark with grease, and smudges were smeared on his white T-shirt. He gripped a beer can between his thumb and forefinger.

"I don't know. It's always in your toolbox," Tocho said.

"It's not there. You used it last, remember? To fix the scooter out back."

"That was weeks ago. I put it back."

Walter's eyes narrowed, and his face reddened with heat. "You callin' me a liar? It's not there. Send your friend home. Find me that socket set, or it's your ass."

Walter crumpled the can and threw it at Tocho, who guarded his face. The can bounced off his head. Droplets of its contents spattered everywhere, and Tocho saw beads of it on Stone's cheeks.

The enraged man left. Tocho's shoulders sank, and he bent his head down. Tears welled up and burned his eyes. He did his best to suck them back, but one escaped down his cheek. He scowled and shook his head. His knuckles turned white from gripping his hatchet so tightly.

"I'm sorry," Stone said.

"Asshole." Tocho smashed the hatchet down on top of his dresser. The blade stuck in the wood halfway. He pulled the blade out and commenced hacking at the dresser top. Wood pieces flew until a sizable chunk of it was gone. Not much was said after that. The silence was awkward.

Then Stone had said, "I'd better go." He'd seen himself out.

Tocho's body stiffened, and he clenched his teeth as the memories flooded his mind. He hadn't thought of Henry Walters for years.

He wished he could have killed Henry like he had James. Tocho had gone through five foster families, and they'd all been nightmares.

Tocho hadn't thought of Stone in an age. He refused to admit feeling the pain of losing Stone as a friend, but it was there. He had been so convinced of Stone's loyalty until Stone had turned on him and refused to leave Parowan.

Tocho tossed a stick into the fire. He had moved past Stone's betrayal—or so he thought. Now that it was resurfacing, it infuriated him, giving him the urge to lash out at someone.

"Tocho?" Jaci approached.

He snapped his head to her, and with one look at him, Jaci stopped in her tracks. "Are you okay? Is everything all right?"

"Stone is helping the white man."

"Oh. Wow. I had forgotten that name. I guess he's still around. Are you worried?" Jaci sat next to him.

"Not at all," Tocho said, shaking his head. "It makes no difference. The gods are on our side, and I will have my revenge."

CHAPTER TWENTY-ONE

The ground was covered with scattered pieces of bloody snakes, still smoking. Chase shivered at the memory of those things crawling at his feet. He hoped Benson would be okay.

Chase stepped over a serpent's corpse and approached Kenny, who was reloading his clip. Kenny's eyes twinkled with a smile that consumed half his face. It was one of the most endearing characteristics of this young man. He continued to impress Chase, who'd had him pegged as a rookie who couldn't shoot.

"You're a good shot," Chase said.

"I grew up shooting. You could say I was born with a pistol in my hand. When I was old enough for my dad to teach me, I took to it like a baby to a mama's bosom. At twenty yards, I knocked a can off a log with my first shot. My dad said I was a natural."

"How good are you at sniping—say a hundred fifty yards or more?"

"I do pretty well up to a hundred, but I don't know about beyond that. Not like you, I'm sure. Miles told me how you were the best."

"Miles exaggerates. I used to be pretty good, but not so much anymore." Chase glanced away.

"If you got it, you got it. It doesn't go away. The one thing my daddy always said is to trust your gut. You let too much get into your head and it screws up your shot."

"We'd better get going. We have to find her by tomorrow night. It's good you have that talent. I may need you."

"You got it, bud. These maniacs have been terrorizing our town for too long. And taking our children. It's not right."

"I just wonder why no one has caught them yet. I get the sense that this is the first manhunt. Why hasn't there been one before, like when Tenley went missing?"

"There's been a couple of extensive manhunts, but they've always come up empty. Once Tocho and his men enter these mountains, they turn into ghosts and disappear."

Locking his jaw and pursing his lips, Chase walked away.

"Not this time, Chase. It's different. We'll find her."

The morning had started off cold, but two hours in and with the sun climbing without a cloud to block its rays, the heat baked Chase and his crew. They continued their journey through the red mountains. The dread in the air thickened with each mile. Chase pictured unseen beings filling the empty spaces around him—crawling and slithering over each other like a pit of snakes. He shivered as if a phantom tickled his spine with its nails. He eyed the fiery cliffs, trees, and rocks as if they were watching him.

Is this really another world? He wondered how they could have slipped into a parallel universe without knowing it. If there was a portal to another dimension, maybe they hadn't gone through it yet but were only experiencing rays of it. Like the rays of the sun—they were miles from the sun yet still felt its heat. The portal was stretching out invisible waves, and that was why the sensations intensified as his group got closer.

That's why they never found Tocho or those missing kids. They reached a point where the rays of the portal hid them from the eyes of our world, Chase thought. It would also explain why the helicopters hadn't spotted them.

Stone halted the train and hopped off his horse to investigate the trail. He studied the ground and placed his ear to it as if the dirt could speak to him and say, "Yeah, they were here, all right." Stone mounted his horse, and they continued. About half an hour later, Stone led them between two monolith red cliffs, into a slot canyon—like a crack in the mountain—no more than ten feet wide. The sun was blocked, and Chase welcomed the shade.

The trail wound between sheer rock faces for miles, and Chase stared at the pillar formations—which could be mistaken for statues—in awe. He heard the steady patter of water ahead, and the temperature cooled as they neared the sound. He recognized the splashing of a waterfall before he saw it. They stopped at its pool.

Chase craned his neck to look at the top of the falls. The crest of the mountain had to be at least two hundred feet above them, and a creek fell off its edge like a slim line of crystal-clear water. It splashed off of massive boulders at the bottom before creating a small pool and disappearing beneath the rock. The mist cooled his body as he approached and dismounted. Roman took a drink, as did Chase and the others, and he refilled his canteen.

"It's beautiful." Miles stood next to him, marveling at nature's creation.

"I don't know this place." Kenny shook his head. "I've been coming to these mountains my whole life. I thought I knew every inch."

"You've never been here before?" Chase asked.

"Uh-uh."

"You'd think this would be a tourist spot. I can see a lot of hikers wanting to come here," Miles said.

Stone was eyeing them from a distance, and Chase caught his attention. "What about you, Stone? Is this place new to you?"

He hesitated. "I've never seen this canyon before or this waterfall."

"Are we still on the right trail? We haven't lost them, have we?" Miles asked.

"No. Their prints are everywhere."

"This is why we had to take horses and track them through the mountains. We'd never have seen this otherwise. Stone explained it to me," Chase told Miles.

"I don't like it. Something is not right," Miles said.

"Nothing's right about any of this."

"I've lost all communication with my team, my satellite phone isn't working, and I haven't seen one chopper—I just don't get it."

"Do you remember what you used to tell me when we were in Kandahar—when nothing made sense, we lost comms, and we couldn't find the leader, Jemaah? 'Keep pressing forward,' you said. 'We know our task, and we'll accomplish it.' And we did."

Miles nodded.

"We have to trust Stone. He knows these mountains, and furthermore, he knows the enemy. There's a lot of crazy shit going on. They attacked us last night. Someone put those things in our tents. I counted at least twenty snakes. They're trying to stop us, which means we're getting close and we're a threat. And I have a feeling shit's going to get a lot crazier."

Miles smiled and placed a hand on Chase's shoulder. "I'm supposed to be comforting you—giving you strength—and here you are encouraging me."

"We're friends. It's what we do. Let's just make sure we both don't lose it at the same time."

His horse pranced nervously, whinnying, and Chase took his reins and ran his palm gently along the side of Roman's head. The other horses neighed and flounced with a threat of bolting. Fear stared back at Chase from his horse's eyes, and the air was charged with an intensity that caused every hair along the nape of Chase's neck to stand at attention.

"What's going on, buddy?" Dillon said, attempting to soothe his animal.

"Shit!" Ike said as his horse took off.

Darkness slid over the path as the horses trotted along the trail. Chase craned his neck, expecting to see a cloud covering the sun, but the sky was clear. The blackness crawled toward them like a mist, swallowing the red cliffs as it went. The aura was as dark as night and appeared to be devouring the canyon along its course.

"What the hell?" Kenny's jaw dropped as he stared at the thing.

The dark fog began to swirl, creating a deep pit within it like a tunnel. Chase couldn't pull his eyes from it as if it had him in a spell. The back of his head thrummed, and the pain intensified like a migraine. Mesmerized by an ugly beauty inside the thing's spinning maw, Chase was tempted to approach and enter, but he knew if he did, it would suck him in like a black hole. An image appeared inside the dark tunnel—a young lady dressed in Native American garb. Her hair was long and black, and her body seemed to shimmer. A smile unfolded on her face, and the warmth of her eyes softened Chase's heart. It was Oakley. She was there, and she beckoned him inside.

"Stay back! Don't look at it!" Stone warned. "Don't believe what you see inside. It's not real."

Appendages stretched from it like massive arms—six of them—and they were wavy like smoke. A hand flew in front of Chase's eyes, blocking his view, and then the hand gave him a shove. Chase stumbled back, pressing his hands to his eyes, and began to shake the spell from his head as he pulled his gaze away.

The hand had belonged to Stone, who was running to each of them and covering their eyes. Stone ran into Kenny, almost knocking him over, waving a hand in front of Kenny's eyes and stretching his other hand to Miles. Kenny pressed his palms against his eyes, crying out, and Miles wavered on spaghetti legs as he shook his head clear. Stone finally reached Dillon, breaking his spell, but he hadn't reached Ike, who was walking toward the thing, arms at his sides and eyes fixed on it like a zombie.

"Mom?" Ike said, sounding close to tears.

"Ike!" Chase hollered and ran after him. "That's not your mom!"

The six arms stretched out to the canyon walls on either side and rose halfway up the rock faces like fast-growing towers. Six heads formed at the top, two glowing green eyes appeared in each, and a strange formation of black sticks stuck out of their temples. No, not sticks—antlers. Three shadow creatures glowered down on them from each side, and a low humming rose and echoed through the canyon.

Chase grabbed the back of Ike's shirt and pulled him back while covering his eyes. Ike fought him for a moment, and then Chase felt his body relax. The horses bucked and whinnied, but Dillon, Benson, Kenny, and Miles were able to keep them from running.

Stone crossed to the center of the trail, keeping his head down but facing the rising black smoke. He raised both hands—feathers and beads clenched in his fists—and began to chant. His incantations came out like a song and a prayer, as if he were asking the gods, or God, to help them and send these foul things back to hell.

Chase prayed, too, for the first time in years. The fear shook his bones, and he would have prayed to anything if it ended the incessant humming. The breeze that blew against them was cold and carried a filthy stench that curdled his stomach, tempting him to vomit.

A loud crack cut the air like the snap of a bullwhip. Chase stared in horror at the canyon walls as splits in the rock snaked their way to the top. Small rocks and pebbles rained to the earth.

Stone ceased his chanting and turned to them. "Run!"

Chase turned to sprint in the opposite direction, the way they had come, but blackness approached from that end as well.

"This way!" Stone pointed toward the original black hole, and Chase's stomach flopped. The swirling inside the dark tunnel had stopped. The black fog had also ceased approaching as if frozen. "Do not look into it. Keep your head down. I can't hold it for long."

Each of the men mounted their horse and kicked their ride in gear. The horses shot forward. Chase held his hand out for Stone, who grabbed on and swung himself onto the back of Chase's horse. The cracking sounds increased, and larger pieces of rock broke free and crashed around them.

"Come on, Roman!" Chase urged his horse, bending his head low.

The mountains on either side slid toward them to sandwich them, closing in fast. As they sped through the blackness, Chase couldn't see the canyon's exit. All he could do was trust his horse to get them to safety. A boulder smashed the ground next to them, and Roman swerved with a whinny. Small slivers of shrapnel pelted Chase's skin.

Finally, the blackness dissipated like wispy smoke, and the sun broke onto Chase's face. He saw the exit ahead. The canyon was six feet wide and closing. The riders shot out of the canyon, into the open, in a cloud of dust and gravel. They continued to race until they were well away from the crumbling mountain and didn't slow down until they approached Ike's horse, who stood idly in a field, eating grass, like nothing had happened.

"I can't believe we made it out of there." Kenny shook his head.

"That was terrifying," Dillon said.

Stone was staring into the distance as if studying the horizon.

"I guess the supernatural is real," Chase said.

Stone nodded. "That was bad medicine."

"Bad medicine is right. I think there was something in that pond at the waterfall. Like a drug or hallucinogen," Miles said.

"Look." Kenny pointed at the crumbling canyon. "Does that look like a hallucination? And if it was, how did we all have the same one?"

"That black shit almost swallowed us whole," Dillon said, trembling.

"I don't know what the hell it was." Miles shook his head.

Chase understood his friend's stubbornness. He was the man in charge and ultimately carried the responsibility for everyone's welfare. He wouldn't allow himself to believe in evil and black magic—he couldn't. Someone had to stay rational.

Miles moved his horse away from the group, and Chase urged Roman after him. As he approached, he saw that Miles was trembling.

"You okay?" Chase asked.

"Yeah." Miles shook his head as Chase patted his back.

The two trotted their steeds back to the group, and they were all on the trail again in minutes.

Chase moved his steed alongside Stone. "So, what was that back there?"

"Evil. It is something from beyond. We are not safe anywhere out here."

"What was that you did to stop it? You seemed to know what to do."

"I did what my grandfather taught me to do. I wasn't so sure magic was real until now, but I'm sure glad he taught me how to fight it."

"We all are. You saved us. Thank you."

"It will get worse. I'm not sure what nightmares lie ahead, but it will get darker. And scarier. We need to be prepared."

"How do we do that?"

"When we make camp tonight, I will bless our surroundings. Then each of us must take turns to stand watch. Last night, they entered our tents and planted serpents. I believe they will do something similar again, but this time, it will be deadlier than snakes."

"I agree. Can you tell if we're close to their village?"

"We are. I'll get us close enough but not so close that they can see our fire."

Chase took a deep breath and blew it out.

"Tomorrow we'll be there," Stone said. "We'll see your daughter, save her, and kill Tocho, or my life is forfeited."

Chase couldn't agree more. Life wouldn't be worth living if he didn't succeed.

CHAPTER TWENTY-TWO

Oakley followed Inola to the center firepit, where Tocho and five other men sat around the crackling flames, passing a pipe back and forth. The chief took a toke from the long wooden pipe, held the smoke in, and passed the pipe to the man sitting next to him. It was the man with the top hat. Tocho's eyes were like steel, and Oakley felt them cut through her as she approached. Inola sat on a log while Oakley halted ten feet away from the leader. She pursed her lips and battled his stare with her own baleful glare.

Smoke drifted away from lips that barely moved as Tocho's eyes bored into her. Then a smile crept up one corner. "Cherokee Oakley," he said, and two of the other men chuckled. "Take a seat."

"I'll stand." She crossed her arms.

"Has your stay been comfortable? Are you getting enough food?"

"What does it matter?"

He grimaced. "Because you are very important."

"Really? And what does that mean, exactly?"

"The existence of our people will not only survive but flourish because of you. We have been abused by society—we have lost most of our Paiute tribes over the centuries. White man has ruled for too long, and they desecrate this earth, the animals, the trees, and the waters. These living things are gifts from the gods and should be honored and respected, not used and abused for white man's pleasure."

"But you're a murderer. I'm pretty sure people are gifts from God, too, and yet look how you're treating us! You killed a man in that store and those three men yesterday. You took me away from my parents. How is that right?"

"I have been given a vision. I have talked to the gods, and I have talked to our ancestors on the other side, and these are my instructions. Sometimes war is needed to have peace—peace that has been withheld from my people for too long."

"Who is the god you talk to? Is his name Uncle Willie?"

The smile erased from Tocho's face, and his jaw locked.

"Is he the one telling you to do this?" Oakley continued.

Tocho was silent for a beat and then regained his wits. "So, you have had a visit from Uncle Willie? This means you *are* special."

Rage fueled her, and her entire body shook with it. She couldn't believe she was talking to this giant barbarian who could tear her body in two with his bare hands, but she didn't have anything to lose. Inola kept quiet with her head down. Tocho's men continued taking tokes from the pipe, staying silent, and watching the argument like a tennis match.

"So... I'm a sacrifice? You're going to kill me?" Oakley's voice cracked.

"You are a means to an end."

A tear ran from her right eye, and she let it run down her cheek without wiping it. "What good will that do? Do you really think that my... sacrifice will give you all this magic? Are you hearing yourself?"

"The gods will reward you. You will sit among them and be showered with gifts you cannot imagine. It is not only my Paiute brothers and sisters I do this for but for all Indigenous people. All the tribes in this country will unite as one, and we will fight alongside our ancestors reborn from beyond the veil. They will rise from their graves by the thousands—millions! We will have an army of incomprehensible numbers and power. We will take back our lands." His eyes widened, and a glow of excitement emanated from him. "So you see, it is not just for the Paiute but also for the Cheyenne,

Utes, Shoshone, Mohicans, Navajo, Comanche, Apache, Mohawk, Pawnee, Wynoochee, Blackfeet, and of course, Cherokee. And hundreds more."

He pointed to Oakley, stood up, and stepped closer. "Do you not wish to see your people find redemption? The Cherokee always tried to make peace and signed many treaties with the white man. After so many treaties, the vast lands of the Cherokee Nation were gone but for a small piece. White man wanted that too. Chief John Ross urged his people to stay on their lands in hopes the treaty would be rescinded. This did not happen. Your people were thrown into stockades and awaited their relocation to the West. Sixteen thousand Cherokee were forced to take the six-month journey to 'Indian Territory' beyond Arkansas. They suffered from sickness, starvation, and the biting cold of winter. Four thousand Cherokee perished and never saw the new land."

Tocho let the words sit heavy in the air as he drove his eyes into Oakley. She shuffled her feet, and not being able to hold his stare any longer, she shifted her eyes away. Tocho displayed more knowledge and intelligence than she'd expected him to. Up to this point, she'd had him pegged as a brutish beast without a brain. Instead, he was a brutish beast with a brain.

"Did you know this about your people?" he asked.

"Of course," she lied. "I mean, it's well-known how bad all Native Americans were treated. But things aren't like that today. Right?"

Tocho snorted with a *humph*. "Not in your privileged world. Your father is white. Is your mother full Cherokee?"

She nodded. "Yes. Which makes me half, I guess."

"Your father's whiteness has given you a free pass. You think we're treated equally today?"

"People see my skin color. They don't know I'm part white. They don't treat me different. Not that I'm aware of."

"You need your eyes awakened."

"Woke?"

Tocho squinted as if not understanding what she'd said.

"We use the word *woke* these days," she said snarkily.

"You're a brave girl. You will need that come tomorrow night."

She swallowed hard.

Tocho turned to Inola, who had been silent the whole time. "Take Cherokee Oakley and get her dressed for tonight's dance."

Inola led Oakley back to her hut. Oakley's eyes took time to adjust from the bright light of day to the dark of the interior.

"What are you *doing*?" Inola exclaimed.

"What do you mean?"

"No one has ever talked to Tocho like that."

"Well, maybe someone should."

"Are you crazy? I'm surprised he didn't smack you across the face and lash your back with a whip. I'm not kidding."

"You're right. I shouldn't do it. He might kill me." Oakley's tone was biting with sarcasm. "Oh wait, he is killing me. I forgot."

Inola flinched as if she'd been splashed in the face with freezing water. "I don't know what's gotten into you, but I'm trying to help you."

"Help me do what? You won't let me try to escape. I'm going crazy, Inola. Talking like this is my only defense. It's the only thing keeping me from losing my mind. You keep saying how you're planning something—so what's the plan? Kill Tocho and all his men and make a run for it?"

"Maybe." Inola shrugged.

"Are you serious?" She moved her face close to Inola's, staring into her eyes. "You're joking, right? Tell me you're joking."

"Not kill everybody, just Tocho. Tonight. While he's sleeping."

Fear grasped Oakley's lungs and squeezed her air out. She felt dizzy and quickly sat down.

"I could slip something in his drink tonight. It will dull his senses and give us a chance. If Tocho is gone, I don't think the rest of this tribe will go through with it. Actually, I'm sure they wouldn't. Tocho is a self-proclaimed shaman and chief, and only he talks to the gods. Only he knows the ritual."

"How do we kill him? Sneak into his tent and do what?" Oakley asked.

"A knife across his throat. He'll bleed out."

Oakley lifted trembling fingers to her lips. *Is this for real?* She asked herself if she could really do it. *What choice do I have?*

Oakley sat outside the hut, waiting for Inola to return with her ceremonial dress. She watched Tocho from afar with her stomach churning. Her eyes followed his muscle-bound, sinewy body, and she asked herself again if she could run a blade across his throat.

Little ol' me? The thought sickened her. Killing someone in the midst of battle was one thing, but this felt more like murder. But battling Tocho was out of the question—she knew she would lose.

A man wearing a headband, jeans, and a leather jerkin approached Tocho. "You called for me?"

"Tate." Tocho stood.

That was the last word Oakley understood as they started a conversation in their native tongue. The intensity of Tocho's voice increased, and the one he called Tate cowered before him with pleading eyes. Tocho pointed to the east, and Tate's eyes followed. He was pointing at a giant tan-and-red boulder. The rock was the size of a Volkswagen Bug. Its surface was mostly flat and angled out, and the sun glanced off it. Oakley cocked her head quizzically at the ropes resting at the foot of the stone.

Three men grabbed Tate, who immediately fought back. He kicked and swung his arms to escape, but his fellow warriors were able to sustain their offense and finally had him in a tight grip. They began to drag him toward the boulder. Tate spat and yelled, and then his last words came out in English.

"I am your best friend! If it wasn't for me, none of this would be."

Tocho casually turned to him. "Accountability, Tate. We came up with those rules together. Neither of us are exempt from it. You will be released in time for our dance tonight."

"What did I do wrong? We planted the snakes like you asked. We got rid of two men."

Oakley swallowed hard. *Two men? Which two?*

The men carrying Tate halted as Tocho approached, pointing a finger at him. "You were supposed to stay and finish the job. You could have killed them while the snakes distracted them. Did you think of that?"

Tate pursed his lips and looked away.

"You are a warrior, Tate. You are all skin-walkers. Use your skills. We are at war. And the white man still comes for his daughter."

Relief spread through Oakley.

Tate spat and cursed more.

"You are still my friend," Tocho said. "Learn from this, and return to the brotherhood."

The men stripped Tate bare except for a loin cloth and laid him on top of the rock, chest up. Using the ropes at the base, which were attached to stakes in the ground, they tied each wrist and ankle. They pulled him taut so his body formed an X. Tate squinted from the sun. Lying there all day—no cloud in sight—the sun was sure to scorch his skin.

Out of the corner of her eye, Oakley noticed Chenoa standing still and staring at Tate splayed out on the rock. Her body hung woefully, and her eyes glistened with tears.

An hour later, Inola returned with Oakley's ceremonial dress. They entered her hut, and Inola spread it out on the floor. It was made from deer hide, and running along the bottom skirt and at each sleeve were tassels. Painted in red on the chest were an elk skull and antlers, and colored beads and turquoise jewelry were embedded throughout like someone had gone crazy with a Bedazzler tool.

"It's pretty," Oakley remarked.

"Chenoa and Jaci made it. They are the best dressmakers. Go ahead and try it on."

Inola averted her eyes while Oakley undressed and put on the new outfit. "It hangs like a drape. Do you have a belt?" Oakley asked.

"Yes." Inola wrapped a leather string around her waist and pulled it tight.

"Much better. I'm sure this would attract all the boys." Oakley laughed.

Inola chuckled. "You're beautiful. I'm sure you don't have any trouble getting boys."

"You would be surprised. What about you? Is there anyone you like?"

Inola rolled her eyes. "There's not many choices out here."

"When we get back home, we'll make all the boys swoon over us." Oakley looked down at her dress. "I've always dreamed of being asked to go to a dance—and one day going to junior prom."

"What's junior prom?"

"It is like... like one of the most magical nights ever. First, a boy asks a girl, usually in a clever way. My friend's older sister was given a bowl of Swedish Fish. They were all red except for one yellow one on top, and the note said, 'Of all the fish in the sea, would you go to the dance with me?'"

"Wow." Inola's eyes lit up.

"The boys dress in tuxedos, and the girls buy a fancy dress. Sometimes you get picked up in a stretch limousine. And the dance is elegant, and you get pictures, and it's like a big Cinderella affair." Oakley didn't know if her friend knew all the references she'd mentioned. If Inola did, it was only because her mother had told her. The thought of that pained Oakley.

"This village has a lot of young people. Are you sure there isn't a boy here that you've had your eye on?"

"There is one boy I like, but he doesn't see me. Besides, Tocho wants me to marry Tate."

"Tate? That guy they strapped to a rock? He's old enough to be your dad."

"I know. Chenoa is his wife, but now Tocho wants to marry Chenoa and make her wife number two. Tate and Chenoa have been trying to make a baby but are unable to. I suppose he thinks it's Tate's fault. So if he marries me, there's no risk of spawning another me." She shrugged.

"That's sick. You're what—thirteen or fourteen?"

"Thirteen."

"That sick bastard. Don't you do it. You're escaping with me. I will do it. I will kill him." A new rage fueled her.

"You can do this?"

"We are doing it. Tonight."

Inola nodded. "First, we have to finish getting you ready for tonight's Ghost Dance."

"I'm in the dress. What else?"

Inola placed a bowl filled with a thick red liquid in front of her. "We have to paint your face."

CHAPTER TWENTY-THREE
Tocho

The casual talk and murmurings ceased as Tocho strode in front of the crowd and swept his eyes across them. People who hadn't noticed him quickly had to be elbowed by others to shut their mouths. The village surrounded the bonfire in a half circle, and a boulder had been chiseled and shaped into an altar and placed before the fire. Tocho took center stage across from them. He stepped onto a flat rock that had been placed on a slight mound. It raised him three feet from the earth—enough to let his people know who was chief and watched over them.

The air was deafeningly silent now except for the crackling and popping of the fire. The night was black and spotted with stars, the moon was full, and the flames danced across their faces. Tocho wore a full chief headdress fanned out with feathers and colors, which draped to his feet. His face was painted with red, yellow, and black marks. Ten men marched in line until they formed a barrier between Tocho and the fire. They turned and faced the crowd like sentries. They wore headgear—although not as adorned—and they, too, had painted faces.

In unison, the ten warriors pounded their chests once and belted out, "Tocho!"

In response, the crowd cried out, "We are Paiute!"

"My Paiute brothers and sisters," Tocho said in their native tongue. "The time we have waited for is nearly upon us. Our ancestors wait on the other side. They have waited for much too long for what they are due. Redemption. Vengeance!"

The crowd cheered and quickly quieted to let Tocho continue.

"The white man has lied to us over and over. They lie out the side of their necks as they pander to us with promises that aren't nearly enough. They treat us like fools. Like lesser men and women." He scanned the crowd and pointed at a woman. "Tallulah. You lived in their world for most of your life. Do you remember how you were treated at school and in the workplace? Did your teachers treat you fair? You told me stories of how your English teacher called you a liar. She didn't believe that you aced your tests and homework without cheating. Then she called you a dirty Indian."

Tallulah's eyes dropped, and she nodded.

"Mahkah." Tocho turned his attention to one of the ten men. "You watched as three men stopped your dad outside the bar and beat the shit out of him before taking his money." Tocho turned back to the crowd. "Mahkah was only eight years old at the time."

Tocho's attention turned to a woman in her mid-twenties. "Halona. You were brave enough to tell me your story, and you said it was okay to share it."

She nodded.

"Halona was attacked and raped on her way home from high school. By a cop no less." Tocho spat. "And later learned that this bastard had impregnated her. Her parents went straight to the police. That's what we're supposed to do, right? They are set to protect us. Her parents talked to his superiors, but they wouldn't hear her story. They told her that it was consensual. Well, my friends, how is it consensual when her eye is swollen and black and her body is covered in bruises? Is it consensual that the rapist has her claw marks on his arms? White man does not protect us. They lie to us, like they have since they arrived on our land.

"Many of you remember what life was like in their world. Some of you who are of the new generation are fortunate to have been born here in your rightful place. This home of refuge. This land the gods made for us and continue to hide from the eyes of our enemies."

Tocho withdrew the tomahawk that hung in his belt and examined it. "The hate that has been shown to us and all the mistreatment burns a fire in your bellies and a thirst for rage. I know it. I feel it too. But rage will lead us to mistakes. As much as you may want to bash their skulls in—like I do—we must withhold that anger. Redemption and justice are what we truly seek and what has been promised to us."

Facing the crowd, he raised his fists and tomahawk high. "Tomorrow night, the gods will grant us our wish. They will raise our long-dead ancestors, who will join our fight. And then we will bash in the skulls of the white man." He said the last words with a growl, and the crowd cheered. "We will be reunited with our brothers and sisters whose lives span hundreds of years. My great-great-grandfather Wovoka first saw this prophecy in a dream, and the vision of the Ghost Dance was given to him. It is only now that we have been given the key that Wovoka was missing: The gods require a sacrifice."

He turned to the south, where Oakley stood next to Inola in front of Chenoa's hut, and waited.

CHAPTER TWENTY-FOUR

Inola nodded in response to Tocho's signal to bring Oakley forward. "Okay. It's time." She hooked her arm in Oakley's and led her to the ceremony. She stopped just short of it and motioned for Oakley to continue. "You'll be okay. I'll be right here."

Oakley approached the center firepit with trepidation. Night had shrouded the world in darkness. She wore a headband feathered with five plumes of an eagle. Inola had smeared her, from chin to forehead, with the red cream. It was thick on her face, and she felt it cracking whenever she talked or moved her cheek muscles. She had demanded a mirror, and Inola had brought her one. She was almost unrecognizable. Her face was dark crimson, as if she'd been dipped in blood.

The entire village surrounded the fire, and not one person spoke. The air was silent but for the sputtering fire. All eyes were turned Oakley's way, and they parted, making a path for her to enter the center ring. Tocho and his ten warriors looked like the Native American tribes she'd seen in Westerns.

Oakley raised her eyebrows at the sight of Tate. He stood on the outskirts—face and bare chest burnt to a bright red—and kept his gaze down. She couldn't see Inola married to him. The thought was disgusting.

Oakley's eyes moved to the tomahawk Tocho gripped, and she swallowed hard. *This isn't it, is it? He said tomorrow night. They didn't move it up, did they? They have to wait for the blood moon. Did they trick me?*

Tocho held out his left hand for her. She hesitated and then took it. He led her to the stone altar next to the fire, and she sat down. Tocho pushed her to a lying position, on her back, and stepped away. He scanned the crowd slowly and then stretched his arms out to each side and addressed his people in the Paiute tongue.

Oakley couldn't translate his words—at least not all of them—but she got the gist. His voice was loud and his tone deep and strong with confidence. She ran her eyes over the crowd—the glow of the fire illuminating them—and saw that they were glued to his words.

He gestured to Oakley several times and then waved his arms about as if alluding to several people. Then he bent to the ground and raised his hands slowly to the sky. Oakley guessed he was referring to raising their dead ancestors. The crowd cried out a boom of excitement.

"We have fed the gods for long enough," Tocho said, switching to English. She wondered if it was for her benefit but quickly dismissed that. Tocho was too much of a narcissist. "Their bellies are full of the souls we have fed them. There is one soul left, and she is our Crimson Queen."

Tocho changed his stance and began a low chant, and three men began to beat a steady rhythm on drums that sat between their legs. Tocho raised his tomahawk and began to march around the fire in a sort of dance. The ten men dressed in ceremonial garb began to follow his dance and chant with him. The chants started out low and then rose and turned into a cry, as if they were in pain and pleading with the gods.

Children in the crowd began to dance in place and chant, and women and other men did as well. The night was filled with their song. Clouds of dust kicked up from their feet, and the fire grew despite no one feeding it.

Tocho lifted his head and weapon high, lowered them, and then raised them again. He continued this with his dance. Oakley felt the chant inside her, filling her entire body from finger to toe, and her heart beat in sync with the drums. Her eyes kept returning to the tomahawk in his hand. Would it crash down on her at any given moment?

Suddenly, Tocho reached inside a pouch on his belt and threw something into the fire. Whatever it was caused a flash explosion—like gunpowder—and the fire turned an emerald green. The crowd gasped, and a scream was caught in Oakley's throat. Her heart surpassed the beating of the drums, accelerating to a fast-paced thumping that threatened to leap out of her chest.

Tocho stopped his dance and stood in front of Oakley. His eyes filled with the green flames. He lurched at her with his weapon. Its blade was striking for her neck. She covered her face and screamed.

She felt nothing. The blade didn't hit her. She was still breathing. She opened her eyes. Tocho was still lurching at her—mimicking his slaughter of her. The crowd chanted one word over and over again, and it sounded like "Yes, yes, yes." Oakley continued to flinch as the tomahawk pretended to cut at her throat, chest, and head.

Tocho finally stopped and withdrew something else from his satchel. It was red and dripping, and he bit into it and thrashed back and forth like an animal tearing meat apart with its teeth. He rose and lifted his head so that all could see the blood smeared on his face and dripping from his teeth and chin. He lifted the red item high—it was the heart of an animal. At least, she hoped it was from an animal.

Will that be my heart?

He howled at the night, and the crowd howled with him. His eyes were crazed and still ablaze with the green firelight. The air was electric with a heavy dread. Something else was there. Those beasts from the forest or something else—something unseen. Something worse. Maybe Uncle Willie had returned.

Oakley was panting for air—her lungs were thirsty for it and not able to catch enough. She turned and caught Inola's gaze. She was in the crowd, but she was not with them. Her stare was fixed on Oakley. She wasn't chanting or dancing. She fidgeted with her fingers, her eyes were wet, and Oakley felt her empathy.

CHAPTER TWENTY-FIVE

Chase couldn't sleep, and it wasn't because of the wolves' howling that echoed through the canyon, which caused him to squirm in his bag. He couldn't get Oakley off his mind. *Where is she, and what is she doing? Is she hurt? Is she falling apart mentally?* She had every reason to be.

But something told him that wasn't the case. His daughter was strong-willed. She had a resilient and rebellious spirit. Her attitude was frustrating to deal with at times, but looking deeper, he appreciated that about her. It meant she had a mind of her own. She had developed her own opinions, and it didn't matter if Chase or Kira opposed them—it didn't change anything. Oakley held her own.

What drove Chase mad was that he hadn't reached her yet. They were far behind, and every minute dropped like oatmeal from a spoon. They had left too late—by a full day—and were not moving fast enough. Stone was doing his best to track them, and every person on his team put in equal efforts and sacrifices. Chase had to keep reminding himself of this to stave off his anxiety.

He had one more day to find her. That was it. He was so close, yet not. There wouldn't be any slowing the next day. He would push everyone to their top speed.

Stone had said they had four to five hours—maybe less—before reaching the village. From the layout of the land and mountains, Stone believed the settlement was in a pocket at the bottom of the crags. Therefore, making camp at this distance was the smart thing to do. They couldn't risk the enemy detecting their whereabouts. Because of the snake attacks, the constant sense of being watched, and the near-fatal event in the canyon, they were failing at hiding.

It was Chase's turn to stand watch. He twisted to look at Miles, whose chest moved up and down slowly as he gave a low rumble of snoring. Miles was in a deep sleep despite the wolf cries. Chase unzipped his bag, slipped his boots on, and left the tent with a flashlight, a handgun, and his rifle.

Dillon was sitting by the fire and staring into it as if hypnotized.

Chase tapped him on the shoulder. "Anything happening?"

"Nope. Just those wolves howlin'. They were close for a while, but I think they're farther out now."

"About how far do you think?"

"A mile or two. Keep the fire fed, and they shouldn't be trouble."

"Get some good sleep, Dillon."

Nodding, Dillon stood and ambled to his tent. Chase took his spot on the log before low-burning embers. He tossed another log in and watched the flames lick at it as if it were covered in sugar.

His right hand began twitching, and he tensed. "Damn it."

He needed to be at his best to rescue her. He couldn't have his gun hand fail him when he needed it the most. *Why in the hell does it do that?* He'd never suffered an injury to cause this condition. It had started after the incident, and people told him that it was induced by PTSD. After all, he had taken an innocent life, and his hand shook to keep him from ever shooting again. The entire police force was in support of his actions—so much so that if he heard one more person tell him that it wasn't his fault, he would vomit.

"Hey, it could have happened to anyone," people told him. His therapist repeated the same sentiment. So why did he feel so sick to his stomach? Why was he haunted by nightmares replaying the scene over and over again?

Maybe because you didn't tell them everything. He knew he should have divulged more, but there was a wall he couldn't get past.

He could still feel the gravel against his belly as he lay on the roof, posted across the street from the Parsons' home. Jake Parson had held his wife at gunpoint and threatened to kill her and their newborn baby if anyone entered. "I'll paint the wall with her brains," he had said. "And the baby too."

Negotiations lasted more than six hours. Jake was accusing his wife of cheating and kept saying that the baby wasn't his but belonged to whatever asshole was screwing his wife. She denied it and begged him to listen to reason, but Jake was bipolar and off of his meds. He wasn't thinking rationally.

At one point, they had nearly convinced Jake to surrender. He was sobbing and apologizing for what he'd put his wife through until he heard one of the officers trying to enter through the back door. Jake twisted and fired shots, hitting an officer in the leg.

Jake roared and began throwing furniture around. A chair busted through the living room window. Through Chase's scope, he could see partial images of the bastard charging his wife. Jake grabbed her, threw her against the wall, and batted her head with his fist.

"Let your wife go, Jake, or we'll be forced to take you down!" Todd, the negotiator, yelled through his megaphone.

Jake turned and fired two more shots out the front window. He didn't hit anything, but it was enough to convince Chase's captain to give him the order to take Jake out the minute there was a clear shot.

Chase readied himself and followed every movement he could see through the windows. Three panes had glass uncovered—two of which were only partially draped—and the bedroom window on the second floor was wide open. The ground crew spoke to Chase through his earpiece, keeping him up-to-date as to what Jake's current position was, according to what they could hear and see.

Twenty minutes later, Chase got his wish. The wife ran upstairs into their bedroom, and the husband followed. Figures moved fast across the window, but Chase didn't have a shot. Then, a minute later, as if by magic, Jake stepped to the window and peered out. In his entire career, Chase had never been given a clearer shot. Chase was only seventy-five meters from his target, with not a trace of wind. Nothing was in the way.

He put Jake's heart at the center of his crosshairs, and just as Chase's forefinger squeezed the trigger, a blur of white crossed the lens as his wife—as if knowing the police were set to kill Jake—lurched in front of him, crying, "Nooo!"

It happened so fast that Chase didn't have a chance. Everyone believed it had all happened in a split second—that Chase had squeezed the trigger at the same moment that she had jumped in the way. That was Chase's story. He even tried convincing himself of it. But was it true?

Every so often, the truth poked its ugly head into Chase's thoughts and reminded him how he'd had a chance to stop. Before shooting, he'd seen her jump. It was a split second, yes, but he could have halted. But he was convinced that he still had the shot. His target sat barely an inch to the left of where his wife stood. The bullet should have hit Jake, missing her entirely.

But life didn't always play fair. The bullet found her dead center. Chase saw red spreading across her white blouse.

"Sylvia! Sylvia!" Jake cried as she collapsed in his arms.

He'd been hit, too, but functioned as if he didn't know it. The round had pierced her chest, exited her back, and lodged itself below Jake's right shoulder. The SWAT team swarmed the house like bees to honey, pulling Jake away from his wife as he howled in agony.

Chase had felt it right then. His right hand had spasmed slightly.

Please, dear God. Please help me get my daughter back safely. Hold my hand steady at the right moment. I need this. I need her.

Chase had been put on leave while the incident was under investigation. It took months, and there was a trial before the board, along with a barrage of questions from the press, who attacked him at every turn. Chase's life came to a halt, including communication and visits with his daughter. The trial was rough, but he was cleared. Captain Jones and the rest of the team were eager for Chase to return, but he wasn't the same. He went on two calls with SWAT to bust a couple of low-level drug rings, but he froze when Jones gave him positioning orders. His captain looked at him, and then his eyes moved to Chase's trembling hand.

He gave Chase a nod and told him to stay back. "I gotcha."

Later, Jones pulled him into his office and directed him to seek counseling with the division's therapist. Chase attended the recommended sessions but never connected with the doctor. Something about the woman's personality clashed with his, and he never felt comfortable coming completely clean with her.

Eventually, Chase made the toughest decision of his life—to leave SWAT. Captain Jones offered him a position as a trainer or doing a desk job, but Chase refused. He didn't have the nerve to tell Captain Jones, but he couldn't be around the men, his former SWAT team, or the captain. They all reminded him of the nightmare that fed his fears and held back the healing he desperately needed.

He took a job selling and installing security systems—something he knew a lot about—and to his surprise, sales came easily. He was a natural and finally making decent money again. Not only that, but he had the potential for doubling his previous income.

Something was missing, though. His soul was empty and sad, and since he'd walked away from the only friends he had known, and no family lived nearby, he was alone. He thought constantly of his daughter and ached for her to be in his life again. He needed her but felt like he didn't deserve her. He had been absent for so long, and even the last few visits he'd had with her, there had been a disconnect.

Chase had called his ex-wife shortly after the incident. He was supposed to be picking Oakley up in a few days, but because of the ongoing investigation, the press, and his mental condition, he had to break those plans. Kira had said she understood and even extended her sympathy, but the next time he called her—several months later—she was cold and short. How could he blame her?

"Please tell her I love her," he said.

"You need to tell her."

Chase paused. "I will. I promise."

"Are you making plans to see her? Take her for a weekend, maybe?" his wife asked.

"I... I'm just not ready. I want to. I really do. But..."

"Chase, I can't carry your love for her."

She was right. He'd known it even then but didn't want to admit it.

Two buddies from SWAT visited him unannounced and dragged him to a favorite local pub. They talked and drank all night, and each of them gave Chase great advice. He needed to reconnect with his daughter before the years flew by and she became an adult with resentment. His good friend Wes told him that he should take her on a vacation. A place where they could connect again, learn about each other, and start a new relationship. Wes said if he didn't do this, he could lose her forever.

"I tell ya, every time I take my daughter for the weekend, she is constantly on her phone," Wes said. "Kids act like they can't survive without those damn things. What you should do is take her camping, where there's no TV or internet to disrupt you guys."

"She's never been camping. I think she'd hate it," Chase said.

"Of course she will—at first. But then she'll learn to appreciate it. It will give her memories for a lifetime."

"Don't expect miracles," his other friend, Barry, said. "She may still be cold and distant by the end of that trip. But, after a while, you'll start to see slight differences. You need to continue to stay in touch. Call or text her, and I guarantee you she'll turn around. You'll see."

Chase had begun researching the internet for places he could take her, and once he came across information about Bryce National Park, Zion, and the Grand Canyon, the plan had seemed perfect.

Chase sighed and looked at his watch. It was 2:57 in the morning. He still couldn't shut his mind off. Sleep would not find him on the eve before the biggest and most important day of his life.

He craned his neck to look at the stars. The black sky was filled with twinkling lights. They were more brilliant this high up than they were back in the city. He caught movement from his right and turned in time to see a shooting star. It was a beautiful flash in its seconds of existence, and he made a wish.

"I hope that star was for me."

He stood up, stretching his legs, and scanned the area. The wolves' howling had subsided a while ago, and he decided to take a stroll. The moon was full and tinted red, and with nothing in its way, it illuminated the canyon with a dim light. There was a chill in the air. Chase zipped his coat all the way up and strolled in the direction of his daughter.

He passed the horses, who were silent and still until they sensed his approach. They pranced in place nervously. Two of them whinnied, and another snorted.

A wolf howl sliced the night—closer than the last ones—and Chase shuddered. He spun in that direction. There was nothing but trees, rocks, and shadows. He flashed his light quickly, but it illuminated nothing but the inanimate objects. No wolf. No creature.

He continued his walk. He didn't have much of a plan other than to make it to a high spot where he could visualize Tocho's village using the night vision on his scope. He'd be stupid to attack it himself or even sneak in to find his daughter. They had one shot, and he wasn't going to foil it by doing something so foolish, even though a nagging part of him wanted to.

He hiked an incline and flashed his light on and off occasionally to illuminate his path. Another wolf cry etched the silence. This one came from the opposite side, sending chills across his bones. He flashed his light but saw nothing but a copse of trees.

This is stupid. Wolves could attack me.

The farther he got from camp, the more he increased those chances. He debated for a minute and then ran his light ahead to see how far a high spot would be. He had fifty or more yards to go, and even then, he wasn't guaranteed to see anything. It wasn't worth it. He had left his post unguarded, putting his men at risk.

He was heading back when he heard a rustling in the pines on his left. He swept his light across the trees. Several branches were bouncing until they slowed and finally stopped. Something or someone was in those trees. He swallowed hard, and his neck felt as if an ice cube slid down it. His body spasmed.

A rumbling growl escaped from within those trees. He stood only twenty feet away. The horses rustled restlessly.

Chase raised his rifle and secured its butt against his shoulder, preparing to shoot anything that moved. His right hand spasmed. "Fuck."

He clicked off the safety at the same moment a beast leapt from the trees, charging on all fours. Chase caught a glimpse of its wild eyes, dagger teeth, and body encased in a rug of bristled hair. He fired a shot from his M1A rifle, which he'd loaded with 175-grain .308 Winchester rounds, heavy enough grain to kill a moose. Despite his right hand, the shot landed. The beast staggered and rose on its hind legs with a cry. Its forelegs were shaped like a man's, bearing razor-sharp claws at each digit. The monster clawed at the air. It stood twice the size of a wolf and regained its speed fast.

The creature rushed him and swung a sweeping blow, which Chase blocked with his rifle. The force knocked the gun from his hands and sent Chase tumbling down the incline. His arms and hands burned from the claw wounds.

Chase rolled to a stop, withdrew his .50 caliber Desert Eagle, rotated to his back, and fired two shots into the creature as it bounded down the hill. The rounds ripped open two bloody holes in its chest. And just as it pounced to finish him, Chase fired a third round, which blew out its left eye in an explosion of blood, hair, brains, and bone fragments.

The creature landed on top of Chase like a lump of dead meat. The air in his lungs was trapped, and his bones threatened to snap under its weight. The thing reeked of mangy mutt and blood.

The wolf-creature thrashed in pain and whined like an injured dog, allowing Chase to push and pull himself out from under it. Crouching over the thing to catch his breath, Chase witnessed the monster shudder and cry out one last howl. Three wolf howls responded in mourning for their lost brother.

"Chase!" Miles ran to him, gripping a shotgun. His eyes widened at the grisly sight. "Are you okay?"

Not having enough breath to answer, Chase nodded. Miles helped him to his feet as the other men exited their tents, fully armed for what must have sounded like war.

"Good Lord." Dillon stood next to Stone, gripping his rifle.

Fear crossed Stone's eyes as if he'd witnessed a million urban legends of skin-walkers coming to light. Kenny held a pistol in both hands as if he'd just entered the O.K. Corral, and his words seemed caught in his throat.

"What the hell is this?" Miles asked.

"There's more. Be at the ready," Chase warned as he reloaded his pistol.

The wolf cries continued for a few more seconds, and then the night sat still. A cool breeze whistled through the brush. Each man stood tense, at the ready, glancing around and waiting for an ambush of nightmares.

Chase splashed the trees with light and ran it slowly along their perimeter, and Miles did the same on the opposite side. The horses grunted, and one of them gave out a small whinny as it trotted in circles, attempting to bolt. Dillon, Stone, and Kenny warily walked through the camp, strobing their flashlights in all the dark corners. Kenny's light shook in his trembling hand.

Dillon passed by all the tents until he got to the last one. "I'm not seeing anything."

"Maybe they left," Kenny said in a quaking voice.

And then it happened—a beast sprang from the dark, tearing through a tent to get to its target. Dillon stood beyond the tent and the creature. The thing split the canvas shelter in two, and shreds of fabric burst in a cloud about it. The monster's deep growl scraped every nerve in Chase's body.

Dillon twisted to face it—the rifle shaking in his hands—and he fired twice before the demon was upon him. The beast swung, and the gun flew from Dillon's hands, and then the creature's claw raked across Dillon's head. It would have taken his head from his shoulders if Dillon hadn't been quick enough to lurch back from the attack. The beast's nails sliced across his forehead and right cheek, and Dillon fell, sprawling.

Ike rocketed out of his tent, wearing only one boot and pants—no shirt—and holding a shotgun. His eyes widened in shock as he watched Dillon fall, and then he stared at the massive beast before him. He pelted the creature with three rounds, running at it and yelling a war cry. The monster twisted and swept his massive arm at

Ike. The blow hit the agent so hard it knocked him back and sent him flying.

Stone and Kenny ran to the rescue as the thing leapt on top of Dillon to tear him apart. Kenny's guns fired, staving off some of the creature's blows, but it didn't stop it. Stone fired twice with his shotgun, which rocked the beast on its feet. The creature turned with a baleful glare that would have turned bones to water and roared.

Chase and Miles moved to help until they heard the padding of rushing paws behind them. They twisted to face the third terror, bristling with dark-gray hair and salivating from its open maw. Chase locked eyes with the creature. Its burning yellow eyes brimmed with madness and violence. Chase secured his stance and fired from his Desert Eagle while Miles blew hot lead from his shotgun, pumped, fired again, pumped, and fired again. The beast reeled and howled then staggered back and glowered at them. Miles fired again, and blood and fur blew from its shoulder. That was enough for the beast. With a frustrated whine, it turned and fled in the opposite direction.

Chase and Miles ran to the other fray in time to witness Stone press the barrel of his shotgun against the wolf creature's head and fire, splitting its cranium apart. Brains and blood sprayed the tent. Dillon lay only inches from the creature, moaning in agony, and Kenny was pulling him away.

Stone turned to Chase. "Quick! My bag!"

Chase nodded and sprinted to Stone's tent.

"Miles. Get me water and towels—or any sort of cloth," Stone said.

Miles left to fetch them.

Chase handed Stone his bag. His gut wrenched at the bloody sight of Dillon's wounds. Skin hung in flaps from Dillon's forehead and cheek, revealing the white of his bones. His hands were drenched in crimson plasma, and his shirt was ripped open and filled with gore. Chase put a hand to his own wounds, thankful they weren't as bad.

Dillon's face was covered in sweat, and his body convulsed with shock. He squeezed his eyes shut and gritted his teeth, looking close to screaming. Stone withdrew a large knife and shoved the handle of it into Dillon's mouth to bite down on. He poured water from a canteen all over Dillon and began dabbing it away with the cloths Miles had brought.

Miles jogged to Ike and helped him to his feet. Ike held a hand to his head as Miles planted a shoulder under one arm and walked him to the rest of the group. Ike sat down next to the tent. His right eye was closed and swollen, and the whole side of his face had started to bruise.

"Let's get him somewhere clean. Lay him down on a bag or a blanket inside the tent. I need to clean his wounds and sew them closed," Stone said.

"I have a med kit. There's bandages and disinfectant in there," Miles said and ran to get it.

Chase, Kenny, and Stone carried Dillon into Kenny's tent and laid him down on a sleeping bag. It was crowded, so Chase stepped out while Kenny stayed to assist Stone. Miles handed them his med kit and exited to stand beside Chase, who was gawking at the slain beast.

Miles followed with his eyes and gasped. The creature, mangled and dead, was transforming. Its hair was receding, and the arms and legs were shrinking. Its claws and paws melded into human hands and feet, and its snout sank like a caved-in cake, yet it couldn't quite form a face because it was split in two. Bones cracked, and a sound came from it like boots pushing through knee-deep mud as its insides must also have been changing. After several minutes, it looked like a human man.

Miles's jaw hung low. He looked like he wanted to say something or throw up, but his body was frozen.

"The legends are true." Chase shook his head in disbelief. "Skin-walkers—shape-shifters."

"Werewolves," Miles grumbled. "It can't be. Something's not right. Stone's stories have messed with our heads, and now we're seeing things. They were human all along. We just thought we were seeing creatures. This is an illusion."

Chase gave him an incredulous look. "Are you off your rocker? We just saw this thing transform."

"We thought we did."

"All of us share the same delusions? And what about those claw marks up and down Dillon's body?"

Then Chase remembered where the stinging sensation in his forearm was coming from, and he pointed to his own wounds—three slashes across his arm and nicks on his hands. "And where did these come from? We have to stop kidding ourselves. This is real. We're dealing with something evil. Remember the canyon? The shadows and the glowing green eyes and how they brought the mountain down on us?"

Miles stared at the ground as if not wanting to meet Chase's eyes, then he looked at Chase's arm. "We'd better get that wrapped up. Stop the bleeding. I'll get some bandages."

Miles entered the tent and came back out. He poured water over Chase's wounds as Chase gritted his teeth in pain. Miles patted them tenderly with a clean cloth.

"I'm just as baffled as you, Miles. But we have to understand our enemy in order to fight it."

"And just how do you propose we fight these monsters and supernatural demons? Hell, I blew enough holes in that thing back there to turn him into Swiss cheese, and it just ran off."

"We don't fight them. We just need to get my daughter back and get the hell out of here."

"You think they'll negotiate?" Miles asked.

"Not from what I'm learning about Tocho. We've gotta find a way to sneak her out. Steal her back. We have to make it to their base and come up with a plan on the fly, but even if we're just dealing with humans, we don't have enough manpower. We're outnumbered."

"If I could just make contact with my men—"

"Contact is lost! They are not here. We are not where you think we are. We've crossed into some fucking twilight zone. We're alone."

Miles locked eyes with him. Chase could see that he was finally getting through to him, even if Miles wouldn't admit it.

"And my daughter is alone. With *them*." Chase hissed out his last word.

Miles ran a hand over his eyes as if to wipe away the exhaustion. He regarded Chase and appeared to want to say something—like it was right inside his mouth, waiting for release—but then he pursed his lips and looked away.

CHAPTER TWENTY-SIX

Oakley waited for Chenoa to fall asleep before making her move. Chenoa had been following Tocho's instructions to house Oakley and feed her, but that was about it. She never talked to Oakley or gave her any looks other than a scowl. *What a bitch,* Oakley thought. *How can she allow this to happen to me? To a fellow woman. Come on.*

Inola was her only friend out there. She would be losing her mind if it hadn't been for Inola. She was truly a godsend.

Oakley eyed the door. She waited—for what seemed like hours—for Inola to approach and give the signal. The door opened just a crack, a form blocked the moonlight, and a hand reached in with a curled forefinger motioning for Oakley to follow. It was Inola.

Oakley peeled away the fur blanket and crawled out the front door. She looked back. Chenoa hadn't moved.

The outside was bright with the moon. It already glowed with a red hue, and the next night, Monday, could quite possibly be her last day on earth. If Inola's plan worked—and if Oakley found the nerve—she could prevent her looming death.

"Are you ready?" Inola asked.

Lying, Oakley nodded. Was anyone ever ready to murder another person? Sure, she had told herself a million times that it was in self-defense, and by all means, it was, but who was she kidding? It was still murder.

Inola motioned to Tocho's hut, and they jogged quietly to it and stood outside his door. They pressed their ears to the entrance and listened. It was dead silent but for the low rumble of snoring. That was a good sign.

"Tocho should be in a deep sleep. I was able to slip some desert star into his water."

"What does that do?"

"It's a plant. My mom taught me how to find it. It will slow his heartbeat and make him sleepy. I used a lot."

Inola withdrew a knife. The metal shone in the moonlight. Oakley's stomach roiled. She took a deep breath and let it out in a stutter of rasps. Her nerves raced at a high intensity throughout her body.

"Here." Inola handed her the knife, and Oakley gripped it in a sweaty palm. "Just run this along his throat. Deep." She demonstrated with a finger across her own.

"Is there anyone in there with him?"

"His wife, Jaci."

Shit. I can't do this.

Inola pulled on the door, but it didn't budge. She crouched and showed Oakley that the bottom corner of it was wedged in the dirt. She carefully lifted the bottom of the door until she could move it freely and open it halfway. They both stood still and listened for any sound. Nothing had disrupted the snoring.

Oakley crouched and peered in. A slice of moonlight illuminated part of a mound of blankets at the far end, and a hand rested next to it. It was a large male hand. It was Tocho, and the rest of him was shrouded in darkness. The way his arm was lying signaled to Oakley that he was lying on his back. It would be ideal for her attack.

It was this or her own death in less than twenty-four hours. She couldn't rely on her dad to show up on a white horse and save the day. *It's the right thing to do*, she told herself. *It's the only way.*

Inola's eyes were wild. She looked as petrified as Oakley felt. Inola impatiently motioned for her to go inside, as if she'd been waiting there for an hour. They didn't have time on their side. Anything could happen. This was their best opportunity. She wouldn't get another.

Oakley entered on spaghetti legs. It felt like an out-of-body experience. She felt like a programmed robot moving against her will. Her right foot kicked something over with a hollow thud, and she froze. Every hair stood on end as she held her breath, hoping it didn't awaken the beast. The body beneath the blankets shuffled. The snoring paused, then resumed after a few seconds. Oakley breathed again.

She looked to see what object had nearly caused her early demise. It was a clay pot. She shut her eyes, clutched the knife, readied herself as best she could, and then reopened her eyes. Inola was glowering in with eyes so white they could have produced two flashlight beams. Oakley gave her a nod to show that she was okay.

She moved to her hands and feet and crawled toward him. Her eyes began to adjust to the darkness, and she saw his outline and profile—short, flattened nose and square jawline. By shuffling slowly forward, she found it easier to clear her path of anything that might be standing between her and her target.

She moved next to him. His snoring made the ground reverberate. Staying on her knees, she raised her upper half to loom over his body. Someone else was next to him—Jaci. She lay on her side, facing away, fortunately. Her long black hair was splayed out behind her.

Oakley watched Tocho's face for any movement. His eyes remained closed, and his mouth was slightly open, emitting the snoring sounds. She moved her knife toward his throat and held it an inch away from his skin. She watched in horror. *Oh my shit, oh my shit, oh my shit.*

The knife in her trembling hand shook so badly she didn't know if the blade would land on its target. *Am I really doing this? I can't be. I can't do this.*

The sharp steel glinted in the dim light. His Adam's apple slid up and down as he took a sleepy swallow and then resumed the snore.

His chest rose and lowered with each breath. There was life. She was about to take it.

Oakley imagined Inola freaking out behind her. She closed her eyes and pictured the horrible things this man did. She saw the body of the store clerk bleeding on the floor, the top half of his head torn off. The group of people around him sobbing and shaking in fear. The three hikers on the hill brutally cut down by his arrows. Inola's mother, who he had killed. Inola being whipped and tortured. Inola being forced to marry an older man.

And how many other atrocities has he committed that I'm not aware of—like sending men to kill my dad? Is he even still alive?

And then she thought of herself lying on an altar as he prepared to hack at her with his tomahawk. But that still wasn't enough. For some reason, it wasn't an image that moved her to kill him. *Am I not afraid to die?*

Then she thought of her mom. She imagined her reaction as an officer told her the news of her slain daughter. Her mom would fall apart, possibly faint and collapse. She wouldn't make it through the funeral. She could hear her screaming in rage at what had been done to her Oakley. She imagined her mom—as she'd heard many parents who'd lost children did—entering her bedroom and burying her face in Oakley's clothes to breathe in her smell.

In many ways, her mom was her best friend. Oakley could tell her anything. Whenever she'd had a difficult day or problems at school—whether it was about sex, drugs, or a mean girl—her mom was the first Oakley talked to about it. Many of Oakley's friends said they would never talk to their parents about sex or drugs. Although Oakley hadn't tried either of them, she felt comfortable enough to have those discussions with her mom. They watched rom-coms together and spent hours shopping at the mall. If her mom lost her—if she lost her mom—it would be crushing.

Oakley's throat tightened, and her sinuses clogged as she began to weep at the thought of her mom. And her dad. *Oh my gosh, my dad.* There were a million things that she needed to tell him. She hadn't had the chance. She wanted—no, needed him in her life.

She thought of her friends and her family and all the people who would mourn her. She thought of her friend Inola and the traumatic life she was living. She was enslaved to this man to do whatever his sick mind demanded. And all these things gave her grit.

She opened her eyes, resolute to do what she came to do. Her knife hand stopped shaking. She moved it to his throat, prepared to make the cut.

"Tocho!"

The scream came from far off—somewhere outside—and she froze.

"Tocho! Tocho!"

Tocho's eyes flew open. For a brief moment she locked eyes with him. She saw the darkness within them and the hatred and rage. Strangely enough, he did not seem surprised to see her with a knife to his throat. Tocho grabbed her wrist in a viselike grip, and she couldn't move.

"I'm sorry," she whimpered.

He threw Oakley off of him, and she tumbled across the ground, her surroundings spinning in her head. Jaci jumped out of the blankets. Her eyes widened at the sight of Oakley.

"Watch her," he ordered Jaci and charged out of the hut.

From within the hut, Inola was nowhere to be seen. If she were smart—and she was—she would have torn out of there the minute Tocho had awakened. Inola couldn't have done anything to help Oakley by staying. Oakley looked at Jaci, who wore no expression but was watching her intently. Jaci's eyes moved to the knife in Oakley's hand.

"You came to kill my husband?"

"I don't know." She shook her head.

"The gods watch him. He is not of this world. Not anymore. You'd have better luck killing a bear with that."

Oakley had no response. She turned and began moving to the door when Jaci stopped her.

"Cherokee girl." Jaci's face had relaxed. There was a sadness in her eyes. Oakley got the sense of her hopelessness. "We are all doomed."

Is she trapped too?

"Tate!" Tocho hollered from outside.

"I'm sorry" was all Oakley could say.

Jaci gave a nod, and then she exited the tent.

A Paiute man approached Tocho, dragging something behind him. Oakley moved to the right to get a better angle. The man pulled a makeshift gurney created out of sticks, and lying on it was a mangled, bloody man. Oakley's heart leapt into her throat at the fear that it might be her dad until she saw the long black hair that hung from his head. It was one of their own.

Torches were quickly lit, illuminating them all.

"What is the meaning of this, Tate?" Tocho pointed at the man on the gurney.

The look of fear on Tate's face told her how frightened he was to explain. Tate was not winning points with Tocho. That meant good things for Oakley and good things for her dad.

"They had guns. Big guns. Delsin needs Honi."

The muscles in Tocho's bare back flexed as he took in a deep breath. He clenched his hands into fists. He turned and called out, "Honi! Bring your medicine bag!" Tocho snapped back to Tate. "How can you fail? You have the strength of ten men. You walk with the wolf. All of you. Four warriors left my camp, and only two return." Tocho moved his eyes up and down Tate. "And yet not a scratch on you. How can that be? One warrior and one girl return."

"It's not like that. I was high up. I ran in to help but... but Wesa and Awan were killed, and they were close to killing Delsin. I saved Delsin and came back here. But he is close to moving to the other side."

Tocho crossed his arms. From her angle, Oakley couldn't see his face, but she imagined fire burning from his eyes.

A man wearing a top hat ran to the injured person and knelt at his side. Tate set the gurney down. Delsin raised a bloody hand, and the man with the top hat gripped it.

"Stay with us, brother. I will call upon the gods," Top Hat said.

That must be Honi, she thought.

Tocho and Tate stepped back to give the medicine man room to work. Honi withdrew items from the bag and rubbed something on the bleeding man's forehead. The ground turned wet with blood, and the man groaned.

Honi began chanting words unknown to Oakley, but they came out in a singing fashion similar to chanting during the weird dance. Holding objects in each hand, the miracle man lifted them and shook them back and forth. They sounded like a baby's rattle. The tone in his chanting deepened and grew louder. He began to dance around Delsin, and then a gust of wind blew past Oakley and swept up a swirl of dirt around the injured man and Honi. She heard a thousand voices whispering in the breeze that surrounded her. There was something unseen that moved throughout the village. A chill ran through Oakley's body.

Honi's voice suddenly changed. Oakley couldn't explain it other than that it wasn't his voice anymore. It was guttural and bellowed out, echoing through the canyon. The man on the gurney rose into the air and floated above it by a few inches. Oakley's mouth went dry, her body trembled, and she felt an urge to pee and vomit at the same time.

Then the man with a torn-up chest of gore, floating above the ground, began to spin furiously like a piece of rotisserie meat turning at a blurring speed. She continued to hear the whispers but couldn't decipher their meaning, and then a hundred beastly growls thundered and melted her bones. She felt dizzy and ready to collapse.

The wind howled and whirled about the shaman and his patient. The growls cried with a whine in their voices and then turned sharp with fury. Two hands gripped Oakley's arms from behind, and she nearly lost it.

"Oakley." It was Inola. "Oakley. Come on."

She turned to her friend, who looked as horrified as she felt.

"This way," Inola said, and they distanced themselves from the horror.

CHAPTER TWENTY-SEVEN
Tocho

The wind died down, and Delsin's body and gurney settled back to earth. The bullets and fragments of rounds that had pierced his flesh now rested on top of his body. Each one sat in blood above where the wounds had been. Everyone watched Delsin and Honi in amazement except for Tocho. He stood inches away from Tate, drilling his eyes into him, as Tate shuffled nervously.

"You have disappointed me greatly."

"I—I'm sorry." Tate shrugged.

"Apologies are not enough. I have witnessed too many mistakes on your part. I have entrusted you with the most important responsibilities, and you continue to fail me. The gods have withheld your seed from procreating, and I have to take notice of this. Perhaps I am not listening to the gods who have given me sign after sign of who is weakening our tribe."

Tate's face wrinkled in anger. "I have done everything you've asked. I have supported this tribe in every way possible. Maybe what's really weakening this tribe is its chief."

A shocked murmur ran through the crowd.

Tocho scowled. "Is that what you believe?" He turned to face the gathering people. "Is that what you all believe—that I am the problem?"

Mutters rumbled through the people, and they each began shaking their heads and answering no.

Tocho turned back to Tate. "Our tribe does not seem to support your theory."

Chenoa ran from her hut to investigate. She froze and stared at her husband. Tate bounced a glance her way. Chenoa shook her head slowly as if to signal to Tate to back off.

Tate pursed his lips. "A chief who looks out for his tribe does not take another man's wife as his own. A true chief does not whip and torture children and women. True gods do not ask for sacrifices of young girls. I have watched for too long how you have poisoned us all with your lies. You are the serpent that weakens this tribe."

Several gasps escaped the audience.

A smirk ran across Tocho's lips. "If I am poisoning this tribe—if I am not meant to be chief—then let the gods answer in the outcome of a challenge."

Tate locked his jaw and nodded.

"Choose your weapon."

Tate withdrew a knife. Tocho held his hand out without taking his eyes off his enemy. Honi quickly stepped up and handed him a knife.

"If I shall fall..." Tocho faced the crowd. "Then Tate is your true chief. You will all follow him. For this will be the answer from the gods. But... if Tate falls, and I still stand, then the gods have confirmed me as the true chief and shaman."

The silence was deafening. Tocho didn't move. He waited for Tate.

Tate studied his foe and began to circle him with his knife held out. Tocho kept his knife down at his side and followed Tate with his eyes. Tocho was confident, and he wanted Tate to know it.

Chenoa raised a nervous finger to her lips as if to hold back a barrage of angry words. She mumbled a soft prayer.

Tate fake lunged and retreated. Tocho didn't flinch. Tate continued to circle, and Tocho remained still.

"If you don't attack, I stay chief."

Just as Tocho finished his words, Tate dove in for the attack. He swept his blade for a belly cut, but Tocho careened away. Tate continued with a combination of blows from a low kick and a left punch. Tocho blocked the punch, but the kick connected, and Tate stabbed the knife at him. Tocho twisted and slashed his knife at Tate. They moved in a blur of attacks and parries and dust kicked up in a cloud. Tate withdrew from the fray, and each took a second to catch his breath. Their chests pumped up and down, and both of them glistened with sweat.

Blood ran from a cut across Tate's right bicep and another one below his pectoral. Tocho felt several stings across his body, and blood ran. There were two deep cuts across his chest and one above his left eye. He wiped the blood from his brow, but more replaced it. Several gasps arose from the crowd. It didn't faze Tocho. He strode with buoyancy.

Tate threw a smile Chenoa's way, but her face was a wreck of fear. He didn't wait long to engage again, and they were quickly interlocked in a mesh of muscle against muscle. They broke apart and then attacked simultaneously in a tangle of feet and fists punching against flesh and bone. Blades flashed and thrust, and more blood was drawn. Tate attacked with the quickness of a cat, bringing his knife down at Tocho, who caught his wrist and plunged his knife deep into Tate's jowls.

Tate's eyes widened, and he began convulsing and choking on the blade that filled his mouth. Blood gurgled and poured out. Tocho twisted the blade savagely before withdrawing. Chenoa let out a shriek then quickly silenced herself. Tate crumpled to his knees, holding his throat.

"While he still holds life, I can save him," Honi said, stepping forward.

Tocho motioned for him to stay back. "No. He has chosen his fate."

Tate toppled face down on the dirt and spasmed for a couple of minutes before ceasing to move. Tocho turned to catch Chenoa's response. Her eyes were wet, and she was trembling and holding back an eruption of emotions. Satisfied, Tocho marched back to his tent.

CHAPTER TWENTY-EIGHT

After securing the camp and calming the horses, Chase found a moment to collapse, and exhaustion dragged him to sleep. He awoke an hour later as dawn was starting to break, and he wandered to Dillon's tent. He poked his head in. Stone sat next to Dillon, dabbing his head with a wet cloth. Half of Dillon's head and face was wrapped in gauze that was already turning red, and his chest and arm were mummified the same way. His eyes were closed, but his body trembled.

"How's he doin', Doc?"

"He just broke a fever. I sewed up his wounds the best I could and gave him medicine. He took nearly all of my thread. If anyone else gets so much as a cut, I won't have enough to stitch it."

"He's going to need antibiotics. With all those wounds, he'll surely be infected," Chase said.

Stone nodded. "I gave him a cream made from purple coneflower. It's an antiseptic, and it has anti-inflammatory properties. It will help, but he'll need more medical treatment than I can provide."

"You're amazing. I don't know what we'd do without you."

Stone shrugged and dabbed Dillon's forehead again. "He can't go on. He'll have to come off the mountain. Cedar City will be the closest."

Dillon shifted, mumbled something incoherent, and coughed. "I'm going on. You need me."

"I appreciate your bravery, but you're in no shape, soldier." Chase patted his foot.

"You're down two men already, and I can still shoot." Dillon struggled to sit up. He winced and clutched his chest.

"You can't even open your eyes," Chase said.

Dillon slowly pulled one open. The other one was hidden under bandages. "I still got one. Let's get your daughter."

Stone gave Chase a disapproving look.

Chase nodded. "I'll go check on the others. We've gotta move." He left the tent.

The disheveled posse rounded up their gear speedily and rode out of camp just as the world was lighting up. Dillon held the reins in one limp hand and rode his horse, nodding in and out of consciousness. Stone had replaced his bandages before they left, but red dots were already starting to appear through the fabric.

Miles pushed his horse and rode up alongside Ike. "How are you doing?"

"I'm alive." Ike rolled his good eye. The right side of his face looked like he'd been hit by a truck and had already turned black and purple.

"You don't have to do this. I can't ask you to. You could stay back. Help Dillon. Take him into town."

Ike turned to Stone, who was in the lead. "How many men are we up against?"

Stone shook his head. "I'm not sure, but the best I can tell... ten, maybe fifteen. Including Tocho. The women are warriors too. I'm not sure how many of them."

"And each one can turn into a fucking werewolf?"

"Yes. They are shape-shifters. They deal in magic and sorcery."

Ike turned back to Miles and hooked a thumb at Dillon. "If he goes on, I go on."

"I never could have predicted all the shit that's happened. I still can't believe what we saw. It can't be real. There has to be a sensible explanation." Miles shook his head and turned his eyes to Chase.

Chase pursed his lips and locked his jaw, preparing for Miles's doubts. He kept his focus on the path ahead.

"So, you really think we're up against evil, demons, fire-and-brimstone kind of thing?" Miles asked.

Chase slowly turned his head. "I'm not going through this again with you."

Miles swallowed hard.

Kenny trotted his horse alongside Miles. "We killed two of them things. If you told me two days ago that I'd be chasing Native Americans, sleeping with snakes, and being attacked by werewolves and a creepy dark mist, I'd say you were crazy. But here we are. And we're still ridin'. We have the best tracker, the best sharpshooter, an ornery ranch hand, and two of the FBI's best. I like our chances."

Dillon scoffed.

Chase grinned. He liked Kenny's optimism.

"How old are you?" Miles asked.

"Twenty-two."

"No offense, but you barely left your mommy's house. You haven't been in the shit like we have."

"I beg your pardon?" Kenny stiffened and glared.

"I was like you at twenty-two. Full of grit and thinking I could take on the world. I wish it were like that, son. But after life slaps you in the face so many times, you tend to get humbled."

"These men killed my dad. That man they call Tocho left nothing of him to look at in the casket. I'd say that's a pretty hard slap in the face."

Puzzle pieces came together in Chase's mind, and he twisted in his saddle to face Kenny. "Sheriff Gunther Reese was your dad? I thought your last name was Lloyd."

"Reese married my mom when I was still a baby. My biological dad ran out on us, never to be seen again. Reese became my dad. He treated me like his own son. I'm in the process of changing my last name to Reese. He *is* my dad."

"I'm sorry," Miles said.

"Nothing to be sorry for. I just have to ask you one question. If you're so negative about our situation and our odds, why are you out here?" Kenny asked.

"Two reasons. My friend's daughter was taken, and this is my job."

"So? It doesn't make sense if you think we're not going to succeed."

"I didn't say that."

"It's definitely what you're saying. You refuse to believe in the supernatural, even when it's staring you in the face, and you keep shooting down positive vibes. You can't get ahold of your men and your helicopters, and I get it. You're scared."

Miles's face heated to red, and he opened his mouth, likely about to argue, but Kenny cut him off.

"I'm scared too. We all are. It's natural. We'd be stupid if we weren't. But being scared and negative isn't going to help us. If your car is sliding toward a truck, and all you can focus on is the truck, you're gonna hit the truck. Look the other way. Focus on the solution, not the problem."

Miles bit his lip and looked away.

"The way I see it, even if it seems ridiculous, the trick is to stay positive. Don't just believe that we stand a chance—believe that we'll get his daughter back. Believe that we'll all return." Kenny shifted his eyes to Chase. "And if we don't make it back, if we die—and we might—then we die. But I will die fighting for my friend's daughter. If I can call you a friend, Chase."

Chase's eyes softened. "You are my friend, Kenny. How can I not call all of you my friends? You don't know me, but you're willing to risk your lives for my daughter. No matter what happens, I will be forever in your debt, and you earn all of mine, Oakley's, and her mother's gratitude."

They rode in silence for a few minutes. Miles dropped his eyes, but it was obvious he wasn't seeing the ground—he was lost in thought. He gave his horse a friendly kick and trotted next to Chase.

"I'm sorry, Chase. I didn't realize that I..."

"It's okay, buddy."

"I am with you one hundred percent."

"I know," Chase said.

Miles nodded in Kenny's direction. "The kid's wiser than his years."

"He continues to surprise me."

"I think he actually has me convinced."

"I don't have a choice. I have to get her back, Miles."

"I know. I didn't want to admit that all the crazy weird shit we've witnessed is true, because I don't know how to fight it. I can't control it, so I stick to what I know."

"That's all we can do," Chase said.

"But the kid's got a point. We're still here, and I keep saying that we will succeed, but for the first time, I really believe it."

They rode in silence for a bit. The morning air was chilly, especially the gusts of wind that kicked up and bit Chase's back, ears, nose, and fingers.

From the rear, Dillon broke the silence. "Hey, Stone!"

"Yes," Stone answered without stopping or turning.

"I just realized something. That werewolf bit me, didn't he?"

"Yes. Not full bites but nips."

The group—except for Stone—turned to stare at Dillon. His eyes were as big as eggs. Blood drained from his face, and his Adam's apple bobbed as he swallowed hard.

"Am I gonna turn into one of them? A werewolf?"

Miles and Kenny let out a chuckle.

"No, my friend. It doesn't work like that," Stone said.

Dillon released a breath of air.

"That's too bad. It could have come in handy," Ike chimed in, and the rest of the group broke out in laughter. It helped with the tension.

CHAPTER TWENTY-NINE

The village was deserted in a matter of minutes. An entire group of fifty or more people was making its way along the trail leading to the southern mountain. It wasn't lost on Oakley how easily organization and arduous work came to these people. She had an appreciation for who they were—outside of this situation—and she saw them in a different light. They were followers, mesmerized—or even brainwashed—by a cult leader named Tocho. She wished he didn't have such a hold on them.

She thought of Jaci—not so much in what she'd said but what had been written on her face. Jaci was a slave to Tocho as much as Oakley was his victim. *Is that true for everyone here?* She believed so. Inola had told her that if they killed Tocho, the rest of the small empire he'd built would crumble.

A short while after Oakley had returned to her hut the night before, Chenoa had entered, cursing under her breath and throwing items around. She had been enraged over something.

"Are you okay?" Oakley asked with trepidation.

Keeping her eyes on the ground, Chenoa ignored her.

Oakley learned of Tate's demise the following morning. Inola had filled her in, and Oakley's heart had sunk for Chenoa.

The evil of Tocho's reign continued, and these people were living in fear. After what Oakley had witnessed—from the werewolf beasts to the dark magic she'd seen in healing the wounded man—she could understand why. Inola's mother had tried to get away, and it had cost the woman her life. Tocho had used that to his advantage, making an example of Inola's mom, and he had done the same with the killing of Tate. Death was a strong motivation to keep them in line with his laws and orders.

A tall man strapped a bow to his back, barked at a woman—probably his wife—then grabbed a bag next to his hut and swung it over one shoulder. The man then jogged toward the main group, who were already leaving the village. She recognized him. He was the man who had been torn to pieces on the gurney. She eyed him for a long time, looking for cuts, wounds, scars, or anything. His chest was bare except for a breastplate made of beads, and there was no sign of physical damage. He walked and ran without any limp or struggle.

A chill of dread ran through Oakley. The growling beasts murmuring in the wind returned, surrounding her. Their incomprehensible chanting and whispers came from what had sounded like thousands of unseen people. They rattled her nerves so thoroughly that she had to shift her attention to something else.

"Hey." Inola appeared next to her. "How are you doing?"

"I'm not."

"Don't worry. I found a way to help you."

Excitement boomed. Oakley was willing to latch on to any fragment of hope. "Really? What is it?"

"I can't tell you right now. I'm still working on it. Did you wash your face?"

Oakley's skin still had remnants of the paint from the previous night, even though she had washed most of it away. "Yes. I couldn't stand it."

"Chenoa's going to be pissed."

"Move it!" a deep voice thundered in their direction. Tocho's head stood above the rest of the men and women in the crowd. His face was painted red, white, and black, making the whites of his eyes pop, and he was glaring at the two of them.

Inola and Oakley picked up their pace. "Tocho put me in charge of you." Inola's mouth spread into a wide grin.

It was the first time Oakley had seen her smile, and she thought, *She must really have something.*

"I'll be with you right up to... you know," Inola said.

Fear roiled in Oakley's stomach as she thought of the end.

Inola took Oakley's hand in hers. Oakley felt strength in the gesture, and as they continued walking hand in hand, it gave her courage. Tocho plowed his way through the crowd, toward the two of them, and Oakley's heart jumped, but his attention was not on them. It was on the man with the hooked nose.

"Delsin."

Delsin turned and straightened to attention.

"Take Nigan. You two, stay back here and wait for our pursuers. Use the rifles. They don't make it past this point, or you won't make it through this night. Understand?"

Delsin nodded and was turning to go when Tocho stopped him.

"I have faith in you, brother. Nigan is young. Make him stand."

Delsin lifted his chin and pounded the left side of his chest with his right fist. He hit it so hard Oakley heard the thump. Then he turned and ran to a man who was farther up in the crowd. Oakley assumed he was Nigan.

As Nigan stopped to listen to Delsin, his face expressed fear. He couldn't have been a day past eighteen. Oakley wondered if this would be his first act as a warrior.

"Your father must still be alive," Inola said.

"Yes." A tear ran from her eye. "For now. I wish I could warn him."

"I don't know how we could do that."

Oakley studied the ground as they walked, and an idea popped in her head. It wasn't a fantastic one, but it was at least worth a try. "Keep watch for me."

"What?" Inola's eyes widened.

Oakley let go of Inola's hand, backpedaled, and stopped. She eyed her surroundings quickly to see if anyone was paying attention and then went to work with her right foot. She dragged her heel—her sneakers had been replaced with moccasins—through the dirt, plowing two inches into the soil. Clouds of dust billowed as she continued drawing interconnecting lines.

She glanced up to see Inola scanning the people ahead. Being in the back of the pack, they didn't have to worry about anyone behind them noticing. Delsin and Nigan had crossed to the west side of the village and disappeared into a hut. Inola peeked over her shoulder.

It wasn't perfect and was far from pretty, but Oakley was finished. The letters were a bit misshapen, but the two words weren't bad, considering the time constraints: *LOOK OUT!*

She jogged back to Inola's side. "We in the clear?"

"As far as I can tell. What did you do?"

"I wrote a warning in the dirt. I just hope it stays and those two guys don't see it."

"Delsin and Nigan are idiots." Inola rolled her eyes. "Your chances are good."

"I just hope my dad sees it in time to help."

"Pretty good idea actually. It's enough to let them know there's a trap."

"Thank you, Inola."

"For what?"

"For everything. For being my friend out here. I would be a mess. I couldn't do this without you."

Inola smiled. "Friend? That has a nice ring to it. I really don't have any. I was about to lose it myself out here. With my mom gone, I've felt lost for months with no one to talk to and no one talking to me. I was ready to surrender until you showed up. Oakley, you are the best thing that's ever happened to me."

Oakley wrapped an arm around her shoulders and squeezed.

"Inola!" a woman's voice yelled. Chenoa broke through the crowd, striding for them.

Inola gasped, and Oakley's neck hairs stiffened. *Oh shit, she saw. We're caught.*

"Inola." Chenoa approached and stopped her. "Go with Tocho. I'm staying with her."

"No." Inola was firm. "I am supposed to stay with her right up to the ceremony. I'm supposed to paint her face. Get her ready."

"No more. I'll do that. Tocho wants you."

Inola's face twisted in despair, and tears welled up. She gave Oakley a frightened look.

"I-I'm more comfortable with Inola doing it. She's always done it," Oakley said.

"I don't care." Chenoa shot her a glare.

Whatever plans Inola had come up with were unravelling rapidly. Oakley didn't know what they had been, but she was sure they were out of reach now.

Inola squeezed her hand one more time before breaking away. "Stay strong."

"You too," Oakley said.

A blanket of despair dampened her spirits, and as she watched Inola trot toward Tocho, she worried about why Tocho wanted to see her. Maybe he'd noticed her writing the warning. Chenoa didn't say anything about the words in the dirt, so Oakley decided she had lucked out there.

A metallic snapping nipped her nerves. It came from back at the hut Delsin and Nigan had ducked into. Nigan stood outside, holding a rifle. Delsin stepped into the sun, carrying a similar rifle, and using the lever action, cocked his weapon.

"Move," Chenoa demanded and pushed Oakley's shoulder so hard she nearly toppled.

Something inside Oakley snapped. Something had held her tongue before, but whatever it was, she didn't hold back now. *What do I have to lose? And who cares if I get hit?* She was sick of her treatment.

"You know something?" Oakley pointed at Chenoa. "You're a real bitch."

Chenoa burned a look at her while her lips curled into a snarl.

"Go ahead. Slap me, push me, I don't give a shit. We're all gonna die anyway. Whatever demons your asshole leader calls up are going to eat all of you alive. And I think you know that. Do you think To-cho knows that he's the only one who believes in his revelation? I mean, how ridiculous, right? Calling up your dead ancestors to take over the country? To start a war? Where do you think you'll end up?"

Chenoa didn't break her glare. She didn't give a sign either way. Oakley had no idea whether she was cracking Chenoa's barriers.

"We're in the back of the group. No one would see us leave. We could just run that way into those trees." Oakley nodded to the west. "Make our way across the hillside. The sentinels won't be there. Everyone is going the other way. The only two people we have to deal with are idiots. We can get past them easy."

There was no reaction on Chenoa's face.

"Really? Even after he killed your husband?" Oakley asked, giving her an incredulous look.

Chenoa grabbed a handful of the back of Oakley's hair and shoved her to the ground. She had deserved it. The comment about Chenoa's husband had been cold.

Oakley picked herself back up and dusted off her dress. *It was worth a try.*

CHAPTER THIRTY

The sun was blistering, and the left side of Chase's face felt like it had been pressed against a hot skillet. A number of clouds drifted across the sky and occasionally blocked the sun, bringing moments of reprieve. Hooves clicked against the shale that formed the hill they climbed.

His gut squirmed with anticipation. He couldn't get to Oakley fast enough, yet he was terrified to reach his destination. *Will I be able to rescue her? Would I be too late?* If they rode into that camp, guns blazing, they could all be shot and killed before reaching her. Then again, they had the advantage of surprise.

He wasn't sure what the right plan of action was. He only knew that he had to get within sight of the village. Then he could devise a plan.

I love that girl, he thought. Memories of past Christmases shuffled through his mind. She was seven. Santa had brought her an Easy-Bake Oven along with an entire play kitchen. Kira had been concerned that she was too young for it, but Chase had known better. Oakley was bright for her age—her reading and writing skills were stellar—and she was reading at a fifth-grade level. She was kneeling on the floor with all of the ingredients displayed in front of her, studying the instruction booklet.

"Okay," she started matter-of-factly. "First, you open the cake mix and pour it into the bowl." She pointed to Chase, who quickly knelt next to her, and followed the baker's directions. He snipped the top off of the package with scissors and poured it into the small bowl. "Then you pour the water in. Did you get the water? You have to measure it."

"Okay. Where is the measuring cup?"

"I'll get it," Kira said, smiling at the two of them. She took the measuring cup and brought it back with water.

"I need the mixing spoon," Chase had said.

"Here it is, Daddy."

Daddy. He sure missed being called that. She could call him that for the rest of his life, and he'd never tire of it. He'd continued being her assistant for hours as they playacted going to the market and then helped each other put the groceries away in the play kitchen.

When Oakley was six, they took a family vacation to Disneyland and spoiled her with every princess dress, toy, and event one could imagine. She met all the princesses, including Belle, her favorite. Of course Oakley was wearing her matching Belle dress, and when it came time to go into the Bibbidi Bobbidi Boutique, where they would do her makeup, face gem, nail polish, and the works, Chase assumed he'd stay back and let Kira do that with her. It was more of a mother-daughter event. Kira felt the same way, but Oakley surprised them.

"Daddy, will you go in there with me?"

"Honey, don't you want to go with Mommy?"

"I'm scared. I want you to take me." She gripped his hand.

How could he resist her brown puppy-dog eyes? He had glanced at Kira to see if she was okay with it. Her giant grin gave him his answer.

"Of course, sweetie." Chase took her hand. "After you, my princess." He'd taken a bow, and his sweeping hand had directed the way.

The memories kept hitting him one after another and tightening his chest.

"You okay?" Stone rode next to him.

Chase didn't realize that he had tears in his eyes until he wiped them. "Yeah. I'm good. Are we almost there?"

"I think so. We should be able to see their village from the top of that ridge."

The top of the hill was thirty yards away. It wouldn't be long.

"Stay our horses. We don't want to be seen." Stone halted and dismounted.

The rest of the group stopped, hopped off their horses, and tied them to a tree. They moved silently to the crest of the hill and popped their heads above the ridge. There it was. At the bottom of the valley, tucked against a red mountainside and surrounded by trees, was the destination they'd fought so hard to reach. The ground was spotted with domed huts, and Ike scrunched his face.

"Where're the tepees? You said they lived like their indigenous ancestors. Wouldn't they have tepees?"

"No. Our people built shelters out of sticks and mud. I'd say they got it right," Stone said.

"Miles, bring me those binoculars," Chase asked.

Miles crept along the hillside and handed them to Chase.

Chase swept his enhanced vision back and forth across the village several times. "What the hell?" He continued his search, slowly focusing on each hut, tree, firepit, and anything he could see. His heart began to thump at a rabbit's pace. "It's a ghost town. Nobody's there."

"Let me see." Miles took the binoculars and looked for himself.

"They've gone on," Stone said.

"Gone? Gone where?" Chase grabbed Stone's shirt and pulled his face to his. "Where did they go? You said they'd be there!"

"Easy, Chase." Miles grabbed his shoulder and pulled him back. "Don't lose it now."

"They've taken her to Angel's Landing. Or—this world's version of it."

"He's right, Chase. Remember he told us that's where the... the ceremony is going to take place."

"Already? It's happening now?"

"No, buddy. Not until tonight."

"At full blood moon," Stone said.

Blood moon, Chase thought with disgust. *My daughter's blood.*

"Let's mount up. Go in slow. We'll find their tracks, and we'll get there in time. Isn't that right, Stone?" Miles said.

"Yes. They'll be easy to track because there's many of them."

Chase sucked in air and let it out. His shoulders relaxed, and he hung his head. "I'm sorry. I lost it there for a minute."

"It's okay. You have every right," Miles said.

"Totally understandable, man," Dillon added.

They led their horses down the hill and into the valley, dust billowing behind them like smoke. The world was silent except for the clopping of hooves and the occasional whistle of the breeze. They passed by each hut. Some had doors and some didn't. Some were built large and others not much bigger than a lean-to.

Pistol in hand, Chase dismounted and began to fling open the door of every hut, one by one, hoping—a fool's hope—that he would somehow find Oakley inside one of them. Miles did the same on the other side. They walked their horses by the reins and cleared each home. At the eleventh one in, Chase froze in the doorway. He stood there for a moment. Something inside was out of place. He saw a familiar color amid a pile of blankets. The material was a striking brick red. He remembered Oakley approaching him with the duffel bag strapped to her back. She'd been wearing a red shirt and jeans. He scampered to the pile, tore through the blankets, and pulled the red material out. It was Oakley's shirt. No mistaking it. He brought it to his face and breathed in her scent—a familiar perfume. He'd smelled it on her when he picked her up. As he searched further, he found her jeans and shoes too.

"What is it?" Miles poked his head in.

"Her clothes." Chase choked on his words. He turned and showed Miles the shirt.

Miles's eyebrows lifted in empathy, and he took his hat off.

Chase took the clothes, marched to where Stone was still mounted on his horse, and held them up. "Why are her clothes here and she's not? What have they *done* to her?" He trembled with fury. His mind sifted through horrible scenarios of the worst kind.

"They would have put her in a ceremonial dress. It's required for the ritual. She must also be pure. I assure you she is untouched."

"Damn well better be," Chase spat. He opened a saddlebag, stuffed the clothes into it, and remounted his horse. "Let's go. She's not here, and we're losing daylight."

"You've got it, amigo." Miles nodded and jumped onto his horse.

They continued trotting through the camp until Stone stopped them. "Look."

Stone pointed at the ground, and Chase was off his horse and dashing to the spot in the blink of an eye. He stood over the area with his eyes transfixed on the words written in the dirt. A lot of it had been blown away by the wind, but there was enough to decipher.

"Look out." Chase turned to his group. "She wrote it."

Miles cocked his rifle. "Find cover! It's a trap!"

A gunshot cracked the air, and Chase felt a round whistle close to his cheek. More shots rang out as the men dismounted and dove for cover. Ike cried out, collapsing to his knees. His hand clutched his shoulder, and blood seeped through his fingers.

Chase ran to Ike and helped him to a nearby hut as a bullet drilled a hole into the ground near his boot. He quickly studied his wound. The round had exited his back, below the shoulder.

"It went in and out. You okay?"

"I'll be fine." Ike nodded.

"The shots came at a downward angle. Sixty-four meters. Approximately thirty-six meters high." Chase studied the hillside. He turned to find Miles and motioned to him in the direction of where the bullets had come from. "Two guys at most."

Based on the number of rounds fired and the quick succession, it was his best guess. Stone and Dillon stood together two huts away from Miles. Kenny jogged from his spot to Chase's flank.

"Kenny. Get my rifle. You and I will make it up that ridge over there." Chase pointed to the west, then he looked to Miles, Stone, and Dillon. "Miles, you cover us from your spot. Stone and Dillon, when it's time, you guys run ahead to that larger hut and draw some fire. Give us ten minutes to find a spot on the mountain, and then let loose hell."

"You've got it," Miles said.

Stone and Dillon nodded.

Keeping his head low, Kenny quickstepped back to Chase and Ike with a rifle and a shirt. He handed Chase the rifle and scooted over to Ike, holding up the shirt. "It's all I've got. I'm going to bandage your wound." He quickly wrapped the shirt over Ike's shoulder, pulled it tight, and tied a knot. Ike winced. "Keep pressure on that." Kenny patted him on the back.

"Thanks."

Chase and Kenny strode behind the hut and crossed the open plane toward the mountain. Shots rang out as Miles sent a barrage of rounds from his .30-06 Springfield rifle. Miles dove behind the hut as the return fire tore up the front of his shelter and puffed dirt up around him. A bullet ricocheted off a rock with a high-pitched whistle.

Chase and Kenny climbed the incline, using massive boulders and shrubs for cover. A piece of shale broke under Chase's foot and crumbled down the hill, but he quickly regained traction. A large, jagged piece hit another rock, flipping it toward Kenny, and he dodged it.

Chase stole glances toward the area of the shooters, but couldn't make them out yet. Twenty-two meters up, he found an outcropping boulder that made for good cover as well as an ideal spot for viewing the valley and mountainside. He should be able to make out his targets from there.

He snuck up the side of the rock and peered over it, scanning the mountainside. Most of it was rolling hills spotted with scrub oak and brush. It wouldn't make a good spot for sniping. But just beyond that was a cliff of jagged rocks and boulders that overlooked the village.

"That's where I would be." He turned to Kenny. "Do you have the binoculars?"

"No. I didn't know you wanted them."

Chase couldn't blame him. He hadn't asked for binoculars before. He gazed down toward his comrades. He found Miles and was also able to see Stone and Dillon. Chase propped his rifle on the boulder, pressed his eye to the scope, adjusted its focus, and began scanning the area for the snipers.

Shots cracked the silence from below. Stone and Dillon had run to the large hut and opened fire. Then Miles joined in.

The return fire started, and within seconds, Chase spotted a series of flashes in two areas. One was a little higher than the other and closer to the mountain. He turned his scope in that direction and soon saw blue amid the gray-and-red rock. It was the shirt of one of the shooters. Then he noticed a feather sticking out of the Native's headband, giving Chase the perfect target for a brain shot.

The scope was suddenly moving everywhere, and he lost his target. "Fuck."

His hand was shaking. Setting the rifle down, he clasped his shaking hand with the other and tried to will his arm to behave.

"What's wrong?" Kenny asked.

He couldn't hide it from Kenny. "It's... my hand. I have this condition."

"What condition is that?" Kenny cocked his head.

"I don't know. I can't figure it." Chase took a deep breath, closed his eyes, and then repositioned himself to shoot. It wasn't stopping. If anything, it was getting worse.

"Damn, that sucks. What can I do?"

"You're gonna have to shoot. I can't."

"Okay." Kenny nodded, although there was a hint of hesitation in his eyes. "Long-range shooting's not really my thing. You're the pro. Are you sure?"

"Yes, dammit. It's not going to stop, and we have to take them out."

Chase slid off the boulder, and Kenny crawled up it and positioned himself.

"Where are they at?" Kenny asked, looking through the scope.

Chase inched next to him and pointed. "Do you see that pile of boulders at the base? Head straight up from there thirty-eight meters. He's at a fifteen-degree elevation."

Kenny gave him an incredulous look. "English, please. I didn't do so well in geometry."

"A hundred and twenty-five feet up. At the center of the mountain. There's a little alcove. Do you see that?"

Kenny slowly moved the rifle up the hill then stopped. "There that bastard is."

Relief boomed in Chase. "Okay. Now look to where his head would be. Do you see his feather?"

"Oh yes. Right there."

Taking in the strength and direction of the breeze, Chase said, "Perfect. Aim the crosshairs slightly above that—as if you're shaving the top piece of that feather off. You'll hit the brain stem."

"Okay."

"Careful. We only have one shot at this. After you fire, we're giving up our location. Also, if you miss him, our target is going to hunker down, and we'll lose him."

"No pressure there," Kenny said with sarcasm.

"Take the safety off. When you have the shot, breathe in and out, then squeeze the trigger slow."

Chase watched him. The soft breeze blew Kenny's bangs to the side. The air was silent and tense. Finally, Kenny let out a small breath, and Chase knew he had this.

Crack! The round echoed through the canyon.

"Now there's red. Just to the right of the feather. Sprayed over the rock. I got him!"

"Nice. Good shot," Chase said.

Two shots burst, and one of them bounced off the boulder in front of Kenny, sending up a ray of shards. Kenny didn't panic. He slowly moved the rifle to where the shots had come from.

"I can't see him."

Guns were fired from their friends below, and clouds of dust and particles exploded around the area of the shooter. The shooter swiveled and returned fire to Miles and his group.

Kenny fired a shot and then a second and a third. The echo of a ricochet rang out. Tiny explosions popped up from rocks that were hiding the man. More shots came from below, and Kenny fired a few more as well. Finally, a man emerged from between the rocks, loping down the hillside, kicking up a cloud of dust that trailed behind him. He stumbled, fell, and got back up again.

Right eye pressed against the scope, Kenny carefully followed him with the rifle, waiting for the right shot. The man made it to the base and started running across the open ground just south of the village. He carried his rifle in one hand while his other was pressed against his side, and it was red. He raised his rifle, and Kenny squeezed off a shot. The man's leg crumpled like paper, and he fell.

"Wait," Chase said, placing a hand on Kenny's shoulder. "We could use him alive. He can lead us to my daughter."

Miles marched with purpose to the fallen man. He had discarded his rifle and carried a pistol. Blood sprayed out the back of the man's head, and it deflated like a balloon before Chase heard the thunder of the gunshot. Miles was firing his Desert Eagle. He didn't stop. He fired three more rounds into the dead man.

"What the hell's he doing? Miles! Miles!"

It wasn't until Chase and Kenny were off the mountain and traipsing through the village toward Miles and the gang that he realized why his friend had done what he had done. Ike was sitting against a post, legs splayed out, hands open on his lap, and head sunk to one side. Blood painted his arms and legs. Chase couldn't figure it out. The last time he'd seen Ike, the man had only been shot in the shoulder.

"Miles?" Chase asked softly as he approached.

Miles crouched next to Ike and caressed Ike's head. He laid him down. Ike had been gut shot. He moved slightly and opened his eyes to slits. His face was pallid as milk.

"There you go, buddy," Miles said.

"I'm sorry. I didn't think..." Ike choked.

"You have nothing to be sorry for. You did good."

Chase approached Stone. "What happened?"

"Bullets surrounded us. The hut Dillon and I hid behind was turning into Swiss cheese. We weren't going to make it much longer. Ike ran into the open to draw fire so we could run for shelter. That's when they got him." Stone hung his head.

Chase's heart dropped.

"Should I get your medicine bag?" Kenny asked.

Chase was sure Kenny knew what the rest of them knew—that Ike wasn't going to make it. They were too far away from medical help, and there wasn't much they could do for a belly shot.

Stone solemnly shook his head.

CHAPTER THIRTY-ONE

In a corner of a cave, Chenoa was spreading red paint over Oakley's face, and she wasn't gentle about it. She dipped her hands into the pot of crimson cream and smacked the contents onto her cheeks. Oakley's head banged against the wall of the cave several times while she did it. Inola had been right—Chenoa was angry that she had to repaint her face.

They had made their way up the mountainside until they entered a cave. Several of the men lit torches to light the way, and they spent the next hour hiking through the cavern. The tunnel wound its way through the mountain, flames flickering their light upon the rock walls, and they stopped at a large opening. The cave's exit was covered by a drape of falling water. The crashing of the waterfall thundered through the cave. The view beyond the waterfall was blurry, and only nondescript shapes were visible.

The people quickly built a fire near the opening and bustled to prepare food. Men stuck hunks of meat onto spits and began to turn them over the flames. Women were mixing something that looked like dough in pots.

After searching through the crowd for several minutes, Oakley finally spotted her friend. Inola was at the far end of the group, cutting vegetables on a flat rock.

"Here." Chenoa jerked Oakley's attention back to her by yanking her arm.

She commenced placing bracelets made of intricately cut turquoise up each arm and setting rings on almost all of her fingers. Then she dressed her neck with several necklaces made of matching stones. Chenoa grabbed Oakley's shoulders and steadied her as if she were a portrait she needed to study. A slight smile rose on one side of her face. It was the first one Oakley had seen on her. If she could call it a smile.

"Tonight, you are the Crimson Queen. The Queen of Fire—the chosen one."

"Chosen to die," Oakley snipped.

"It is a great privilege. The gods have chosen you to be the redeemer of all our people. Your people too. You should feel honored."

"Forgive me if I don't feel the same."

"I need to get your headdress. Don't try running. It won't be good for you."

"You mean, worse than what you're already going to do to me?"

Chenoa glared at her but said nothing. She stood and walked away.

Oakley turned around and searched for Inola again. She continued to watch her as she cut vegetables and swept them into a large pot. After a couple of minutes, Inola lifted her eyes and caught her gaze. Her face lit up with a smile. Oakley lifted her hand and gave a timid wave. Inola sent a quick one back.

Her heart swelled. She wished she could have Inola by her side. She didn't know how she was going to do this without her.

Chenoa returned and placed a headband adorned with smooth turquoise gems on her head. It was different from the one she had worn at the dance.

A little later, the entire group of people feasted on a plethora of food, potatoes, vegetables, bread, and what looked like wine. Oakley's stomach churned so badly that she couldn't find an appetite, but Chenoa made her eat, forcing her to finish at least half of her food. Then she handed Oakley a large cup filled to the brim with a red liquid. To her relief, it wasn't blood—it was more the consistency of wine. She took a sip and scrunched her face from the bitter taste.

"Go on. Finish the whole thing," Chenoa said.

"I can't. It's awful."

"You must. The Crimson Queen must have all of this."

"And what if I say no?"

"Then I'll have one of the men crane your head back and force open your mouth, and I will pour it down your throat."

Oakley sighed and continued to drink and choke it down until it was gone. She set the empty cup down and pushed it toward Chenoa, who gave a nod then stood up and walked away. The air was muggy and sweltering, and the sweat dripped down Oakley's back.

She stood and made her way to where she had seen her friend, but Inola wasn't there anymore. The crashing water thundered before her. She approached the waterfall and stared through it, becoming mesmerized by it. Water had always been peaceful, but on this day, it had to work extra hard to give Oakley's anxiety any rest.

She tried to look beyond the curtain of water, wanting to see what lay ahead for her. *Where is our destination?* Her body trembled with jittery nerves that she couldn't shake. *Where is my dad? What's my mom doing right now?* Oakley's time was running short. How much longer she had, she didn't know. She only knew she wouldn't make it into the next day. Chances of escape or rescue were slim. She told herself she had to prepare to die.

How do I surrender? My dad isn't yielding. He is still searching for me.

She had half a mind to leap through the waterfall and run, but reasoning stopped her. She didn't know what lay beyond the water portal. It could be a sheer drop to her death.

She studied the faces of the people around her. All of them were busy with their preparations. Women adorned themselves with jewelry and bright colors, and men dressed themselves from head to toe in Native American wear and headbands filled with feathers. No jeans or outside clothing were present anymore. It was as if they were preparing to attend an elaborate affair. She also noticed there were no guns. The only weapons they carried were bows and arrows or tomahawks.

They're all dressing up to watch me get murdered. How sick are these people?

She weaved her way through the crowd, searching for Inola. If there was any time she needed Inola, it was now. Oakley combed the crowd again for several minutes but couldn't find her.

CHAPTER THIRTY-TWO

Ike continued to lick at his cracked lips as he lay trembling on a pile of blankets the men had gathered. Miles fed him water, which he gulped down thirstily, and Stone gave Ike medicine that he said should help with the pain.

Chase approached Kenny, who was searching for something in his saddlebags. "That was some shot you made on the mountain."

"Thanks. You did the spotting and walked me through it."

Chase shrugged. "You did what I couldn't. You saved lives."

"So did that start happening after the incident in Phoenix?" Kenny pointed at Chase's right hand.

"How did you know about that?"

"Sheriff had me run a background check on you. It's standard."

Chase dropped his eyes and looked away.

"You were cleared," Kenny said.

"I still took an innocent life."

"That's what haunts you, isn't it? You can't fire a rifle again because you're afraid the same thing will happen," Kenny said.

"I don't know why, really. It's not that I'm afraid it will happen again. My hand goes into spasms even when I'm not shooting."

"Did you mean to kill her?"

"What?" Chase snapped, giving him an incredulous look. "No, for hell's sake. What kind of question is that?"

"Something similar happened to a friend of my dad's. He worked on the force with him and accidentally shot someone who he thought was armed. It turned out the perp was only holding a cellphone. My dad's friend came to our house one night. I heard my dad talking to him. He said, 'We are only guilty of our intentions, whether they are acted on or not. You shot an innocent person by accident, not by intent.'"

It wasn't that Chase didn't know that already—or hadn't been told that in so many ways—but something in that phrase *intentions* clicked with him. It rang with clarity.

"Intentions, huh? I suppose you're right."

"I know I'm right. My daddy was always right."

"Still... you'd better hang on to my rifle. I'm going to need you before the end."

"If I'm going to be posted as a sniper, that means you're going to be up close in the fight and deep in the shit," Kenny said.

"Most likely. I can't trust anyone else to grab my daughter, and I can't trust anyone but you to shoot the enemies around me."

"I gotcha." Kenny nodded and withdrew a large, shiny knife from his saddlebag. It was at least twelve inches from handle to point, and the blade was wide and shaped like a meat cleaver.

"Good hell. Do you kill moose with that thing?"

"I could." A sly grin spread on Kenny's face. "I made this myself. I've been learning the trade of a bladesmith. This is the first knife I've ever made. Take it. It's always given me luck."

"Thanks." Chase took the knife, sheathed it, and attached it to his hip. It was so heavy it pulled his belt at an angle.

Stone approached after scouting out their trail. "They went up the mountain."

"Up that?" Kenny pointed and pulled a face.

"The mountain is steep. We'll have to leave our horses," Stone said.

"Leave them with me." Dillon sauntered over. "I'll stay and watch over Ike."

"How are you feeling?" Chase asked.

Dillon's face was pasty and wet with sweat. "Like shit warmed over."

"Any more fevers?" Stone asked.

"I broke one a bit ago. I'm just really weak, and every bone aches."

Half of his head had swelled up more since the morning. It was anyone's guess how much internal damage he sustained from the werewolf's blow.

Chase ambled to where Ike lay. Miles was placing a wet cloth to his head.

"How are you doing?" Chase felt stupid asking the question but was absent of anything else to say.

"I'm dying. I know you're all afraid to say it, and I get it. But no one needs to stay with me."

Dillon plopped down next to him. A cloud of dust kicked up as his butt hit the dirt. "I'm staying with you anyway. I feel worse than I'm letting on, so you're stuck with me." He held out his right hand, and Ike clasped it. Stone had just finished replacing his bandages, and blood was already seeping through.

"I'm so sorry," Chase said. "You shouldn't have been out here."

"It's my job. Blame the assholes who shot me. It's not your fault." Ike fell into a coughing fit and spit blood. "Just get your daughter back, man. You do that, and it makes it all worth it."

Chase reached a hand toward him, and Ike took it. "Thank you for everything. I will never forget."

Ike nodded with a smile.

"You too, Dillon." Chase turned and shook Dillon's hand. "Take care of this man and the horses. We'll be back."

"You got it."

Chase withdrew and walked away.

Miles knelt by his friend again. Ike looked into his eyes. "Tell my wife."

Miles nodded. "I'll make sure she knows," he choked out.

As hard as it was, the men pulled away and headed for the mountainside. No one said a word. After a few minutes, Chase closed in on Miles and placed an arm over his shoulders, and Miles leaned into his friend.

The hill was steep, and the trail snaked. They stepped over large and small rocks, and sagebrush rubbed against Chase's arm like sandpaper. The sun was well past noon and scorching the right side of his face. He thought of Oakley. *Where is she? What is happening?*

His thighs burned as the incline increased, and sweat ran into his eyes. He rubbed it away, but more wetness drained down his cheek onto his lips. He tasted the saltiness. There was a plateau ahead he hoped would show a clear direction to take. He couldn't imagine Tocho's people climbing to the top of this mountain. It didn't make sense. There had to be a trail that led to the east or west around the mountain. The thought of traipsing around the width of this massif was too daunting to think of. He and his men would never make it by nightfall.

Once they stepped onto the ridge, the trail flattened out and turned to the east. Scrub oak grew over the trail, and when they'd cleared those leafy branches, Chase saw the gaping maw of the mountain. It was a cave. The footprints and drag marks led straight into it.

Kenny stepped back, placing his hands against his lower back, and craned his neck to look at the mass. "Huh. Do you think it comes out somewhere? Like on the other side?"

"Only one way to find out." Stone marched inside.

Their flashlights illuminated their way. Kenny ran his light along the rocky walls in awe. "I hope there's no bats in here. I hate bats."

Chase let out a slight chuckle. "There's worse things to fear ahead than bats."

"Don't know about that. I've always been scared of 'em. My brother convinced me that they'd dive atcha and bite your neck. He definitely scared me early on."

"Don't worry. I'll save ya." Miles slapped Kenny's back with a grin. "The way things are going, I wouldn't be surprised to find vampires."

"Don't say that," Kenny said.

The cave burrowed deep into the mountain. Chase ducked under a group of low-hanging stalactites, and he heard a distant rumbling. This thunder didn't boom and go away—it was constant.

Stone led the way and stopped when white flakes floated around them like snow. He snatched one out of the air. "Ash," he said, rubbing it between his fingers.

Then Chase smelled the campfire. "They're close."

"Maybe. I don't see smoke. The fire is out already. They could have moved on, but stay quiet and ready just in case."

They slowed their pace and eyed every step they took.

"Keep your flashlights pointed at the ground. Use them only when needed," Chase whispered. *Are they up ahead? Will we reach them before they get to Angel's Landing?* Chase could only hope. *Hang in there, baby.*

The cave turned downward, causing them to stop and study the way forward. The ledge was fenced off by stalagmites, but there were a couple of spaces wide enough to squeeze through. Chase flashed his light below. It was a twelve-foot drop, and the footing was too sketchy to attempt jumping.

"Follow my lead," Stone whispered and, holding on to a stalagmite, lowered himself onto the face of the small cliff, finding footholds and outcroppings. He made the descent look easy.

Chase followed carefully until he stepped on a rock that gave way and tumbled. He twisted and fell, but Stone was fast and caught him in his arms. With Stone's help, Chase was able to bring himself to a standing position again.

"Thank you."

It took a few moments for Miles and Kenny to make it down, and the group continued marching forward. The thundering sound increased enough for Chase to discover its source.

"A waterfall inside the mountain?" Kenny asked. "Do you think they're cannibals like in that movie *The Thirteenth Warrior*?"

"You watch a lot of movies," Miles said.

"I love 'em."

"I've seen that movie." Stone patted Kenny on the shoulder.

"You have?"

"It's a good movie."

Miles shrugged.

They trekked on for another thirty minutes until they saw the waterfall covering the exit like a curtain, and a reddish glow emanated from beyond, lighting up the cave. There were objects all over the ground near the gaping hole but no sign of Oakley or the rest of them. Chase ran ahead and halted at the exit.

He turned back to his group as they neared. "I can't see beyond it."

Stone stood at the edge and studied the falling water. Images on the other side were blurry.

"They were just here. It hasn't been long." Miles knelt at the remnants of a fire and placed an open palm above it. "It's still hot."

Kenny picked up a pot that sat against a wall, peered inside, and then took a whiff. His face twisted in disgust. "Whatever they ate sure stinks."

"She was here. How long ago?" Chase turned to Stone.

Stone crossed to the fire remnants and crouched next to Miles. "No more than an hour."

Excitement and anxiety raced through his bones. "We've gotta pick up the pace."

"Hold on, Chase." Miles patted the air in a calming motion.

"Hold on? That's all we have been doing—waiting, holding. We'd be on them right now if we hadn't been dragging our feet the whole way."

"That's not fair," Miles said. "You're upset."

"You're damn right I'm upset."

"Just hear me out, Chase. If we catch up to them now, they will have the advantage. They'll hear us coming a mile away and pick us off one by one."

Kenny stepped forward. "He's right."

Chase took a deep breath and let it out. "What do you suggest?"

"Let them get to their destination, set up camp, and get comfortable. Then we can scope it out and devise a plan. We can do like you said—sneak in, grab Oakley, and get the hell out of there."

Chase let the words run circles in his mind and then nodded. "You're right. That would be best."

"What do we do now?" Kenny asked.

"Let's take a breather. Get a bite of protein into us. We're gonna need it."

CHAPTER THIRTY-THREE

Stone handed out pieces of jerky, and Kenny passed around a bag of trail mix. Chase sat and chawed on his piece, staring off into nothing. His mind raced. The adrenaline pumping through his veins made him want to bust through those bastards who took his daughter and kill them all single-handedly. With the amount of rage that fueled him, he believed he could do it. Rationality told him otherwise.

"What's this Angel's Landing like?" Miles asked Stone. "You said it was a mesa."

"It is a mesa, but the path is very narrow and dangerous. There's a little more space at the top, but not enough to hold all of their people."

"Maybe it's not really at Angel's Landing," Kenny said.

"My grandfather is not mistaken. It is there."

"Maybe it's different in their world. You know, like how we've run into so many things on this journey that aren't part of our world," Kenny said.

"Is that what that is?" Miles pointed at the waterfall. "Once we go through there... we're officially entering the other world?"

"Yes. I can feel it. Can you?" Stone said.

"What do you mean?"

"It's what we've been feeling this whole time." Chase took a swig from his canteen and set it down. "The air is alive with it. It feels like being held under water and charged with electricity all at once. It's gotten stronger the closer we've come. I feel a million living things swimming all round us, crawling on us, biting us, but I can't see them."

"My grandfather says other worlds are all around us," Stone said. "That they live in one space, like one giant sphere. Occasionally, we bump into them—where the veil is thin—and when you feel the chills up your spine or along your neck and arms, that's them touching you. I believe the veil has been thin during this whole trek. This portal"—he pointed at the waterfall—"is generating enough energy and spreading it through this entire canyon that it has cracked the veil that protects our world."

Kenny shivered. "That's a creepy thought."

"It's also dangerous. If we don't stop Tocho and close this gate, whatever is in there is going to be in our world."

"You still have doubts?" Stone locked eyes with Miles.

"I don't know what to believe. I'd rather get Chase's daughter back and forget this whole place. Them too."

"I hear that," Kenny said.

"Tocho will continue to raid our towns, steal our daughters, murder innocent people. He will gain more power after tonight. Tocho must be killed." Stone took a drink.

"I get that, Stone, but we don't have an army. To kill him, we'd have to start a war." Miles crossed his arms.

"Getting my daughter back is priority. If we get a chance to kill him, great. No one wants to cut his head off more than I do. But if it risks our rescue, then we kill him another day."

"I will kill him," Stone said. "We'll get your daughter back, and I will stay behind to kill Tocho."

Chase furrowed his eyebrows. Stone seemed to prioritize killing Tocho over getting Oakley back. Chase prayed whatever the man was feeling didn't get in the way of their first goal.

They stretched after eating their protein snacks and performed a quick ammo inspection. They laid out their weapons, which consisted of Miles's .30-06 Springfield rifle, Chase's M1A SOCOM 16 rifle, Stone's 12-gauge shotgun, Kenny's two 9mm Glock pistols, Miles's M9 Beretta, and Chase's Desert Eagle 50 AE.

They were getting slim on ammo. Stone had ten shotgun shells. Chase had fifteen rounds left for his rifle and twelve rounds for his pistol. Miles had eight rounds left for his rifle and eighteen rounds for his pistol, and Kenny carried two fifteen-round magazines.

"Miles and Kenny, you guys will be manning the rifles," Chase said.

"Are you sure? You're the best sharpshooter we have," Miles said.

"Kenny is just as good." Chase handed him the rifle and the box of rounds. "I'm going to be down on the ground, getting my daughter."

"I will be with you." Stone snatched up the shotgun and sheathed it.

"Here." Kenny handed Chase one of his pistols.

"I have my fifty cal," Chase said.

"You might need something lightweight too. Easier to handle," Kenny said.

"Stone, you could use the Glock." Chase held it out for him.

"I'm good." Stone withdrew a tomahawk from his pack and stuck it into the back of his belt.

Chase took the Glock from Kenny and jammed it into the back of his pants.

Miles picked up his rifle. "What are the chances of getting them all to stand still?"

"I'm not so worried about them as I am about whatever they're calling up from hell. Do you know what it will be?" Kenny looked at Stone.

"Demons." Stone's words were like teeth running against bare bone.

"Did your grandpa give you any advice or magic words to battle these things?"

"He gave me one word."

"What was that?" Kenny asked.

"*Poyoha*. Run."

"Shit," Miles said.

Stone crossed to the edge of the cave and stared through the rushing water. Miles tied a rope around Stone's waist and wrapped the other end around a stalagmite. Chase and Kenny held on to the rope as well.

"We've gotcha in case you fall." Miles nodded.

Stone strapped the shotgun case to his back and carefully stepped through the wall of water, which splashed as the weight of it hit him. His feet slipped slightly. Stone leapt—Chase held his breath—and the slack of rope ran with him. The slack ran out, and the rope pulled taut in their hands. The only sound was rushing water.

"Stone! Stone! Are you okay?" Chase called.

No response came for a few seconds. Then Stone called, "I'm okay. You have to jump, but there's solid ground below."

"How far below?" Kenny mumbled.

"It's not far," Stone said as if he'd heard Kenny's question.

"I'll go." Chase gave Miles a firm look.

Stone detached himself from the rope, and the guys retracted it and tied the end around Chase.

"You're good." Miles nodded.

Chase followed Stone's steps and walked into the waterfall. The weight of the river was crushing and attempting to throw him off the ledge. He stuck his left foot out, searching for any other ledge to cross to—it met empty space. His left foot slipped, and he caught himself.

"Jump!" Stone hollered. "Trust me."

Chase crouched, preparing to propel his body forward with the thrust of his legs.

"Jump out at least five feet."

Five feet. Chase repositioned himself, took a step back—the cascading aquatic force pushing at him—and took two quick steps. He used his right leg to launch himself into the air.

He flew through the water and out the other side, and his body dropped. Everything was a blur. Chase couldn't adjust his eyesight quickly enough. He saw dark objects, a massive form below that might be the ground, and the blur of Stone's face and hands.

His feet landed, but because his boots were wet, they slid out from under him. The ground was uneven, consisting of crevices and bulges and angling down to either side. Stone's arms were clasped around Chase and kept him from tumbling. Focusing his eyes, he looked into Stone's smiling face.

"I've got ya," Stone said.

Chase untied himself and told them they could pull the rope back, which they did.

Kenny leapt next. He popped out from the waterfall careening, his arms and legs flailing in the air as if that would help him fly. He landed just on the edge, and Chase grabbed his belt and pulled him in.

"Miles! Tie yourself in the middle of the rope, throw us one end, and keep the other end tied off!" Chase called.

"Got it!" Miles answered.

One end of the rope popped out of the waterfall, and Stone caught it. They waited for a few minutes, and then Miles's blurred form appeared through the waterfall. He stumbled then leapt. He made it all the way to whatever ground they stood on, and Kenny grabbed him in his arms.

Chase couldn't help but wonder how his daughter had done it—along with the rest of the tribe. They would all have had to leap the same way. Then again, the Natives were more used to this route than they were.

Chase took in his surroundings by first deciphering what it was they stood on. It wasn't ground. It was made of a hard, earthy material, and he crouched down and felt it.

"This is bark. Is this a tree?" He stood up and scanned the area.

They were standing on a tree limb at least fifteen feet wide. The edge of it bent downward, then the limb twisted and narrowed itself into a point far below. All around them, filling the sky above and below, were massive arms of the giant tree, which turned and dove, rose and curved, but none of them had leaves, and each limb's tip disappeared into thin air as if plugged into something invisible. Blue sparks popped around the spots where they vanished.

Chase's jaw dropped as he took it all in. Each hair on his body tingled and straightened. The air felt like soup. His mind spun in a euphoric way. Something unseen rubbed against his arm and then slithered across his lower back, and he shuddered.

Kenny's eyes widened. "What the fuck was that?"

"Did you feel it too?" Chase asked.

Kenny nodded.

Miles turned his head slowly, taking in the sights around him, and when he turned to face Chase, his skin was pale, his mouth hung open, and his bottom lip quivered. It was clear that he wanted to say something, but the fear must have gobbled his words.

The sky was dark except for a spot that glowed fiery red and orange. Stars were popping out, and the sun was burning its last rays. Or so Chase thought. He looked again. It wasn't the sun at all—it was the moon. The blood moon.

Filling the sky around them and as far as they could see were hundreds more trees like the one they stood upon. They weren't the evergreens one would expect to see in these mountains but deciduous trees—like giant oaks. But there was something odd about them. Chase couldn't place it until he saw the trees that were miles away. They were at a far-enough distance to make them appear small, and he could see them whole. They floated in the air, unmoving and completely upside down.

He looked down at the limb they stood on. It wasn't a branch. It was one of the roots of the tree. Peering over the edge, far, far below, he could make out the branches that formed the canopy. It still wasn't filled with leaves, but there were a few patches of foliage in sporadic spots.

A flash of light in his peripheral vision caught Chase's attention, and he twisted to see the source. Another flash came. It was lightning. It cracked the sky like a rock fracturing a windshield. This electricity was a deep reddish hue—almost purple. The rumble of thunder followed, and black clouds crept across the sky.

Chase studied the roots of a distant tree. There was still something peculiar about how the ends disappeared into nothing. Then, like a lightbulb turning on, he realized what it was. The roots of these trees were planted in his world. They were *feeding* off of his world. That pissed him off on a whole other level.

Preparing for their return, Stone tied their end of the rope to a branch so as not to lose it. "We'd better move." He turned and marched forward. The group followed, and no one said a word.

CHAPTER THIRTY-FOUR

They traveled along the wide bark road as it curved and dipped, ducking under wooded arms that crossed their path and stepping over occasional bulges in the roots. Chase tried to keep his eyes off the vast emptiness below them. One small slip would be fatal. The roots of the tree surrounded them above and below, and the dark sky and red canyons served as their backdrop. It was a picturesque scene in a strange fantasy world, and the silence was deafening. He didn't hear a bird chirping or a squirrel scurrying. Not even the whistling of a breeze passed them. The temperature was warm with a slight chill, which was not uncommon for an evening in the desert.

As they passed smaller roots that jutted out, Chase ran his hand over their surfaces and saw purple light run along the lines of the wood like fast-moving snakes. It would disappear and reappear farther up the root branch and, like sparks of life, throughout the entire tree. *That's why the air feels electric. These trees produce electricity—along with the lightning.*

The giant red mesa of Angel's Landing emerged in the distance. They were getting closer. They transferred to wooded paths—hopping from one root to another—to stay on the trajectory toward their destination. The roots they walked on were narrowing and becoming not much wider than the width of their bodies. They held their arms out to keep balance.

Another tree stood adjacent to them. Studying its giant limbs, Chase could see a straighter and safer path to the mesa. Stone must have seen it, too, because he leaped to the new tree, and the rest followed. Miles's right foot slid as he landed, and Chase snatched his arm, halting his fall. Miles's eyes were huge as he breathed a sigh of relief, steadying himself.

Before long, the monolith of Angel's Landing was in front of them. It stood as a single, titanic rock—like a monster's tooth—protruding from the ground far below. Red-and-brown mountains encircled the mesa. Two gigantic trees floated on either side of the mesa, like massive claws reaching toward the rock. Chase scanned the trees through the binoculars and saw tiny figures inhabiting the roots and limbs. They were using the trees as an amphitheater, the center stage being the point of Angel's Landing.

The trail to the point was only a few feet wide. It rose, curved, and angled down again like the spine of a brontosaurus. The trail was spotted with evergreens and shrubs. The view was breathtaking. Steel fence posts had been installed in various spots along it, and a chain connected them in areas where people stood a greater risk of falling. The guard chain hung at waist height so one could hold on to it for security.

Stone faced the group. "Tocho will have the altar placed at the point. That's where the ceremony will be held."

Chase appreciated how everyone was referring to it as a ceremony instead of what it was—a sacrifice. A murder. Using calmer language didn't change the direness of the situation.

"There's a tent up there. I think. Right next to that large rock at the top." Miles lowered the binoculars and handed them to Chase.

Chase raised the binoculars and studied the area. After a few seconds, he focused in on what looked like deerskin hanging off the side of a rock. The fabric was pulled taut as if to create an enclosure. "I see the tent. That's where she'll be. I'm sure of it." He nodded.

"That sounds right," Stone said.

Chase turned to the group. "Stone and I will hike the trail to the top and get in that tent. If we're lucky, she'll be in there and we can pull her to safety. Kenny, you make your way through that tree on the left side, and, Miles, you take the one on the right. Each of you, find a spot where the point of Angel's Landing is clear so you can take a good shot. If we don't make it in time and they take Oakley to the altar, don't hesitate to kill Tocho. Also, clear a path for us. Shoot anyone in our way."

"You've got it, brother." Miles patted him on the shoulder.

Kenny was gripping a branch with white knuckles and staring into the vast open below.

"Kenny," Chase said, approaching him, but he didn't seem to hear. "Kenny."

Kenny turned with a look as if he were ready to vomit. "I don't do so well with heights. This is... extreme. But I heard ya. Make my way to the left. I'll find a spot, and I'll cover you and your daughter."

"Thank you. It looks like there's a path to that tree from here. These branches intersect with the big one on the side of the mesa. Will you be okay?"

"I will."

"Try not to look down. It messes with your head," Chase said.

Chase and Stone stepped off the tree and onto the stone path of Angel's Landing and, utilizing the chain railing, commenced forward. Both Kenny and Miles were crossing through the mazes of winding roots to their destinations, and the crimson moon eyed them from above. Its reddish glow illuminated their way. Chase had seen a lot of bright moons in his life that lit up the night, but this one was a beacon charged to three times the wattage, radiating a glow that turned the world a dark bloodred.

Gusts blew against them, strong enough to rock Chase's balance. He white-knuckled the chain and breathed a sigh of relief as it kept him from falling. The path was not much wider than his form.

"Is there a moment that marks the exact time when Tocho will... will execute?" Chase asked with trepidation. "Have we missed it? Can you tell?"

"He will strike when the moon is at its peak. It must be directly above us."

Chase glanced again at the bright orb. It sat at eleven o'clock. He had no idea how fast the moon moved, but he quickened his pace.

The path angled steeply then dropped slightly and snaked its way up the mountain. They passed several Utah junipers with strange and twisted shapes, each no more than fifteen feet tall. The men and women sitting in the gnarly roots on either side of the mountain were coming in clearer. Their movements caught Chase's attention as several of them stood and walked around.

They disgusted him. How could these people take part in such a diabolical plan to murder an innocent girl—and furthermore, to raise the dead and summon creatures from hell? It made him ponder what really might happen.

Could Tocho's vision really come true? Chase had seen enough to make him question rational beliefs, so he preferred not to find out.

Stone halted and raised his hand for Chase to stop. He didn't say a word. They stood frozen, listening to the night. A slight rustling of brush came from twenty feet ahead and then ceased.

Stone craned his neck to Chase and whispered, "There's someone behind that tree."

Chase strained to see and saw a shadow between the limbs of a juniper.

Stone held his forefinger to his lips in a shushing motion. "I will go around the right of the tree—you go to the left."

Chase nodded. Stone was courteous enough to give him the side of the path with the chain railing rather than making him risk the edge only inches from a deadly drop-off.

They crept forward. Stone kept his shotgun sheathed and withdrew the tomahawk from his belt. Chase holstered his gun to keep his hands free. They couldn't risk the sound of a gunshot alerting the crowd. Chase thought about using the knife Kenny had given him but felt safer using hand-to-hand combat.

Stone careened right and, holding fast to a branch hand, wielded the tomahawk with his right, while Chase stepped around the tree to the left. Their opponent was in focus between the branches. The man wore deerskin pants and a colored breastplate. He was at least six feet tall and muscular.

The enemy's head jerked in Stone's direction as a twig snapped. Chase stepped quickly. Stone swung low with his weapon and struck the man in the leg while the Native pounded down at him with an object. Chase dashed up behind the man and seized a hank of his hair. He snaked a hand under the man's chin and hip checked him, tossing the Paiute to the ground like a wet sack of laundry.

The Paiute rolled and slammed his back against one of the iron posts holding the chain rail. His eyes widened with fright after his narrow escape. He started to rise, but Chase didn't give him the chance. He snapped a front kick to the man's chin—hearing the crunch as his opponent's teeth clashed together—and the enemy flipped over the chain and dropped into the dark abyss. The man didn't scream as he disappeared. The chain he'd flipped over swung back and forth with a rattle.

Chase quickly ran to assist Stone, who was hanging on to the edge of the cliff with one hand. The foot Stone had barely resting on the trail slipped as Chase arrived. Chase grabbed the thickest branch he saw and lay stomach down, a hand outstretched to Stone. He looked into the man's wide eyes and gritted teeth. Blood ran from the upper-right corner of Stone's forehead. Stone lifted his right hand—still holding the tomahawk—upward to Chase, who grabbed the weapon just below its blade and pulled. The muscles in his arms, and down his back and legs and core, tensed as he used all his strength.

He pulled Stone up until the man was able to grab the edge with his right hand. Chase set the tomahawk down, grabbed the middle of Stone's arm, and pulled. Stone dug into the mountain with his feet; crumbs of rocks fell. Once Stone's upper torso was on the mountain path again and able to pull the rest of himself to safety, Chase breathed in relief. He stayed lying on his side while Stone rolled to his back, and they both panted until their breathing was controlled.

"You okay?" Chase asked.

Stone nodded. "Is he taken care of?"

"Unless he has wings."

CHAPTER THIRTY-FIVE

The beating of drums rocked the night, and Chase and Stone increased their pace. Chase occasionally glanced left to right in hopes of seeing his partners, but there were too many branches and shadows in the way. Stone wiped at his brow—it was at least the fifth time he'd done that.

"Stone, are you okay? That wound looked pretty bad."

"I'm okay. He hit my forehead with his weapon. It's a bleeder. Nothing serious."

"Stop for a minute. Let's bandage it."

"We don't have time, Chase."

"We can't have blood running in your eyes when we're trying to fight either. It just takes a minute, and then we'll run like bandits."

Stone halted and Chase wasted no time in taking his shirt off and tearing one long sleeve away. He handed the fabric to Stone, who wrapped it tightly around his forehead like a headband. Chase threw his shirt back on, with one sleeve missing. Then, muscles straining and thighs burning, they ran up the incline. Chase's lungs labored at this altitude and level of exertion—sucking in copious amounts of oxygen—and the air burned away as soon as it entered.

Chase wiped sweat from his brow and looked ahead. Several drums were being played, and the rhythm of their music inspired the audience to rise to their feet and cheer. The tent was closer. A section of its deerskin flapped in the wind, and its sides billowed in and back out like a lung. It, too, seemed to be grappling for breath.

Lightning cracked the night, one bolt right after the other, and on both sides of the mesa, clouds slipped in. The point of the mesa wasn't in sight yet. Once they cleared the peak and were past the tent, they would be able to see it.

Chase and Stone pushed on to twenty-five feet, then fifteen, then ten. Something caught Chase's eye, and he turned to his left. There was a figure high above in the gnarly roots who stood out from the crowd. He wore a blue and white shirt.

Chase paused for a moment to bring the binoculars to his eyes. It was his friend Kenny, planted on his stomach with his rifle at the ready. Using his first two fingers shaped in a V, Kenny pointed to his own eyes and then toward the point of Angel's Landing.

Chase's heart skipped a beat. *What does he mean? Is he warning me of something?* He gave Kenny a thumbs-up and jogged toward Stone, who had stopped short of the tent. It leaned against a giant rock that blocked their view beyond. Chase ran past Stone, and the moment he crested the hill and stood next to the tent, horror gripped his throat.

A young woman with long black hair and a headband was walking the path away from the tent toward the point. She wore a deer-skin dress, and jewelry adorned her arms. Several men parted to make a path for her. A giant of a man stood next to a stone altar at the point, watching her with a steely gaze. A bonfire blazed next to him, and two men sat behind him, beating on drums.

"Oakley," Chase mumbled as if the air had been sucked out of him. He also recognized the man from the store. He wore a chief's headdress that hung to his ankles. "Tocho."

Several men stood between Chase and her. He was moments too late. Ten or fifteen minutes earlier, he could have snuck her out of the tent—if it hadn't been for the fight or Stone going over the edge or them bandaging his wound or their failure to leave sooner or a million other things.

Don't beat yourself up. Stay calm. Think this through.

He wanted to call out her name. He itched to bolt for her, tearing through these men like paper, because nothing could stop this father from saving his daughter. Stone's hand gripped Chase's shoulder. The calmness in his touch prevented Chase from doing anything foolish.

"You won't make it. They'll kill you first."

Chase sucked in air and released it. "What, then?"

"Let our friends do their job. They have their scopes on Tocho."

CHAPTER THIRTY-SIX

The air was thick and electric. The gnarly brambles on either side of the mesa reminded Chase of the briar patch that Br'er Rabbit begged not to be thrown into, and purple sparks continued to run along their black arms. Thunder added to the ambience, and lightning crackled, lighting up the scene in flashes.

He couldn't see his daughter's face. She kept her head down as she sat on the altar. She finally lifted her head to reveal a face painted in dark crimson from her forehead to her neck. Chase's stomach twisted. Tocho stepped in front of her, blocking Chase's view, and directed the young woman to lie down.

Don't touch my daughter, you son of a bitch. Chase clenched his fists until his nails almost drew blood.

Eight men stood in his way, including the drummers. Four torches, stuck in the ground, burned and splashed light that flickered across the Natives' bodies. The men were all armed with either bows and arrows or tomahawks.

No guns, Chase thought.

One man stepped toward Tocho. He wore a top hat. Chase remembered the fight with him at the store. Top Hat shook rattles in each hand and began to dance—lifting one knee up and then alternating it with the other—and chant.

"Oye ya ya-ta-hey-hey-oye ya ya-ta-hey hey."

Tocho began a chant opposite to Top Hat's. It was filled with several unfamiliar words and came out with a passion and a cry as if pleading with the gods. He raised his hands high, craning his neck and holding a tomahawk. More drums filled the night as members of the audience joined in and began to drum and chant along with them.

A strong gust of wind blew against Chase—more like through him—turning his skin to gooseflesh and rustling the hair and tassels of the Natives. The night felt as heavy as molasses, and then the voices came. A thousand incoherent whispers and mumblings were carried on the wind. The crowd suddenly grew in size as Chase felt the presence of a million evil beings that slithered invisibly against his arms and back. One snaked across his neck, making him shiver. He tried to catch them in his hand but came up empty.

Stone flinched as if being touched and sent a look of fright to Chase.

In the far corner of the plateau grew a dark cloud—a shadow of sorts—that stood out blacker than the sky around it. A rancid scent reached Chase's senses, and an unnerving mechanical hum rattled his nerves. Out of this dark mist, a face formed—two crazed eyes as white as snow—glowering with menacing intentions—and beneath it a twisted smile. Its teeth were misshapen, crooked, and yellow. Whatever it was began to laugh. There was no sound, just a mouth giggling.

The evil that radiated from this demon raked across Chase's nerves like icy fangs against bone. There was an evil about this creature that surpassed Tocho or anything else Chase had witnessed. Stone's grandfather had said the words *atsa* and *asaakwasi*. Evil. Devil. If there was a devil, this creature was it.

"Uncle Willie," Tocho said, and the demon nodded.

Chase looked for Kenny but couldn't see him. "Shoot now, Kenny. Shoot him now," he murmured.

He couldn't wait any longer. Chase withdrew his Desert Eagle, clicked off the safety, and pointed it at Tocho. He didn't have the best shot. Men—their backs to him—were in the way, so he had a very narrow window, not to mention that Oakley was on the other side of Tocho, and Chase couldn't risk hitting her.

Tocho continued to chant and pump his arms in the air, calling to the sky.

"Hang in there, Oakley. Just a little longer." He hoped Kenny and Miles were perfecting their aim at that very moment.

How is she just lying there so still and calm as if nothing was going to happen? Does she know what they're going to do? Maybe they didn't tell her. Maybe she was drugged.

Tocho stepped closer to the altar, lowering the blade of his tomahawk to her throat. He now blocked Chase's view of her. Chase's heart was about to explode. His gut wrenched.

Tocho's body jerked—the crack of a gunshot thundered—and the crowd and drumming were silenced. Red blossomed next to his shoulder blade. The chief stumbled sideways.

Yes. Chase's heart thrummed with an ounce of excitement.

Tocho twisted to glare in the direction of the shot. Kenny's rifle fired again, and Tocho stumbled but didn't fall. Kenny's aim had been even better that time. Blood exploded from the center of Tocho's chest.

The men in front of Chase twisted their heads back and forth in search of the sniper.

Tocho still didn't fall. Raising his weapon, he stepped closer to the altar.

"Oakley!" Chase hollered.

She rolled off the altar and turned, scanning the scene, weighing her options. She made a move to run past Tocho, but the barbarian strode to block her path. She hesitated then turned and ran in the opposite direction.

"Oakley!" he yelled again with more pain in his voice.

She was running for the edge of the point.

Life moved in slow motion, and images blurred. Chase's mind swam with confusion and fear as he watched his daughter leap from the edge and into the open air. His heart stopped. He felt as if a black hole had opened inside his chest and sucked his heart, organs, and entire life deep into its portal. He couldn't be seeing this. This wasn't happening. He couldn't accept it.

But she was nowhere in sight. She was gone.

"Oakley!"

CHAPTER THIRTY-SEVEN

As Chase shouted, all of the men spun to face him. Tocho's eyes glowed with an unnatural white fire, and he burned his glare at Chase. A shot came from Miles's rifle and hit Tocho's thigh, but it might as well have been a mosquito bite. Some kind of magic was within him, keeping him from feeling the damage of the bullets.

In other situations, Chase would have been scared—or at least nervous—by the number of enemies he faced, but none of those emotions crippled him. His body was fueled by rage, vengeance, and adrenaline. Chase withdrew his giant knife, holding it in his left hand and the gun in his right. He pointed and fired at the closest man. Blood exploded over the Native's face as his head snapped back. The recoil from the powerful handgun normally would have required that two hands fire it, but not that day. The anger of a father who had just lost his daughter numbed Chase from physical pain and gave him extra strength.

A blast from Stone's shotgun knocked a man on Chase's left off his feet. Tocho's men charged, and Chase did too. Chase fired his gun again, blowing a hole through the next man's torso, and then finished him with a side kick to the chest, propelling him off the edge of the mesa.

Chase twisted to face the next oncomer, who was swinging a tomahawk, but a shot from Miles hit the man's right shoulder blade and stopped him in his tracks. In one swift movement, Chase arced his knife upward, slicing through the man's throat and nearly cutting his head off. Blood pumped rhythmically from the enemy's carotid artery as he crumpled.

Kenny picked another man off with two rapid rounds. The shots propelled the Paiute back until he stumbled off the ledge. Stone blasted lead at another man—pellets bit into the man's side, and he staggered.

Something smacked hard against the back of Chase's head. He caught the blur of the tomahawk that had struck him and the man holding it. The Paiute warrior prepared to swing again, gritting his teeth, and Chase pointed his gun and fired into the man's stomach.

Chase touched the back of his head, and his fingers came away bloody. He felt liquid run down his neck. It was deep but not enough to kill him.

No, not today. He was fighting his way to Tocho. Chase was going to cut his head off and fill his body with bullet holes, but more importantly—although it might be fruitless—he was going to look for his daughter. He still couldn't believe she was gone.

Maybe there's a ledge just below or a tree that she jumped to. Could she be playing a trick? His gut told him no. There were no trees, branches, or roots that stretched anywhere near the spot where she had jumped.

Another man leapt from a nearby tree root to join the fray—Top Hat—and Stone was caught in a struggle with him. Each held a tomahawk, and Stone's gun lay on the ground. Their arms wrapped up with each other as they grappled.

An arrow passed Chase and stuck into Stone's side, making him drop to one knee. Chase popped a shot at Top Hat. His head snapped back, his hat flew, and Chase fired another shot into Top Hat's chest, propelling the man off the ledge.

Another arrow raked across Chase's hand, causing him to drop his gun. It skittered across the solid surface of the mesa. The wound burned. Chase turned, saw the man arming another arrow, and charged at him. Chase passed the knife from his left to his right. Although his hand felt crippled from the arrow blow, he wasn't going to allow the pain to keep him from handling it.

Realizing that he wouldn't be able to arm his bow in time, the Native dropped it and withdrew his tomahawk. Chase swung his knife down. The Native drove his weapon toward Chase's head. Chase caught his opponent's wrist, and the man caught Chase's wrist, and they were deadlocked.

Chase dug a front kick to his enemy's gut, which released the hold on his wrist, then he thrust the blade toward the man's head, but the man ducked and came at him with a blow of his own. His tomahawk met Chase's knife in a rattling clash.

The warrior swung two more quick bursts, which Chase expertly parried. He stepped back from the man, and they squared off, pacing back and forth like tigers preparing to strike. Chase leapt in with a combination of blows, and switching the blade to his other hand, he wielded an arcing blow—which his combatant blocked—and sent a low kick that made the man's knees buckle then slammed a punch to the guy's left ear. The man stood on the verge of crumpling.

Chase dove in for the kill with two blurring slashes of his knife. The blade cut open a wound across the man's chest, and a second one opened his gut. The man hunched over and gawked at Chase as blood poured from his mouth and his guts splashed onto the ground. Chase sent a final backhanded blow with his knife to the side of the man's head and watched as he tumbled off the cliff.

After a quick search, Chase found where his pistol had fallen and snatched it up. He turned at the growling of a beast. The man Chase had shot earlier in the gut was not dead and was transforming. His fingers extended, claws popped out, and his face pulsed and swam as his bones readjusted and sharp teeth grew. Chase fired two shots into his head, one in his throat, and a fourth into his chest. The transformation stopped, and the body fell still.

Stone gritted his teeth and held the wound where the arrow was stuck. He gripped the shaft but didn't pull on it. Tocho approached, and he and Stone stared at each other.

"You help the white man?" Tocho asked.

"I help humanity."

"What about our people?"

"You hurt our people. You disgrace our Paiute ancestry," Stone hissed.

"And you have come to destroy me?"

Stone gave a single nod.

Tocho placed a palm against the bleeding wound on his chest, smeared the crimson plasma across his torso and then his face, and bellowed out a war cry.

Gripping his tomahawk, Stone approached him with a limp.

Tocho sprang, attacking with his tomahawk, and Stone parried it. Stone kept his stance, allowing Tocho to attack while he defended himself. Stone blocked a downward stroke, and his arm shuddered from the force of it. He held his own for a bit, but he was no match for the strength and skill of Tocho. Their tomahawks clashed, and Stone's snapped in two. Tocho raked his blade across Stone's chest and then sent a backhand blow against his head. Stone crumpled to the ground.

Chase was locked in battle with an enemy, holding back the man's hand that held a blade inches from his throat. It took all of his strength to keep the knife from cutting him. He didn't know how much longer he could hold it off. Chase tried to hit him with his free hand until the man clasped his wrist with an iron grip.

While Chase stared into the angry eyes of his opponent, the man's body suddenly spasmed as if an invisible blow had slammed into him. His grip loosened, and his eyes rolled. Blood spread from the wound in his ribs. Miles had fired a perfect shot. Chase pushed his assailant off the cliff.

Panting heavily, he turned to see his friend bleeding on the ground. At first glance, Chase thought Stone was dead until the man began to crawl. Tocho towered over him.

Chase quickly grabbed Stone's hand, pulled him away from Tocho, and helped him to his feet. Stone's face glistened with sweat, and his eyes were half-open. He was fighting to stay coherent.

Chase turned to face Tocho. The massive chief stood ten feet away. His face was painted with lines of red, white, and yellow, and his eyes were encased in black paint. His pupils still burned with that otherworldly fire. Tocho held a tomahawk at his side. The shadow figure he had called Uncle Willie began to disappear along with the humming.

"Tocho." Chase burned a glare at him.

"White man."

"You took my daughter from me," Chase ground out between gritted teeth.

"She stole my destiny," Tocho spat.

"Fuck your destiny."

The wind picked up, and the whispers being carried by it grew louder. Several strikes of lightning lit up the sky simultaneously, and thunder shook the air. An ominous green light rose from the depths around the mesa. The light came with a mist, and figures appeared in the haze—thousands of them. Chase guessed that these were the creatures that the whispers belonged to. They floated in the air with the light and fog surrounding the mesa and trees. They were not much larger than an average man and were shaped similarly as far as legs, arms, and head went, but that was where the resemblance ended. Their faces were shaped like a V, with a long snout that hung low and no visible mouth. Their yellow eyes held a mystery and slanted downward. Long, wiry hair poked out from their heads and grew along their backs but didn't move with the wind—each strand stood stationary as if styled with glue. Sticking out from each temple was a rack of antlers like one would see on a large buck or an elk.

Stone shuffled to Chase's flank, holding his bleeding side, the broken shaft still sticking out. They were really outnumbered now, and fear shook Chase's bones to water. He figured that his life was forfeited, but that was okay as long as he took down Tocho.

He cut his eyes back to the evil leader. Tocho's eyes hadn't moved from him. Chase gripped the knife and lifted his pistol.

From behind Tocho, beyond the point's cliff, rose a rack of antlers larger than any elk could carry. The span had to be close to twenty feet from point to point. The grand horns sat on top of another one of these creatures, but he was three times the size of a man. His face, too, angled down like the snout of a humble dog but was encased in a bare-bone skull that resembled a giant elk. Inside the skull's sockets glowed yellow eyes. Flowing about him was a massive cloak made of dark animal fur that Chase guessed was a bear's hide. He wore necklaces of ornate design and sparkling jewelry that rested upon his bare chest.

This titanic creature approached Tocho, who slowly turned to meet him. The creature spoke in a foreign tongue with a tone of thunder and the hint of a growling beast. Then Chase noticed the sliver of a mouth just beneath the snout. It pointed at the empty altar.

Tocho gestured with both hands as he talked. "I had it. She was here. She leapt to meet you."

The creature glowered at him with disbelief.

"Forgive me." Tocho knelt to one knee, bowed his head, and raised his hands high. "I will provide for thee another sacrifice. A fresher one. One of great innocence."

The creature grunted out a few more words.

Tocho lifted his head as if perplexed. "What of my ancestors? Are they here amongst you?"

The monster shook his head slowly.

"But… you said… you promised me my ancestors."

The thing only stared.

"Give me another chance. Please. Just a little more time."

No response.

"I don't—I don't understand."

The yellow fire of the monster's eyes flared with intensity as if stoked from within. The sliver of a mouth drew open wide, revealing rows of sharp teeth, and the creature bellowed a massive roar. As quick as lightning, the netherworld creature grabbed Tocho—a claw on each side—and bones cracked as he squeezed him. Tocho howled in pain. Then, like an evil boy with a doll, the thing tore Tocho's body in half. The wet tearing sound sent shivers through Chase. Blood, organs, and guts plopped to the ground, and all that remained of Tocho was his ghost floating between the monster's hands, its face twisted in confusion and fear.

The thing from hell lowered his gaping maw to Tocho's ghost and devoured it whole in one easy gulp. The creature's massive body convulsed, its eyes rolled, and it let out a satisfied slurp.

A bloodcurdling cry scratched the night. A woman stood on the edge of a branch, staring down at the nightmare. Her face was distorted with anguish. "No! No! My Tocho!"

His wife, perhaps, Chase thought.

CHAPTER THIRTY-EIGHT

Oakley awoke with an ache pounding between her ears. It thumped with the rhythm of her heartbeat. Gunshots cracked the silence, as did yelling and the sounds of a fight. She peeled her eyes open and sat up. Beneath the chaotic noise, fabric flapped in the wind. It was the makeshift door of the tent she sat in. It was small and dark. She sifted through her recent memories to discover where she was and how she had gotten there.

Images of a cave and a waterfall splashed in her mind, and she recalled Chenoa forcing her to drink something nasty. She recalled jumping through the waterfall and being caught by one of the men and then walking along a strange path. There was something to do with trees and branches, but her memory became blurry at that point.

"Oakley." A woman's voice spoke, and Oakley turned.

Chenoa sat in the corner with her hands in her lap and meekness in her eyes.

"Chenoa?"

"How is your head?"

"Where am I? How long have I been asleep?"

"We are at the Temple of Sinawava."

"Is that where I'm supposed to be?"

She nodded.

Oakley swallowed hard. Her stomach churned like an ice cream machine full of sludge. Chenoa was one of *them*. Oakley didn't expect much help or information from her but was going to ask anyway.

"Where is Inola?"

Chenoa's eyes dropped, and a darkness crossed her face. "She is gone."

"Gone? Gone where? What do you mean?"

"She is with God. She took your place on the altar."

So many thoughts spun that Oakley couldn't understand what she was hearing. She looked at her hands. They were empty of the jewelry Chenoa had placed on them, and she wore a deerskin top and jeans. It was not the ceremonial dress she had been wearing.

"What do you mean?"

Chenoa took a deep breath. "Tocho is the chief of our people, but he is not a good man. I have known this for a while. He speaks like he's helping us, but he hurts more than he helps. He claims to speak to the gods, but he does not speak to our gods—he does not speak with God. He speaks to gods from another place, an evil place. I had to pretend to be with him—to act like I was loyal—to gain his trust. I couldn't tell you. Nor could I tell Inola until it was time."

Oakley's fear of what she believed to be true sank to the bottom of her gut. "I'm confused. What do you mean 'tell Inola'? What did you do? What did Inola do?"

"I gave you medicine to make you sleep. Inola put on your ceremonial dress, and I painted her face red. She is your same height and has the same length of hair and darkness of skin. You are wearing Inola's clothes. Tocho didn't know the difference. He believed Inola to be you."

"So... Tocho sacrificed her instead of me? He killed her?"

She shook her head slowly. "She jumped. We couldn't allow the ceremony and Tocho's destiny to be fulfilled. It would have brought evil into our world. It would have destroyed us all."

Oakley's heart raced a million miles an hour, and her breath was caught in her throat. "Jumped? Off a ledge? Why? Why couldn't she have just run? Why didn't you *help* her?" Her body heated with anger. Tears ran down her cheeks, and she started to shake.

"It was her choice." Chenoa lifted a folded piece of paper and held it out for Oakley to take. "She left this for you."

"No." Oakley shook her head. "Nooo! Why? Why? She didn't—she didn't need to."

She broke into uncontrollable sobs, and Chenoa approached and wrapped her in a tight hug. Oakley felt Chenoa's warmth, and she wet the woman's chest with bouts of tears while mumbling Inola's name and the word *why*. She cried for a good long moment until she was empty of sobs, at least for the time being.

She sat back, and the clarity of the chaos outside the tent reached her ears again. "What's going on out there?"

"Your father is here. He is fighting Tocho and his men."

"My dad's here?" she cried, and her heart leapt.

Oakley jumped to her feet, and despite Chenoa trying to stop her, she bolted from the tent. Quickly inspecting her surroundings, she saw the trees, the narrow mesa she stood on, a greenish light, and a massive number of people fighting. She moved toward the fray, heart thumping, and then she saw him. His back was to her. A gruesome horror stood on the other side of him, but all she focused on was Dad.

She ran and stopped. "Dad!"

Chase's back stiffened as if he'd heard something, but he didn't turn.

"Dad!" she yelled louder, and he twisted to face her. Oakley would remember the expression on his face for as long as she would live—it lit up like a lighthouse, and he sobbed, running to her.

She ran for him and plowed into his chest. She wrapped him, and he wrapped her. With her face plastered against his chest, she smelled her dad's rustic scent. He was warmth, comfort, and love.

"Oakley. Oakley," he wept. He pulled back, lowered to one knee, and held her in front of him. His eyes wandered across her face. "Oakley. Is it really you? You're... you're *alive*."

She nodded. "It was..." She thought of her friend. Her heart ached. "It was someone else. Not me."

"Oh, thank God." He embraced her again.

CHAPTER THIRTY-NINE

Chase pulled away from Oakley to look at her. He still couldn't believe his eyes. "Are you hurt?" His eyes wandered over her, searching for wounds.

"No, I'm fine."

"You said it was someone else, not you?"

"Yes." Oakley's lips trembled, and tears bubbled. "Inola. She was my friend. I wouldn't be here if it wasn't for her."

"I am so sorry." Chase hugged her again.

Screams scratched the night, chilling Chase's blood. The chaos wasn't over. Swarms of the evil things attacked the people in the giant roots like bees at a hive, slicing, munching, biting, and sucking down the souls of their victims. The villagers ran to escape, but one woman slipped and fell to her death, and a young man ran into a low-hanging branch that knocked him down, making him an easy meal for the demons. Others fell prey to the beasts. Chase cringed as one demon latched its rows of teeth around one woman's neck, cutting off her scream, and blood poured.

A young man's arm was torn from his shoulder and tossed as a demon bit into him hungrily. A woman was running until a creature's claws dug into the back of her calves—stopping her in her tracks—and she fell face down. A human head bounced into the air, and tatters of clothes flew as the beasts ripped into their bodies.

A single chant began. It came from Stone. He stood in front of the giant thing that ate Tocho, holding his arms high with two fists clenched. He threw the contents in his hands at the thing—a white, powdery substance—and the creature squealed in pain. Stone dug his hands into the pouch that hung from his shoulder and spread a line of the powder in front of him from one edge of the cliff to the other. He turned to each floating tree, threw more handfuls of the stuff into the air, and called out more Native chants.

The creatures in the trees froze as if receiving an order from their commander. They turned their attention to the giant demon who was their leader, blood and flesh dripping from several of their maws. The surviving Natives wasted no time in running. Stone was calling upon whatever greater power opposed these demons, creating an invisible barrier of sorts, and threatening pain from whatever magic dust sat in his satchel.

Without changing his stance, he twisted his head toward Chase and extended a second leather pouch to him. "Take it. Throw its contents at these devils and run. Run, and do not stop!"

Chase gawked at the satchel, realizing that Stone had planned this all along, withholding the information from them.

"No. Not without you."

"Save your daughter! Now! Run!" Stone growled, and his eyes widened in anger. His order was so forceful Chase couldn't dispute it.

He took the pouch and strapped it over his shoulder then grabbed his daughter by the wrist and pulled her close. "Stay with me. Do not let go."

She nodded.

They ran. Chase was careful not to sprint so fast that they would lose their footing. Death sat at either side of the trail.

Four demons leaped from a tree, landing in front of them. Their eyes glowed with hunger. Instinctively, Chase fired a shot that hit the first creature in the cheek. Its head snapped back, and a hole appeared, but no blood ran, and the devil didn't fall. Chase quickly dug into the pouch, grabbing a handful of the substance, and threw a cloud of it at the thing just as it lurched for them. The demon reeled, squealing and grasping at its face as the powder burned it like acid and vapors rose from its wounds.

Chase quickly grabbed two more handfuls, and Oakley fisted an ounce in her hand too. They ran toward the other three and let them have it. The white grains covered most of their bodies, and writhing, they crumpled. They squealed, scratching their bodies in a mad panic to wipe them free of the substance. They weren't dying, but they were hurting.

As Chase holstered his gun, another creature popped out of the dark and attacked his daughter from behind. It clutched her arms and opened its jaws to take a bite. Oakley fought to get away—its chomping teeth came within inches. Chase grabbed its head with hands full of the dust and pulled it away from Oakley. It screamed as steam rose from its temples and black blood ran. Chase tossed the thing aside.

Oakley wasted no time in arming herself with another handful, and they ran. Another demon attacked. She spun and hit its face with the powder, and Chase sent it off the ledge with a kick. They sprinted, and as they approached the tent, Chenoa stood in their path.

"Dad. We have to take her with us. She saved me."

Chase nodded.

"Chenoa. We've gotta move. Hold on to me," Oakley said.

Chenoa gripped her hand, and the three of them careened around the tent until they came to the chain railing. They each took hold.

Where are my buddies? Chase wondered, worried.

A loud crack split the night like the sound of a bat hitting a fastball. He looked behind him to see a large limb breaking away and falling. Several more limbs snapped and busted away as the demon things attacked the trees. If the trees fell, so did the people.

Kenny. Miles. He couldn't see them among the running hordes or hear their calls through the shrieks of the people. And he thought of Stone, who was busy saving them. *Will he be able to save himself? Will he have time to turn and outrun them?* Chase felt like he knew the answer, but he didn't want to explore it. Saving Oakley was his priority.

The ground below them shook. He felt the mesa quiver as if something massive—like a wrecking ball—had hit the side of the mountain. Rocks crumbled.

"Stay on the path! Hold to the chain!"

They hurried down the trail. Chase clutched Oakley's hand in a sweaty but tight grip. Her right foot slipped, but he pulled her back to balance. Fragments of shattered tree limbs rained down on them, and sawdust blew into Chase's eyes. He wiped at them, getting rid of some of it, but they still itched. He felt the particles sitting on his right eyeball.

The ground quaked again, and the two of them faltered but remained upright. Lightning struck all around them, and one of the bolts hit a giant limb. Sparks flew and ignited a fire, and the branch crashed through other boughs as it toppled. Out of the corner of his eye, Chase saw several figures tumbling through the air.

Twenty feet ahead, a large limb hung close to the mesa, and a man was running along its arm. The man warily leaped from the branch, landed on the mesa, and grabbed hold of the chain to keep himself from sliding.

"Kenny!" Chase called, barely holding his excitement.

Kenny stood up, brushing himself off, and pulled a sly grin.

Chase wrapped him in a quick hug. "You made it! Thanks for saving me up there, brother."

"I missed a couple of shots, but yeah, I guess I got a couple good ones in." Kenny turned to Oakley. "You must be Oakley, right?"

"Yes."

"I thought I saw... well, hell, never mind. I'm glad we got you. We better get off this crazy train fast." He caught Chenoa's attention and gave her a nod and a smile.

They started forward. "Have you seen Miles?" Chase asked.

"No. What about Stone?"

"He's staying back—he's protecting us."

They made quick work along the spine of the mesa and reached the tree limb where Chase and Stone had stepped from. They crossed to it. Minutes into the tree, a familiar face appeared—a wide-eyed Miles approaching them.

"Chase. Kenny. You guys okay?"

"Miles." Chase hugged him. "I'm glad to see you're still alive."

"I am for now. This place is going to hell."

"It is hell," Kenny grumbled.

"Do you have any rope left?" Chase asked, and Miles nodded.

They strung the rope among them, tying each person's waist to the strand so they were all connected, and pushed forward. Chase updated Miles on Stone's status. Within minutes, more people surrounded them. The surviving villagers ran along the arms of the trees' roots on either side, and some of them stepped down to the same wooded path Chase and the others were on. Most of them were women and children, and a handful were young teens. There was one young adult male Chase guessed was seventeen.

He didn't see them as enemies anymore. They shared the same goal of survival, and instead of fighting, the two groups helped each other. Chenoa tearfully hugged several of them.

A massive bolt of lightning hit one of the trees behind them—the one to the left of the mesa—and an explosion roared. Fire and sparks blew, and the rest of the limbs ruptured. Fragments and chips shot out and showered the group. The limb they walked on shuddered back and forth. Wafting smoke curled about them, and the burning scent of wood filled Chase's senses.

Oakley erupted in sobs and panic. "We're not going to make it."

"We're going to make it, honey. Hang tight. I've got ya."

Each minute dragged like syrup, and anxiety and fear mounted layer after layer, but they finally arrived at the waterfall. The rope they had tied off inside the cave and to a tree branch was still intact.

The men took the lead and worked as if they had done this a million times. Kenny went first while the others untied themselves from each other. Next were the kids and the women. Kenny helped pull them all through. Oakley stayed back with her dad and Miles. Chase tied off the last woman, and she leapt to the rock face beneath the showering water. She gripped outcroppings and held fast, and Kenny pulled as she climbed.

"It's your turn, sweetie."

Oakley nodded, and Chase tied the rope around her. Miles turned to stare at the way they had come—probably searching for Stone, though there was no sign of him. Lightning hit the tree they stood on from several feet away. An explosion of sticks and sparks blew. The wood beneath them shook so hard they nearly toppled.

Miles spun to Chase. "The tree's on fire."

"Hurry," Chase told Oakley, and she nodded. Blood drained from her face, and her eyes widened with fear. "I've got you. And Kenny's got you."

Oakley hesitated for a minute and then leapt. She bounced off the face of the mountain, but when she swung back to it, she latched on. Kenny and the others helped pull her to safety.

The limb vibrated hard, and cracks thundered. Chase thought they were done for, but the bough hung on. He tied himself off to the rope, called out to Kenny, and then flew across the gap. Straining his muscles to the max, and with the help from above, Chase climbed the face with speed.

He was up in minutes, and soon Miles had the rope and tied himself off. The limb beneath him snapped and dropped him fifteen feet. Miles tripped and fell then wrapped his arms around the branch and hung on. He quickly stood up, repositioned himself, and leapt for the mountain.

Chase held his breath. The rope strained, and strings snapped. "Quick! The rope's not going to hold much longer!"

The rope was unravelling fast. Miles reached the ledge just as it gave out. Chase grabbed Miles's arms and pulled him to safety.

He shook the water from himself, and they each breathed a sigh of relief. Chase turned to his daughter and, holding her tight, wept. Although there was still a long trek ahead, he breathed a sigh of relief.

CHAPTER FORTY

Ike was dead, and so was Dillon. Chase could see them from a distance as he and the others stepped from the hill onto flat ground. A strong wind blew from the west, and it had left a coating of dust on the two men, nearly covering their legs with dirt an inch thick. A tumbleweed beat against Ike's body, trying to pass him. His hands lay, limp, at each side. Dillon's body leaned into Ike's, with his head resting on Ike's shoulder. Dried blood mixed with dirt painted Ike's chin, hands, and stomach.

Miles and Kenny jogged toward them and, once they arrived, reverently laid Ike's and Dillon's bodies down.

"Who are they?" Oakley asked.

"Good men. They didn't have to be here, but they chose to help. I couldn't have saved you if it weren't for them."

"So... they died because of me?"

"No." Chase was quick to correct her. "They died because bad people shot them. Everything that happened here is because of that man Tocho and the people who followed him. Understand?"

She nodded.

The remaining tribe members dragged themselves to their homes and slowly gathered their belongings. Chase wasn't sure what their intentions were now that they'd lost their leader. He chose not to speak to them. He didn't know what to say. He also didn't know exactly how he felt about them. Clearly, they'd stood by and allowed his daughter to be taken and nearly killed. Chase wouldn't forgive them for that.

Oakley had told him that Chenoa had saved her. He didn't know the specifics, and he didn't ask. Oakley would tell him when she was ready, once they were out of this canyon and safe. Would she ever feel safe again? That was a question that plagued him. Only time would tell.

His right hand quivered. He studied it, surprised that it hadn't acted out once during Oakley's rescue—he'd made it through without his hand shaking. *Progress? Maybe.*

With curiosity, Chase lifted the satchel Stone had given him. There was a tiny bit left, and he grabbed an ounce of it. He sniffed it and then tasted it with his tongue. "Salt. Huh. That's not what I expected."

Chenoa walked past them and entered her hut. A few minutes later, she exited and approached Miles with armfuls of blankets. "Here. For your men."

"Thank you." Miles took the blankets, and with Kenny's help, they wrapped the bodies in them.

Chase took Oakley to find the horses. He would never let her leave his sight again. They found the steeds munching on grasses near the creek. Chase patted his horse on the back and caressed his head. The animal snorted.

"This is Roman."

"Roman?" Oakley smiled and approached. She began to pet him. "He's pretty."

"He's a good horse."

Roman nuzzled his snout into Oakley, and she chuckled.

"He likes you," Chase said.

Chase and the others brought all six horses back to the village, saddled them, and wasted no time packing. They hung their dead friends over the backs of their horses. The sight was grim, but there wasn't another way. They didn't want to spend time building a gurney to drag behind the horses, and it was important to bring Ike and Dillon home to their families.

"So, where are you going to go now?" Oakley asked Chenoa.

"Back to the city. I have family in Cedar City and St. George."

"Do you want to come with us? I'm sure my dad would—"

"No. Thank you, but I will make my own way. With my people. It's best this way."

"So, are they all going?" Oakley asked.

"There are a few who will stay here. It's the only home they've ever known, and they're frightened of what's out there." She pointed to the west.

"This isn't a safe place." Chase stepped in. "It's not exactly in our world. What if those things come back?"

"Then they do." Chenoa shrugged. "They will have to deal."

Tears filled Oakley's eyes. "I don't know how to thank you. I still can't believe that you and... and Inola..."

"It was the right thing to do. I was never going to allow him to take your life." Chenoa gripped Oakley's shoulders and held her gaze.

"But Inola—"

"She made her choice. She was at peace with it. She wasn't happy here. She is with her mother now, and she is happy. You must always remember that."

Oakley nodded and embraced Chenoa long and hard, and Chenoa reciprocated. Chase hugged her next and thanked her.

Then Chenoa withdrew Inola's letter and handed it to Oakley. "Don't forget this."

"Thank you. I'll read this later." She stuffed it into her pocket.

They said their goodbyes. Chase helped Oakley onto Roman and then mounted the horse himself, sitting behind her. Miles and Kenny each led a horse behind their own with one of their dead comrades.

The group slowly exited the village, passing by huts that were ablaze. Several people were burning their homes. One older woman stood in a daze. Her eyes stared into nothing, and she seemed lost. Their entire world—everything they believed in—was gone. It was as if they were now realizing how they had been duped. Chase couldn't help but feel that this hadn't been so much a tribe of Native Americans paying homage to their ancestors as people hypnotized and manipulated by a cult leader.

Several miles into their trek, Kenny took them in a different direction. They didn't have to travel the entire route back the way they had come. Kenny knew these mountains well and brought them into Kolob Canyon, which led to Cedar City. It was dusk by the time they arrived at the mouth of the canyon, and before long, Miles tried his satellite phone and contacted his FBI team. He gave their coordinates as Kenny dismounted, built a fire, and sat on some logs.

The group sat in silence for a while, and then Kenny struck up a casual conversation with Miles. Oakley sat next to her dad, and he wrapped them in a blanket as the night doused the sun and a chill tickled their backs. Oakley snuggled into him, and Chase's body relaxed. He found himself in shock and disbelief that she was actually with him. He felt like he needed to pinch himself over and over again to make sure he wasn't dreaming. Chase caressed her hair.

"I love you, Dad."

Her words bounded in his heart, and he fought back tears. "I love you too."

"I missed you."

"I missed you so bad." He kissed her on the back of her head.

"You never gave up, did you?"

"Never. I never will. And neither did you. I'm so proud of you."

"It was... like a weird dream. I was so scared, and yet I wasn't. Like something inside took over and held me. You know? And I met Inola, my friend." Her voice cracked.

"I wish I could have met her." He craned his neck and looked at the sky crowded with stars. The silence, the cool breeze, and the crackle of the fire filled him with peace. He thanked God quietly. "Look at this sky."

Oakley lifted her head.

"It's so beautiful. You don't get to see the stars like this back in the city," he said.

"This is what you wanted to show me?"

"Yes. Some of it. This world has some breathtaking creations, and I wanted to share them with you."

She nodded. "But I think I'm done with these canyons."

Chase caught her humor and laughed. "You've seen enough, huh?"

"Definitely."

"Yeah, I don't think we need to come back," he agreed.

"Not ever."

"Disneyland next time."

"Or Six Flags. I'm not a kid anymore."

"You'll always be my kid. I'm glad I have you back. In more ways than one. I will never let anything happen to you again."

"Promise?" she asked.

"Cross my heart."

"I'm going to make you hold to that promise. You know Mom will."

He chuckled. "Oh yeah, she will. If she doesn't kill me for this."

"I'll protect you."

They both laughed, and he patted her on the head.

"There's the Big Dipper." She pointed at the stars.

"Oh yeah, I see it. Too bad it's the only constellation I know."

A distant animal cry echoed, and Oakley stiffened. "What was that?"

"A coyote. Just a coyote."

Miles's team arrived with a train of SUVs, four ambulances, a fire truck, a Ford pulling a trailer for the horses, and several reporters, both local and national. Miles was in top form, ushering Chase and Oakley away from the media to an ambulance, where two paramedics immediately began to treat them.

"Oakley!" a woman's voice cried out. Oakley and Chase turned to find Kira racing for them with her arms held out.

"Mom!" Oakley cried and plowed into her chest. They hugged, kissed, and hugged again.

"Oh, are you all right, honey?" She ran her eyes and fingers over Oakley's face and body as if searching for wounds, cuts, or bruises.

"Yes. I am totally fine. No one hurt me. They were actually kinda good to me."

"Good to you?" Her tone lowered, and she stood back, aghast.

"Well, with the exception that they wanted to kill me."

Kira gasped. "Oh my—" She pressed Oakley to her chest again.

Chase approached carefully, hands in his pockets, and gave her a nod. "Hi."

"Hi." Kira opened her mouth again, but no more words came out.

Chase stiffened and looked away then moved his eyes back to Kira. "How are you doing?"

"Better now. How are you? Are you okay?" she asked, focusing on his forehead, which had a cut across it.

"I am now." He gestured to Oakley. "I'm so sorry. First day out and..."

She shook her head. "It's not your fault. I wanted to blame you, and I did at first. I was so angry. But I also knew you were her best chance of getting back alive. I had to believe in you."

"She held her own. She's a brave girl."

Kira nodded. "Yes, she is."

"We lost phone service on the first day. You must have been going crazy."

"You have no idea." Kira rolled her eyes and sighed and then turned to Oakley. "I can't imagine all that you went through."

"I'll have to tell you sometime. But when I do, you won't believe it."

"Let's get out of here," Kira said.

"I can't wait." Oakley nodded.

They turned and were about to walk back to Kira's car when Chase stopped them. "Kira."

Kira turned.

"Mind if I go with you?" He motioned with his eyes to Oakley. He did not want to let her out of his sight again.

"I wouldn't have it any other way." Kira smiled.

CHAPTER FORTY-ONE

Chase stood alongside Kenny and Miles on Larry Mayo's front porch to deliver the news. It was a strange feeling for Chase, knowing they wouldn't be alive if it hadn't been for Stone. He had led them where they needed to go, had known what to do when Benson was bitten by the rattlesnakes, and had the medicine to treat him. And when those wolf beasts attacked, Stone saved Dillon, or at least extended his life. And in the end, when they were all about to be devoured by a horde of demons, Stone had used his magical talents to protect them, all while sacrificing his own life.

How do I thank his grandfather for that?

Chase knocked. After a few moments, he heard the shuffle of someone approaching the door. When the screen pushed open, a cloud of marijuana smoke escaped and covered them. Larry Mayo's sharp but kind eyes, buried deep in his leathered face, greeted them. Wisps of his white hair blew in the soft breeze.

"Mister Mayo," Chase started but didn't know how to finish. He decided to rip the Band-Aid off. "Stone didn't make it."

Mayo's expression didn't change, as if he already knew. "My grandson came to me in a dream. I saw him battle the evil, and I saw him fall. He has moved on, and he resides with his father and with my parents. They are very pleased, and he is happy. There is another child, and she and her mother are with Stone. This child is no older than your daughter." Mayo pointed at Chase. "Her decision was extremely courageous, and her sacrifice was honorable. It is because of her that we are saved from that evil. At least, for now. Everyone who lives in this world owes them a debt of gratitude."

"Stone was a fierce warrior and a good friend." Chase's eyes filled with tears, and his voice cracked. "He saved us, and I will miss him. Thank you."

A wide grin spread across Mayo's face. "It was always meant to be this way. Stone knew of his destiny before going with you. He knew what needed to be done, and he did it. Don't live with the sorrow of his absence but revel in the joy of having known him."

Chase nodded and then wrapped the man in a tight hug. Kenny and Miles offered their condolences and gratitude as well. Then the three of them stepped back into the truck and drove away.

After leaving Mayo's house, they traveled to the hospital to visit Benson. Both he and Jon had made it out of the canyon alive, and Benson was still being treated for his wounds and dehydration. He was swollen and in pain from the bites. His right arm and leg were numb, and the doctors wanted to keep him for a few more days for observation. They wanted to be sure he regained full mobility and his organs were healthy. Jon had met them there, and Benson's wife was by his side.

After leaving the hospital, Miles drove them to the body shop where Chase's truck had been taken after it had been pulled out of the river. Chase felt pretty sure the insurance company would total it, but he'd have to wait and see. They picked up his belongings, and then they headed to the police station, where Kira and Oakley waited for him. Chase's friends helped him transfer his stuff into Kira's SUV.

"I guess this is it." Kenny smiled and turned his attention to Oakley. "I feel like I know you already. Your dad told us so much about you. I'm glad we got you back."

"I don't know how to thank you," Oakley said.

"A hug will do."

They hugged each other, and then she hugged and thanked Miles. Kira did the same. Chase left with Kira and Oakley, and they headed for a hotel in Cedar City. Chase shared a room with them that night. He couldn't leave his daughter, and Oakley had felt the same.

A chilly breeze blew against him the following morning as he hugged his daughter tightly. Kira watched with a smile, entering her vehicle and starting the motor. Chase let a breath out as he pulled away and looked at Oakley.

"I don't want to leave you," Oakley said.

"I have to stay and wrap up a few loose ends. My truck is still in the shop, and I want to pay my respects to the families of the people we lost."

"I want to too."

"No. You need to go home and be with your mom. It's important. She needs you."

"Give them my love," she said.

"I will."

"So, when will I see you again?"

"Soon. After this, I'm coming up to Boulder to scope out a new home and a job."

Oakley's eyes grew larger, and a huge smile spread across her face. "Really?" She hugged him again.

"Yes, really. I don't want to be far from you, and I still have some catching up to do."

Oakley brought a hand to her mouth as she choked back a cry, and her eyes flooded.

"It's going to be good." Chase nodded.

"The best."

After attending the funerals in Parowan, Chase traveled to Salt Lake City with Kenny, where they met up with Miles and attended Agent Abraham Ike's funeral. He received a full police escort and the traditional law enforcement treatment. The three of them headed for a bar after the service. They sat at a table in silence and nursed their beers.

"We really shook the pillars of hell, didn't we?" Kenny finally said.

"That sounds like a line from a movie," Miles said.

"Sort of. I changed it a bit."

"This whole experience could be a movie," Chase said.

"Write the script, and turn it into one. Kurt Russell can play me." Kenny smiled cockily.

"He might have trouble pulling off a twenty-year-old at his age," Miles said.

"Twenty-two."

"So, what now?" Miles nodded to Chase.

Chase took a swig and wiped his lips. "I've got to find work in Boulder."

"Are you going to go back into police work?" Kenny asked.

"I don't know what I'll do. I have a lot of options."

"I could always use you here. It's not that far from Boulder," Miles pointed out.

"Nah. I'm not a Fed man. I was getting pretty good at selling security systems. I'll definitely install one for Kira and Oakley."

Miles turned to Kenny. "What about you?"

"Me? I'm a good ol' boy from Parowan. That's my home. Someone has to watch the borders of hell so nothing like this ever happens again."

"Cheers to that." Chase took a drink.

"This was too many funerals to have to attend in such a short time," Miles said.

"I agree," Kenny said.

"To our friends." Chase lifted his bottle. "Ike, Dillon, Stone, and Inola."

They clinked their beers together, and each took a swig.

"Are we going to see each other again?" Kenny asked with a tone of hope.

"Not in Parowan." Chase chuckled. "You can't get me to go back there."

"How about we pick a place far from here where us three can meet? A year from now or sooner," Miles offered.

"Hawaii sounds good." Kenny grinned.

They all laughed. "Sounds good to me," Chase said.

After another round of beers, they headed to their cars.

"Kenny, you're a good man and a good officer. Your father would be proud." Chase gave him a firm handshake and a hug.

"It takes one to know one." Kenny smiled, and they smacked fists.

"See you, brother. Be good." Miles gave Chase a tight hug.

"Don't be a stranger. I'll be just on the other side of the mountain."

Miles and Kenny got in their vehicles as Chase headed to his, which was parked in the back. He couldn't wipe the smile from his face any better than he could remove the lump from his throat. He turned and gave a last wave.

CHAPTER FORTY-TWO

Three months had gone by—nearly to the day—when Oakley and her dad traveled back to Parowan. They had promised never to return, but Oakley had said there was one last thing she needed to do that was more important than anything. Her dad had obliged.

Oakley's hands fidgeted, and her body stiffened as they drove down Main Street. The city sat like a monster in the back of her mind—a firm reminder of the horrors they had suffered.

"It's so weird being back. It gives me chills," she said.

"No love lost here," Chase said.

There wasn't a day that Oakley hadn't thought of Inola. She'd watched the movie *Forrest Gump* several times. She also listened to Billy Joel, the Beatles, Bob Dylan, and the Beach Boys. Since Inola wasn't there to enjoy them, Oakley did it for her. It had been therapeutic, and she felt her friend's spirit when she listened. Oakley still struggled with Inola's decision, despite what Inola had said in the letter. It could take months—years—before Oakley would come to terms with what had happened.

Chase drove through neighborhoods toward the east mountain until they arrived at a cemetery on a hill. It took them a few minutes to find the headstones. The Paiute Indian Tribe of Utah had donated two tombstones in honor of Stone and Inola, and they sat side by side. Although Stone and Inola had never met in this life, Oakley was sure they knew each other in the next. Her dad had told her about the dream that Stone's grandpa had and how he had seen Inola with her mother. Their memorials sat beneath the shade of a chestnut tree, and a cool breeze blew through.

Chase set an arrangement of flowers on each headstone. He and Oakley stood in silence as they read the engravings and reminisced. Oakley's throat tightened, and something heavy tugged at her heart. She withdrew the letter and read it aloud.

"My friend, Oakley. I know what you must be thinking, and I am so sorry to have done this to you. I would have loved to go home with you, go to school, attend dances, and go on dates with boys. But it wasn't meant to be. I can't explain it any better. Just know that this was not a suicide, and I didn't come to this decision lightly. Chenoa told me of the grave danger that would happen if Tocho went through with it. The ceremony would unlock a doorway into our world for whatever nightmares lived on the other side. Everyone was at stake."

Oakley wiped tears from her eyes, swallowed hard, and continued. "I wasn't going to jump unless I had no other way. I was going to play it out and see if I could escape somehow. If you're reading this, I guess that didn't happen. I am okay with this decision. One life for many—that's what I kept telling myself.

"I had a dream last night, and my mom was there. It was real. She was with me in that dream, and we hugged forever. She told me how brave I was and said not to be scared. I think it was her way of telling me that it was okay to do this. I also know I will be reunited with my mom, and that is comforting. It was the first time in a long time that I didn't have nightmares. This dream was filled with joy and love."

Chase extended his arm over her shoulders and pulled her tight.

Oakley continued reading. "I loved our talks. I never had any friends, so although our time was short, I loved being with you. And I will always be with you. I wrote a poem. It's not much, but I like it.

"When you can't fly, I will be your wings. When you can't run, I will be your legs. When life is dark, I will be your light. When life is hard, I will be your angel. I love you always. Your friend, Inola."

Oakley broke into sobs. Chase kept silent and let her get her cry out. Once the sobs subsided, she took deep breaths and composed herself.

"Did you bring it?" Chase asked.

Oakley nodded and withdrew the offering from inside her jacket, and Chase helped her tie the string around a flower stand mounted on the headstone so the item could hang. Oakley had searched many places until she found the right dreamcatcher. This one had spoken to her. It was round with several crisscrossing designs inside, and feathers and beads hung from the bottom.

"I bought two of these. The other one is hanging from my bed. May this keep the bad dreams away so that you can rest in peace. I love you always, Inola, my friend."

At that moment, a monarch butterfly fluttered and landed on Inola's headstone. It was as big as her palm and fiery orange outlined in black. Oakley gasped as she took in its beauty. Another butterfly landed next to it. This monarch was slightly smaller. Tears were released from Oakley like waterfalls.

"They're her favorite. She loved butterflies," she told her dad. She wiped her eyes and bent to get closer to the butterflies. Surprisingly, her approach didn't scare them off. Her heart filled with joy. "Hello, Inola and Mai."

About the Author

When Brett McKay isn't conjuring demons and bloodthirsty psychopaths to put on paper, he sells landscaping. He loves all types of music, but hard rock and heavy metal fuel him the most. He enjoys the outdoors, spending time with friends and family, and curling up in front of a good movie with his wife and a bucket of popcorn.

Brett lives in Utah with his wife and two sons. Fall is his favorite time of year because he gets to decorate his house for Halloween much too early for his neighbors.

Read more at https://www.brettmckaybooks.com/.

About the Publisher

Dear Reader,

We hope you enjoyed this book. Please consider leaving a review on your favorite book site.

Visit our site to find more quality books!

Read more at https://RedAdeptPublishing.com.